Lethal Impulse

by

Steve Rush

Dedication

To my wife Sharon.

Chapter 1

Neil Caldera studied every detail of seven potential murder victims. Each a haunting echo of life perched on the brink of tragedy. The NYU students, dressed in an array of bright colors, engaged in animated chatter as they waited to place orders at the diner. Life continued its relentless march forward, even as the scent of a looming threat hung in the air, casting an eerie shadow over Greenwich Village on this Tuesday before Thanksgiving.

The drone of their conversation quieted when a haggard man burst into the deli. Neil turned his attention back to observing an apartment building south of Washington Square Park. The newcomer slammed a grimy hand on Neil's table, while his other hand pressed against his side, obscured beneath a tattered coat. Breathless, he said, "He's at the tavern on MacDougal Street, Detective. He has a gun."

Neil pocketed the hour-old notes from his interview with NYU junior, Saniya Carta. Saniya's family's influence, and important information about her friend's murder, led him to set up in the deli. He put two twenties in the man's palm and sprang off the stool. He zipped his jacket on his way out and called in the sighting.

Procedure and common sense dictated each choice Neil made on the job. He planned out his strategy through the block-and-a-half jog to his destination. Adrenalin fueled his approach. His jacket's zipper jammed as he angled across the street to business façades analogous to five-o'clock shadows on ruddy faces. Two men in overcoats rounded the corner. They moseyed toward the tavern.

The tavern's front door ruptured open. The person Neil sought erupted onto the sidewalk like spewed vomit. He crashed into one man, staggered three strides, and darted past a hand-truck-wheeling delivery person into the street.

Neil ripped open his jacket and sprang off the opposite sidewalk in pursuit of the person responsible for the murders of five NYU foreign-exchange students in an eight-week span. The man fled in a direct line for two blocks while Neil closed the distance to ten yards. Pedestrian traffic increased at Washington Square. Cold air stung his cheeks. The wanted man shoved an elderly woman off a crosswalk. She stumbled into the path of a sedan and angled right across the intersection from Washington Square onto Thompson Street. Vehicle horns blared. Tires screeched.

Neil slowed. Two men rushed to the woman hunched over the car's hood. Neil continued his pursuit when the woman waved them off.

The alleged killer strobed in and out of sunlight on the vacant, tree-lined stretch of Thompson north of Bleecker. At sun-blazed Bleecker Street, the thirty-nine-year-old ex-con faded left. He veered right, spun 180 degrees, and whipped out his left arm. Neil's warning alerted nearby pedestrians. The blast from the killer's handgun scattered them.

Instinct told Neil what to do. Training taught him

how to do it. Calculated motion. Full awareness of the gunman and his surroundings. No immediate threat to bystanders. Two shots. Center mass. The killer sprawled in the intersection.

A scream relayed a message Neil hoped never to hear. A young woman crumpled in the gutter on Bleecker in front of the pharmacy. A middle-aged woman threw herself on top of her. The woman's shriek and sobs reverberated between buildings.

Neil holstered his pistol. He put two fingers on the downed man's neck, confirmed no pulse, collected the killer's weapon, and rushed to the women. Sorrow flushed his chest when Saniya Carta, the twenty-year-old daughter of the Genovese family's consigliere, touched her mother's face. It worsened the moment he dropped to one knee and grasped her hand. Her gaze fixed on him. Saniya's smile sliced through his heart before her body wilted on the asphalt.

An NYPD cruiser slid to a stop on Bleecker. Two uniformed officers hopped out. The sergeant raced up to Neil and the women. She radioed for emergency response. The other officer secured the killer's weapon from Neil. Three additional officers cordoned off the intersection and ordered people back from the scene.

The mother lifted her head. "You're that detective. Neil Caldera, right? I recognized you from the press conference." She extended her hands and pressed his hand to Saniya's. "I'm glad you are the one who killed the man who shot my daughter, Detective. I've been following the story on the news." She released his hand and dabbed her eyes. "Saniya was just telling me about the interview you did with her. She expressed her belief that you are an honest cop."

Neil frowned. "He did not shoot your daughter, Mrs. Carta."

The mother's body morphed from somberness to outrage. She pried off his hand from Saniya's and flailed her arms. "Get away from us. How dare you act as if you care? I hope the full wrath of what's coming terrorizes you for the rest of your life."

The sergeant touched Neil's shoulder and motioned him across the street. She strode alongside him. "What were you thinking, DT? You just admitted to killing a member of the most notorious crime family in the city. Did you not see them?"

Neil fought to not give away his emotional turmoil through his body language. "I can't say how it happened with any certainty. They approached from the right. Neither was anywhere near the line of fire."

"No matter, DT. It's people's perspective. Right now, the blame is on you. My advice to you is to contact a rep." She stepped up on the sidewalk and faced him. "Do you have anybody in mind?"

"Never had a need for one."

"I've heard that about you. You are a good person based on things I've heard at the house. I'll take care of it." She pulled out a notepad and pen. "I need the facts for a scratch report. How did this go down?"

****

Arlo Messana, a sixty-one-year-old tamed beast, watched the incident unfold from a loan-shark's third-floor office on the northeast corner. The elevation and angle offered a perfect line-of-sight between the shooter and his target. A grunt escaped his chest as if someone stabbed him. Arlo tightened his face at the sight. His niece, Saniya, pitched forward off the sidewalk.

Arlo hurried toward the door. "Get someone outside the pharmacy before the police shut down the block." His voice issued a formidable tone. "Saniya's been shot."

His brother blocked his passage. "You can't go down there. You know what will happen if people see you."

Arlo turned back to the window. He watched the increased response on the street as he studied the lines of sight from his location. The scene replayed in his mind. The outcome remained the same each time. The plain-clothes officer shot after the person he chased turned and fired a weapon at him. A bullet from the detective's firearm somehow struck Saniya. Arlo considered the shooter-to-victim alignment. Any variation in the shooter's position showed no consequential difference.

The raised scars on his face reddened in anger. Garlic on his brother's breath wafted over Arlo's left shoulder.

"The mayor and police commissioner will oust that detective. See to it he gets what he deserves." Arlo turned. "I want a copy of his personnel file. Spread the word, Zeno. No one touches him." He sat behind his brother's desk, opened the center drawer, and pulled out a writing tablet.

Zeno squeezed in an armchair in front of the desk. "The family won't like you taking this away."

The fountain pen made a scratching sound on the paper. "Get this to Guido Carta. My regards for losing his daughter. I want no misunderstanding between us. If he questions anything in my note, tell him I'm calling Declan."

Zeno pleaded. "That copper shot and killed his daughter."

"I watched it happen, Zeno. No one will deprive me of this opportunity. I won't allow it. I have my own plans for Detective Neil Caldera."

Chapter 2

Eighteen months later

The time had come for the wife of Madison's police chief to mutilate the town's pride. Tess Fleishman ensnared her first victim in a manner likened to a Southern belle in the best small town to live in Georgia. She inhaled the humid air ripe with pine scent. The fringe of success released an adrenalin rush. Tess braced on the repossessed sedan as she filmed Vanessa Flack running through the thicket.

The sun's rays conveyed a strobe effect on Vanessa's yellow tee and orange shorts. The eighteen-year-old raced across uneven terrain, fought low hanging limbs, and craned her neck to look for her assailant. Vanessa cut over to the dirt road and hustled up the red clay embankment. She heaved breaths and rested her hands on her hips.

"How was that?" Vanessa puffed out the words. "I need realism for the school project."

Tess clapped. She hobbled along the side of the car. She ducked through the open passenger's window and backed out, holding a towel and an insulated tumbler. "You showed me I made the right choice."

Vanessa draped the towel around her neck and dabbed her face. "Thank you for this, Tess."

Tess set the camera on the rear seat. She pictured the murder scene planned at the barn. "You can thank me when it's over. I need your help with this next part because the doctor told me I'm not to lift anything over twenty pounds. This leukemia drains me." She popped open the trunk.

"I heard about your diagnosis." Vanessa embraced Tess. "I thought about going into oncology once I complete medical school. If I get accepted. That is a long way off. What has the doctor said about your prognosis?"

"We view my future differently. I'm hoping for remission." Tess gestured to the trunk. "Climb in."

Vanessa glanced inside the trunk. She retreated two strides. "Do I have to get in there? It looks grimy. Why did you not bring your car?"

"We're documenting an abduction and murder, Vanessa. We can't let anybody see my car or you with me. It will ruin the surprise. It's only until we get to the barn."

Vanessa clambered into the trunk. Tess swathed towels around Vanessa's wrists and ankles before she bound them with paracord. Vanessa thanked Tess for the use of towels to prevent ligature marks on her skin.

Tess grinned. "A killer must focus on details, Vanessa."

The repossessed Impala bounced and swayed through Fairview Cemetery five minutes later. Tess parked in the shadow of trees on the north side. She donned tactical apparel and opened the trunk. Vanessa squirmed and strained against her restraints. Twilight robbed her face of color. Her skin appeared gray. Tess pictured her at the crime scene sans the restraints, her clothing, and a pulse.

Vanessa lifted her head. A puzzled expression

formed on her face. She wiped sweat from her eyes with her fingers. "Why are we in the cemetery? Where are Katie and Chad? You told me the murder-mystery party is supposed to be filmed at the barn."

"It is, Vanessa." The tactical-garbed Tess sat on the lip of the trunk. She grasped Vanessa's hand to calm her. "I sent Chad a message to prepare the scene. Katie and the others will join us after I get you set in place."

Vanessa looked at the cemetery. She struggled against the restraints.

"Have you ever known me to lie to you?"

"No." Vanessa stilled. "You've always been sweet to me."

"Then trust what I tell you, Vanessa. I'm taking you to the barn where Chad will make a video of me killing you. He's agreed to edit our project. I'm counting on Katie for bonus imagery."

Vanessa flinched when Tess flicked open a tactical knife. Uncertainty filled her eyes. "That knife is just for show, right? You're not really going to hurt me."

Tess waved the knife a foot from Vanessa's face. "The effect of a tanto blade is one experience a person never forgets. Keep that look. I want to capture it."

Vanessa reached out once Tess lowered the camera. "Please let me ride up there with you. I'll hide behind the seats. Nobody will see me."

"Relax, Vanessa. You agreed to do this. It will look authentic if one of your friends sees me hauling you out of the trunk. It will be over soon." Tess slammed the trunk lid.

Tess drove the Impala from the cemetery to the west side of town. No one gave her a second look. Darkness consumed them when she shut off the lights.

The sedan rolled to a stop beneath a hundred-year-old oak tree behind Fletcher's barn on Washington Street. Tess eased along the side of the car to the trunk. She felt for the lock. Inserted the key.

Vanessa jerked away when Tess's gloved hand touched her arm. "Where is Chad?"

Tess shushed her. "I told you he's waiting for us inside."

"Then why is it dark in there? You lied to me, Tess. Untie me."

Tess gripped Vanessa's shoulder. She slid her hand to Vanessa's throat. Vanessa squirmed. The second her mouth opened Tess stuffed in a gag. "This is reality, Vanessa. It's time to die for your sister's betrayal."

****

Chad Stoltz opened the door to Fletcher's barn at 9:30 p.m. He winced at the unpleasant smell inside. He sprayed the open space with his flashlight app. A glow came from the wall to his left. Chad covered his nose, skirted around a rusty truck hood propped against three bales of hay, and stepped up to a four-foot-high image painted on the weathered boards. The portrait appeared crimson up close. When his fore and middle fingertips touched it, he jerked away and rubbed his thumb across them. The goo gripped his skin and threaded when pulled apart. He sniffed it.

His throat seized. Chad focused on the crimson-and-weathered face while he shuffled two short steps in retreat. Who would do a thing like this?

The exposé held his gaze long enough for him to remember where he was. This was an old barn full of ominous shadows and places to hide. He anticipated seeing the creature from *Jeepers Creepers* in the loft.

He expected any moment to catch sight of the monster's grin and hear its tantalizing snuffle. An All-American linebacker at Morgan County High School, Chad saw nothing except more bales of hay stacked floor-to-roof on one end and three-to-four high nearest the ladder.

The boards behind the portrait creaked from a gust of wind. Chad shuddered at the sound. A tingle crawled up his neck. A strong acridness enveloped him. The next breath knotted his stomach. His pulse battered his eardrums and punched his temples. That same smell—the smell of death—once nauseated him. It was when he saw his mother's body slumped behind the steering wheel of her crashed SUV eighteen months earlier.

Chad's left foot thumped a truck hood as he hurried to get out of the barn. He stumbled and fell forward onto the dirt floor. Two empty feed buckets banged and rattled on the side boards after his right arm struck them against the outside of one stall. Dust rose from the clay floor.

Death's stench reeked at ground level. Chad looked around and located the source fewer than three feet away. Blood saturated the sawdust-covered floor. Spatter and smears stained the slats of wood separating the stall from the one adjoining it. Never had he observed so much blood.

Chad scrambled to his feet, fumbled his cellphone, pulling it out of his pocket as he ran toward the double doors. He paused long enough to pick up the phone. He shoved open the left-side door, scrolled to the number for Neil Caldera, and pressed his thumb to the screen. He leaned on the barn. He held the phone tight to his ear, bounced on the balls of his feet as he heard the first three rings.

Four rings.

A voice answered after the fifth ring. "Caldera."

"I need you to come to the barn. Now."

"Who is this?" Neil spoke in his Long Island accent.

"It's Chad. Chad Stoltz."

"Chad, try to calm down so I can understand you, okay? You're breaking up. Take it slow and tell me again."

"I'll t-try." Chad peered around the edge of the barn door. The image on the wall stared back at him. "It's just…Somebody has to be dead. This can't be real. There's blood everywhere. I ain't ever seen anything like this. There has to be a crazy monster running loose around here somewhere."

"Where are you?"

"I'm outside Fletcher's barn on East Washington. Please. Please hurry, Bishop. You have to see this."

"Did you say bar?"

"No, not a bar. *Barn*. I'm at the old barn close to the apple orchard."

"Okay, got it. Stay right there. I'm on my way."

Chapter 3

Neil glanced at the dome-glassed clock on the mantel—9:42 p.m. After a change into black attire, he grabbed a flashlight out of the nightstand next to his bed. He flipped the switch to check the batteries. The bulb threw out a solid beam. Satisfied, he put the flashlight in his left hip pocket. He reached for the Smith & Wesson 9mm, hesitated, and slid the drawer closed.

He walked through the leased house, turned off every light except one over the kitchen sink, and exited through the back door. He checked the door lock and even though he planned not to drive his decade-old Acura, Neil pressed the unlock button on the key fob, which also activated a video security-system link. He manually locked the door.

His ten-speed mountain bike stood propped against the wall around back. A trip on foot meant a greater chance of being seen on the road. He risked leaving evidence of his presence if he rode the bicycle to the barn.

The thermometer nailed to the outside door frame showed a near normal sixty-seven degrees on this first Saturday in May. Humidity made it feel more like seventy-five.

Neil chose to walk.

Two hundred yards into the trek he met a dark

vehicle headed in the opposite direction. The Impala slowed to a stop in the roadway. The driver rolled down her window. "You're out late, Padre."

"Hi, Tess. You are the last person I expected to see. Did you trade your vehicle?"

Tess Fleishman sat slumped in the driver's seat. "It's a loaner. I didn't want Rob to see mine about town. I'm supposed to be at home."

Neil stepped over to the car and leaned his left forearm on the door. The thumb on his left hand swiped a roughness in the paint. He glanced at a half-moon-shape scratch an inch below the trim. His heart saddened at seeing the woman's pallor and a walker in the footwell on the passenger side. Six months ago, Tess enjoyed health and a semblance of happiness. They were her life of luxury, not her and Rob's amassed material possessions. It was then she reported leukemia had invaded her body and forced out the richness of her thirty-six-year existence.

"I guess he's not there."

"I needed to get out of the house for a bit. Those walls close in on me. I feel trapped. I can't just sit there, Neil. Life is whizzing by me and I'm missing it because of my senseless disease."

"No words exist, Tess."

She tucked strands of chestnut hair behind her left ear, twisted in the seat, and laid her hand on his arm. Her right arm lifted her breast visible beneath the sheer eggshell tunic wet from chest to waist.

"Words I can do without, Neil. If I weren't such a mess, I'd invite you over for some pat and frisk. Although, be warned. I am armed. You may have to take me into custody."

"You're a married woman."

"Somebody needs to tell that to Rob. He seems to have forgotten." Tess shook her head. She sighed. "It really doesn't matter to me what he does anymore. I'll be gone soon and he can do whatever he wants." She squeezed Neil's forearm. "I want to feel special again, Neil. I want to feel loved."

Neil put his hand on hers. "I'll talk to him."

"No. Please. He shouldn't know we talked."

Neil nodded. He removed his hand from hers and straightened.

Tess waved goodbye. She turned right at the first intersection and in moments the Impala's taillights faded in the darkness. Eleven minutes passed before Neil arrived at the barn. The acrid scent of blood permeated the air.

Chad stuck his head around the corner.

"Thank you for coming."

"Have you notified the police?"

"No. Vanessa Flack called me this afternoon about getting together to do a mock murder scene. I was supposed to meet her here after it got dark. I called her phone several times, but they all went to her voice mail. You've got to help me. Please. If something happened to Vanessa, the police will think I did it."

"Why would they think that?"

"I just assume because we've been talking?"

"Boyfriend-girlfriend talks?"

"No. It's nothing like that. We're just friends."

"Call them. I'll wait."

Chad's hand trembled as he gestured to the door. "You'd better look in there first."

A metal bar fit over a latch to secure the barn doors

on the outside. Neil rotated the bar clockwise and let it hang toward the ground before he let go of it. He tugged on the left-side door. Its lower edge caught on clumps of crabgrass. He lifted the door enough to clear the obstacle and allow enough space for him to squeeze through.

"You want to show me?"

Chad covered his nose and backed away. "Not a chance. I'm not going back in there."

Neil thought about his decision not to bring his pistol. Three years ago, he never would have gone anywhere without one. Besides, any threat in Madison, Georgia compared little to those in New York City.

He stepped through, pulled the door shut, and turned on the flashlight. The stench overpowered the smell of old hay and musk. He aimed the beam leftward. Three bridles hung on hooks between the two stalls on that side. A singletree dangled from a nail above them. Three supports lined the right side, spaced the same distance apart. A ladder leading to the loft abutted the middle post. The space under the loft housed a green tractor and related farm gear.

The rear wall contained double doors similar to those on the front. Neil eased forward. His footfalls made no sound on the dirt floor. A quick check with the light confirmed the first stall was empty. He crept on to the second. A worktable lined two walls. Hand tools lay haphazardly on its surface. A pitchfork and two shovels propped alongside the wall to the right.

The stench intensified with each step. The source was somewhere in the darkness beyond the second stall. He discovered it in the third. A three-by-five-foot blood-soaked spot on the sawdust. Neil had observed enough crime scenes to identify the familiar sight and smell of blood. Light revealed blood on three of the four walls and on a few boards overhead.

He strode to the rear space amidst various farm implements. The flashlight beam revealed nothing unanticipated to the right. The light revealed more to him than he foresaw. Happenstance played no role in the display now before him. The artist's rendition displayed evidence of a warped mind. Malevolence flaunted in the form of a portrait painted with blood. Neil widened the beam of light with a left twist of the flashlight's head. Shock jolted him. The likeness on the barn wall stared back at him with remarkable resemblance.

"Holy mother of Moses. I understand why you didn't want to come back."

Neil looked at the front and rear doors. Light from an approaching vehicle rose on the front of the barn. Gaps around the door allowed enough streaks of light through to make shadows look as if the light infused them with life. The vehicle continued onward. Every shadow around Neil returned to stationary ominous forms. He half-turned toward the front and listened. The whine of tires on pavement diminished. Silence again filled the barn.

The hinges squawked against Neil's shove on the right-side door. Chad turned his head in Neil's direction. He was sitting on the ground with his back to the weathered wood. Knees drawn up, arms wrapped around them and his right hand clamped on his left wrist.

"It's you." Chad shuddered, tilted his head toward the barn. "In there. The picture on the wall looks like you."

Neil glanced inside. The image renewed in his mind. "Is that the reason you called me? To have me look at someone's depravity smeared on a barn wall?"

Chad shook his head. "No, sir."

"Then why?"

"I know what you did."

For fifteen months, Neil kept his past behind him. No discussion necessary. He made known his willingness to serve the church upon arriving from New York City. The church's leadership approved and recommended to the membership that they accept him as their minister.

They did.

Now this.

"Clarify."

"I know you killed somebody."

Neil squatted in front of Chad. "Come to church tomorrow. We'll talk about this afterward. Until then, keep whatever you think you know to yourself. You got that?"

Chad dropped his arms, pressed his left hand to the ground to push upward. He hesitated. "What about that in there?"

Neil stood and offered his hand to Chad. "Not a word to anyone."

Chad took Neil's hand. He pushed up with his left hand. After they shook, he brushed off the seat of his jeans.

"Okay. I'll see you tomorrow."

Chad strode toward home. Neil watched him fade into the night. He took the next ten minutes to look around the barn. He remained far enough away from the sides to not disturb potential evidence. He needed to see the inside and the outside under better conditions.

He must consider every scenario and prepare himself for the onslaught he sensed coming at him.

Chapter 4

Chief of Police Rob Fleishman aimed the headlights of his city-issued Dodge Charger toward the dip in the landscape near the right corner of the barn on East Washington Street. Pale flesh illuminated by the light left no doubt as to race and gender. He knew the girl's identity without getting out of his car—Vanessa Flack. Vanessa attended school at Morgan High. She was a senior of honor roll status. Her peers saw her as ambitious and beautiful. He agreed.

Chief Fleishman keyed the mike on his portable radio. "Dispatch, we have a body outside Fletcher's barn on East Washington. Contact the coroner's office and Neil Caldera. I want them both here ASAP."

"You want the fire department on the scene?"

"Just rescue to assist with transport and hold all calls until I get to the office."

He reached for the trunk release, heard the thump of the latch as it released and saw the rear deck lid pop up in his rear-view mirror. He flicked on his Maglite and strode to the rear. He stared at the black body bag folded on one side of the trunk for a few seconds. There was no reason for hurry. He closed the trunk and ambled to Vanessa Flack's body.

Abrasions, contusions and slashes marred the otherwise unblemished form from her neck down. The face remained as before her soul fled her body. Eyes clouded and pupils dilated, never to capture another moment of her surroundings or the face of her killer.

Fleishman returned to his car. He opened the trunk a second time and removed a roll of crime scene tape. He began at the rear of the barn on the same side as Vanessa's remains. He walked thirty feet west, rounded a pine tree, strung the tape north across East Washington. He circled a hardwood sapling twice, turned east beyond the eastern wall of the barn, circled another hardwood tree, and turned south to the barn's rear corner. He stowed the roll of tape in the trunk.

The Department's limited resources pressed Fleishman to call the GBI—Georgia Bureau of Investigation—for assistance. His pride suggested he let his people handle the initial stages and request outside help later on. In the meantime, he did have one resource available to him.

Neil Caldera.

****

The death of the teenage girl captured the interest of everyone in Madison within a half hour of its discovery. Most of the town's citizens knew of Vanessa Flack's murder by eleven thirty that evening.

Neil nosed the front of his Acura TL sedan between the rear of a fire rescue truck and a police car at eleven thirty-five. He shouldered open the door after the first attempt with the interior release handle didn't open it. The hinges squawked in protest and gave way to his will. Edges of cracked leather snagged at the legs of his slacks as he slid off the seat. He grabbed the window frame and heaved the unwilling door back to its habitat.

Red and blue strobes slit the darkness in an eerie

rhythm. A line of yellow crime scene tape cordoned off an area in front of a barn and down both sides.

The discovery haunted him. He knew the Flacks. This was near their home. Loss rumbled through his body. He witnessed scenes such as this one many times in the city. Flashes of disbelief trekked in multiple directions. Each one faded into despair. Neil saw this as a premonition and feared for the townspeople.

Experience taught him to consider anyone as a suspect. No one, not even the police, may be exempt until the evidence led in another direction. Happenstance in this case did not fit a legitimate scenario. Others would fall. He sensed it in Chief Fleishman's voice when the chief called him and asked for his help.

Neil understood his role in the case. Doing it was another matter. How could he restrict himself to duties of clergy and consultant? How might he offer comfort and guidance to those in need when his focus stayed on finding the killer? Vanessa's murder reminded him of his past. Some of it he preferred to forget. Things he would remember no matter how long he lived.

Eighteen to twenty bystanders crowded the line of yellow tape at the street. Others huddled in front yards of the neighbors' houses and outside vehicles parked along the shoulders on both sides of the road.

Neil stopped short of the tape. The side of the rescue truck shadowed him from the blue and red lights' whipping lashes, reminiscent of similar incidents in New York City.

The exception was location. In Madison, not a single building rose above six floors. Families dwelt in homes where the nearest neighbor lived farther away than the thickness of a semi-soundproof wall.

By eleven forty-five, the crowd outside the crime scene tape doubled in size.

A couple of teens roamed between the crowd and a group of six teenagers around a yellow Honda. Katie Moore occupied the driver's seat of the car, face buried in her hands. A male knelt facing her whom Neil did not recognize. The rest of the group watched in silence. They faced the central part of everyone's focus: the scene of their murdered classmate.

Neil turned his attention to the gathering in the street. Friends. Acquaintances. Neighbors. Strangers. Face-to-face-to-face he studied their expressions. He studied them to interpret each one's body language. Many appeared somber. Some dabbed at their eyes. Heads leaned on others' shoulders. A few hands covered mouths. Sobs and moans escaped them.

In time, Neil expected many of them to darken the door of his office. A few would visit more than once. Want answers. Ask, "Why?" and hope he could give a satisfying answer. A few needed consoling. He doubted any would confess to having committed murder.

Neil recognized everyone in the crowd except five: three males, two females. One man looked to be in his early sixties. A female clung to his left side.

The second female talked with two women whom he knew lived in the other side of town. She held the second male's hand. The foursome formed a circle, heads bowed.

He saw Chad nowhere in the crowd.

A mid-to-late-twenties male lingered in the street behind the crowd. Salon-styled hair and attire included creased dress slacks breaking atop loafers, starched shirt tailored to house broad shoulders and a trim waist. He stood out among the more casually clad townspeople.

Madison boasted of a population of forty-three hundred. Strangers spending time around town usually were tourists.

Something about the man irked Neil. Wariness increased as Neil closed the distance between them. He detected the man's cologne while cutting across downwind and circling behind him. Now, three feet away, Neil planted his feet on the dusty soil a half step behind and to the man's left. He crossed his arms and waited.

The stranger maintained his posture. Arms hanging at his sides, nose pointed straight ahead.

Neil watched the man in his peripheral vision. "Tragedy, isn't it? Young. Pretty. Smart. Academic scholarship to Duke. She planned to be a doctor. Did you know Vanessa?"

The stranger tightened his jaw. Neck muscles bulged above the shirt collar. His carotid artery pulsated under olive skin.

"Vanessa Flack." Neil continued his scrutiny. "She attended St. James Presbyterian here in town with her family."

"Man of the cloth." The voice reminded Neil of rosin. Clear and harsh. The accent indicated New England. The man's tan suggested a much warmer climate.

"Yes."

"Newcomer?"

"Fifteen months."

"Not long enough. You need more seasoning to be

effective in ministry."

"How about you, sir? Is God a part of your life?"

"Does a balance between good and evil exist? Secrets often are construed as lies. If so, what's the difference? Your God, be He so inclined, can uncover your secret. Your mannerisms betray you, Caldera. You should acknowledge your sins to your congregation."

Neil shrugged off the chides. "You did not answer my question. Did you know Vanessa Flack?"

"How does one define knowing? What constitutes understanding? Tell me. Look around. Chaos thrives because our system of justice allows it. We are no better than the predators we decry if our choices lead down paths of deceit and ruin. Are we not the Creator's handiwork? Think about it. Where is equality in birth? What becomes of fairness in life? Consider this tragedy. How many children will perish because Vanessa will never become a pediatrician?"

Neil interrupted the stranger's diatribe. "When did you meet Vanessa Flack?"

Still staring ahead, the stranger said, "Unfortunately, I never had the pleasure."

Neil circled around to face him. "Unfortunately suggests regret. What do you regret, sir? Not meeting Vanessa or something else?"

"Every person lives with regret." He had yet to make eye contact with Neil. "My *one* regret so far is being unable to fulfill a specific undertaking."

Neil caught the emphasis. "One?"

"One taunts me."

"And prods you to do what?"

The stranger shifted his eyes. They locked onto Neil's in a frigid gaze. "Expose secrets."

****

Chief Fleishman lowered the corner of the sheet covering Vanessa Flack's body. He crossed the barnyard to where Neil stood.

The retired naval officer lifted the tape. Neil scooted under it. "Thanks for coming out on a Saturday evening, Padre. I hated to interrupt your sermon prep time, but I've seen nothing like this. Not even the day a band of pirates intercepted one of our transports."

"Where is the family?"

"They're at the station. That's not why I called you. I need your input here. Detective Darren Huber will handle the case. I don't know if you've met him or not. Anyway, what we have I hate to admit, is way above us and I want to keep this local. I prefer not to call in the GBI."

I need your input here. Input had nothing to do with Neil's status at the church. The chief wanted expertise from someone capable and willing to offer assistance. Neil held a master's degree in forensics with minors in art and theology. He spun and headed to his car.

The chief called after him, "One look, Neil. That's all I'm asking."

Neil paused half-turned. "Why?"

"We're sunk with this case if we don't solve it. The city council has already threatened to take away two positions despite the town's growth. If we bungle this investigation, they'll bare-bones the department. Give me something to work off of."

"Nothing more?"

The chief raised his right hand. "That's it."

"Show me."

"We've charted a path to minimize contamination. Follow me."

The chief waded across a thick stand of fescue in need of mowing. A hint of women's cologne wafted in his wake. He circled the covered corpse.

"Who found the body?"

"I was the closest, so I responded to the dispatch. The complainant wasn't here. We had to hunt him down."

"Who reported it?"

"Chad Stoltz."

"You think he's involved?"

"Officers found him curled up in the corner of his bedroom shaking like it was thirty below zero. When they got him calm enough to understand his jabber, he told us a story that I find impossible to believe. Right now, he's our number one suspect. He's the last known person to have seen her alive."

"Where?"

"The church parking lot. He gave a story about some theatrical performance they had in the works."

Mutilation described what Neil Caldera saw when the chief held up the side of the sheet facing the barn. Supine, the torso sliced in diagonal ribbons, thighs split midline to the knees. Arms dislocated at the elbows, angled upward with hands, palms up, underneath the head. Faint bruises discolored wrists and ankles. Perimortem bruises crossed the armpits. No injury above the shoulders. Her hair was dry.

Neil gazed into Vanessa's death stare. Guilt showed him the young woman dead on a New York Street after he killed her. He mouthed, "I'm sorry." No apology ever relieved his agony.

"What kind of deviant are we dealing with here, Neil?"

"An attention-getting monster." He offered no further details. In his opinion, anyone who deprived a person of life in the manner committed against Vanessa Flack existed outside the realm of mercy and deserved swift justice and exact punishment.

"Who should we be looking for?"

He studied the injury patterns. "This is a crime of passion. It was personal. Vanessa knew her killer."

"How could somebody not notice them? Chad claimed to have discovered her in the barn. The body was here."

"Blood should have saturated the ground based on the amount of blood loss. The ground shows no evidence of vegetation trampled on or misdirected from someone dragging the corpse and leaving it here."

"That's quite an astute observation, Padre."

"Somebody washed Vanessa's body and wrapped her in something to transport her. See the faint lividity pattern on her shoulder? At some point she was semi-prone. Blood pooled beneath the skin. The killer repositioned Vanessa on her back in this open display. Have you checked the barn?"

The chief gave a look of disbelief. "Where have you been since you left the bar and grill? Yeah, I heard. Huber told me what you did. It was rash for you to get involved with two armed thugs. We could be working two murders."

"You ask for my help and then treat me as if I am a suspect?"

"In the time I've known you, I've never heard you say anything I thought to be untrue or misleading."

Fleishman motioned to the body. "Does this not repulse you?"

"What's in the barn, Rob?"

Rob jabbed a finger toward the barn. "Forget the barn. You knew Vanessa. You know her family. You're supposed to be their spiritual leader. Where's your empathy?"

"Compassion exists in a person's heart even though it's not expressed in every circumstance. Mine gets trampled when I see things like this. Look at it this way. Vanessa was God's child. A malevolent person desecrated her. No matter how my reaction to her demise may appear to you or anyone else, this murder scene is not a place for empathy. You want justice. I want to see the responsible party pay for this atrocity. What do you say we cease with this nonsense and focus on why we're here?"

"You're right. It's just…This thing's gotten to me."

"This? Or Tess?"

The chief bowed and bobbed his head. "It's Tess. I took her to the oncologist for chemo yesterday afternoon. She refused to allow me to go in with her, again. I only know what she's told me because I've never been allowed in the exam room with her for any of her appointments. Her doctor won't discuss anything with me because of doctor-patient confidentiality. They won't do any more treatments according to her. They claim the leukemia is too far advanced. I might think she was lying to me except for the obvious symptoms. Now I have this to deal with."

"You discovered something in the barn, didn't you? Was she killed in there?"

Fleishman looked toward the barn. "I told you

Huber is working on it. How about we do our jobs, Caldera? Let Huber do his."

Neil rose to his feet. He stood motionless while he stared at the double doors. He pictured the blood-portrait beyond.

"You asked for my opinion, Chief. I offered my thoughts."

"Yeah, okay. There is one more thing."

"What's that?"

"Stay away from Chad Stoltz."

Chapter 5

Neil sat in his car and studied the swarm outside the crime scene tape. Onlookers who remained included a few stragglers and the media. The well-dressed man was not among them.

Neil thought the man looked out of his element. New Englanders visited Atlanta or passed through there on their way to Florida. Not here. Not in Madison. Once named the number one Small Town in America, the historic town sits sixty miles east of Atlanta. People from around the world visited Madison to see the hundred-plus antebellum homes. Neil concluded the well-dressed stranger was not a tourist. The chat he had with the stranger stimulated Neil's curiosity. He vowed to learn the man's identity and his purpose for being here.

The door hinges squawked when he pushed the door open. He headed straight to the uniformed sergeant who had photographed the scene. Thirty-seven-year-old Sloane Azevedo leaned on the back quarter panel of the department's crime scene SUV. She had her elbows tucked to her sides. Her right thumb scrolled through photos on the camera's screen. Her black hair coiled on the back of her head.

Neil leaned on the SUV next to her. "I need a favor." Sloane's shoulders came near to his. She did not hide the screen as she continued to scroll through her photos. Eyes peered at the pictures through black-rimmed glasses on a slender nose.

"Will this favor lead to any chance of intimacy?"

"I want a copy of your photos."

"You know I can't do that." Seven or eight photos of the painted image flitted by. Sloane acted as though she noticed none of them.

"I just want the ones showing the onlookers."

Sloane turned to face him. Out of the Madison Police officers he'd met during his fifteen months stint in Madison, he trusted her. Her smile unlocked his heart. Unlike Tess Fleishman, Sloane Azevedo was single. Her accent suggested she had lived somewhere in the upper Midwest.

"I got plenty of those. Discreet-like, you know. Just in case the perp showed up. Those I can let you have."

"How long?"

Sloane leaned rightward and touched her shoulder to his left upper arm. "For you, give me an hour. I'm about to head to the station. I'll copy the ones you want to a flash drive and leave it at the front desk."

"No need to leave it. I'm on my way there to meet with the Flacks. Let me know when they're ready and I'll stop by your office on my way out."

"And then?"

"I'm going home."

"How about coffee?"

"How about we do lunch tomorrow?"

"Will this be a social lunch or a working lunch?"

"We could make it both if that is a stipulation."

"I have one condition. We limit work to twenty percent of the time, or less."

"I'm for less."

Sloane kissed his cheek. "I'll see you at the station."

The awareness of her kiss lingered on his skin minutes after the warmth faded.

****

The Madison Police Station on North Main Street employed fifteen sworn officers to cover the nine square miles within the city limits. In a city where the annual homicide rate is 0.25 per every one thousand residents, Vanessa's murder rattled the townspeople.

The trauma to her body indicated a crime of passion by someone she knew, not stranger-to-stranger. The killer murdered her in the barn based on the amount of blood present in the stall. He or she used blood to paint the image on the barn wall and then placed Vanessa's body where someone could discover it. Time spent at the scene defined the killer's comfort level there.

Neil believed this was only the beginning. The cause of death by sharp force convinced him of more to come. Superficial slices increased in depth based on the injury patterns. The manner in which the killer inflicted the injuries assured prolonged pain and suffering. When finished, they basked in their success. Their focus extended beyond the deed and fulfillment drove them to feed on that contentment.

He parked in front of Bank of Madison on North Main, crossed the three lanes void of traffic and crossed High Street to the police station. An officer Neil knew only by sight ushered him to an office where Bob and Juanita Flack sat with their fourteen-year-old son, Zachary.

Face grim, Bob Flack got to his feet and extended

his hand. They shook. He held on several seconds. "They won't tell us anything other than Vanessa's been killed."

"There's no more I can add, Bob," Neil said.

"Did she suffer much?" Juanita said. Her eyes were teary and reddened. Her hair looked as though she combed it with her fingers.

In reality, yes, Vanessa Flack experienced immense conscious pain and suffering, although Neil dared not speak of it.

"It's difficult to define how long, Juanita. We should wait for the autopsy."

"But you saw her. You should be able to tell us something."

"Take comfort in knowing Vanessa is in a place where pain does not exist. She would want you to know she's at peace."

"I just hope they catch who did it," Zachary said. "I want them to die the same way she did."

"That's enough of that," Bob said to his son. "We want him caught and punished but that punishment will be up to the courts."

"Yeah, then maybe he'll rot in prison or somebody will shank him."

"Zachary," Juanita said.

"Okay. I was just saying."

"I think we should head on home," Bob said. To Neil, "Thanks for coming, Preacher. And thanks for your prayers. It comforts us knowing she's in Heaven." They again shook hands.

Neil said goodnight to Bob, Juanita, and Zachary. He stopped by Sloane's office to pick up the flash drive. The overhead florescent lights were off. The corridor lights brightened the ten-by-ten room more than did the computer screen on her desk extension. The screen angled away from the door.

Sloane sat hunched forward with her chin on laced fingers a foot away from the monitor. Light emitted from the screen colored her copper skin an Avatar blue.

"Close the door. I want you to see something." Only her mouth moved.

He rounded the desk hoping to see a photo of the crowd and getting an enhanced view of the stranger. The photo displayed on the screen was one Sloane had taken at the crime scene, but not of the stranger. He dropped to one knee, propped his left forearm on the desk, leaned forward, and gazed at a photo of the likeness painted on the barn wall.

Sloane leaned back in her chair until her left scapula touched his right shoulder. Her fingers remained laced as she lowered her hands to her lap.

"What are your thoughts?" He detected the fragrance of citrus body wash or lotion.

"It's good. There's no doubt who it's supposed to be. You need protection, Neil." She called him by his given name and not by his title. That was the first time since they met more than a year ago.

"I have protection."

"You carry. I know. Glock or S&W?"

He said nothing.

Sloane swiveled a quarter-turn leftward in her chair. She unlaced her fingers and laid her right hand on his left. Shadow darkened the left half of her face. The right side remained blue in the screen's light. "Whichever one, I know you know how to use it."

"How could you know?"

She lowered her voice. "You're not a cop anymore, Neil. You are a civilian and you need our protection."

He stared at the mockery of his likeness on the screen.

She continued. "NYPD. Thirteen years. Rank of detective, a gold shield until two years ago."

"How long have you known?"

"Two weeks after we first met."

"You ran a check on me?"

"No. I phoned a contact I have in New York. She told me everything I wanted to know. She said I should trust you. Not could, but should. She stressed that point."

"This friend, is she on the job?"

"FBI. She and her partner investigated the shooting on their end."

"What prompted you to call her?"

"You did."

"Me?"

"The day we met I sensed it about you. I figured you came here from the northeast. We have a way about us no one on the outside can ever figure out. Civilians have no idea what it's like to work in law enforcement. There's no way they could ever understand the bond that binds us together. New York, LA, Chicago, and every other city and town we are an extended family. Those thoughts of you played over and over in my mind until I had to make the call to find out for myself. From what my friend said, you had no choice in the matter. It was either shoot or be shot. The unfortunate result was the young woman's death."

"Who else knows?"

"Nobody. I've locked it away in a safe place." She

touched her chest. "Not even an autopsy will wrench it out of me."

"That means a lot."

"That. Or me?"

"Both," he said without pause. Sloane captivated him with her presence.

"Good. And I'm glad you didn't have to think about your answer. That means a lot to me."

"Like you said. That or me?"

"You." She pulled a flash drive out of one port in the CPU. "I copied the photos you wanted on this. I added a few others." She motioned to the image displayed on the monitor.

"I want to ask you about the detective assigned to the case."

"Darren Huber."

"Never met him."

"You know those detectives who never get in the limelight, but have the knack of solving the complex cases? That's Huber."

"So, he's okay."

"Yeah. He's okay."

Neil pushed to his feet and pocketed the USB stick. "One more thing. How long have you worked for Madison PD?"

"Three years, why?"

"I believe you worked for another agency before coming here. Am I correct?"

"Yes. Chicago PD for nine years."

"Then you know this killer's just getting started. Every detail displays meticulous behavior."

"I got the same feeling when I saw the body."

****

Vanessa Flack's murder added another weight on Neil's guilt. He trudged through the side door of his home leading into the kitchen at five minutes past two. He let the keys fall from his hand onto the counter and tugged open the refrigerator door. Nothing appealed to him. He closed the door and turned away.

Neil pulled out his shirttail on the way to the den. This was his place of refuge from a world of clamor and turmoil. The oversized leather chair supported his hundred-eighty pounds with a cool wraparound welcome. He thrust off his shoes one at a time and slid them aside with his right foot. He reached for the remote control among a variety of reading materials on an end table to the right of the chair. Novels by Child, Koontz, and the latest by Lisa Gardner took up part of the room on the thirty-by-twenty-four-inch table. They lay there for whenever he finished the Alex Cross novel sitting next to his laptop.

He aimed the remote at the TV and pressed the button. A beep signifying the set was on preceded the scene of the Wicked Witch of the West taunting Dorothy Gale after the house landed on the witch's sister. Dorothy's mannerisms and response to the threat made against her reminded him somewhat of Vanessa Flack.

His mind drifted away from the movie and wove through memories of Vanessa. From the first moment he'd met the Flack family, Neil had taken notice of Vanessa's spiritedness and her servant's heart. That desire to serve led her on the path toward medicine. Evil ruined her chance to make differences in children's lives. Malevolence sent her on the way to a stainless-steel table at the GBI morgue on Panthersville Road.

Chief of Police Rob Fleishman warned him to stay away from Chad Stoltz.

Why?

The chief had refused to let him go into the barn.

Maybe the refusal was to prevent further contamination of the scene. Crime scenes were nothing new to Neil. He knew how to exercise care and protect against spoiling any evidence within the confines of the affected areas. Of course, Chief Fleishman possessed no knowledge of Neil's credentials beyond the classroom. No one in Madison knew of them. He wanted to keep it that way.

Instinct prompted otherwise. Lumps in the chair's cushion irritated his legs. The coolness of its leather turned warm and uncomfortable. Neil tried to push Rob Fleishman's demeanor at the crime scene out of his thoughts. The chief wanted him to stay away. The man's behavior in the past couple months betrayed Neil's trust in him as police chief. This was not political. In his opinion, Rob Fleishman was hiding something beyond the infidelity to which Tess hinted. Neil sensed it and determined to do everything within reason to find out what.

He needed to have a look inside the barn—tonight. Tomorrow might be too late.

****

Light diffused on the wall above the headboard in the bedroom shared by Rob and Tess Fleishman. Tess turned to her left side when the car's engine died. Red 4:11 displayed on the clock catty-corner on the nightstand on her side of the bed. She stared at the numbers until the eleven became twelve.

The side door opened and closed. Feet slogged on

the carpet in the hall to the bedroom door. The bottom of the door burbled on the carpet when it swung into the room. Tess closed her eyes. She felt the mattress quiver beneath her. The bi-fold door to the closet shrieked in the tracks. A boot clomped to the floor. The other one dropped three seconds later.

"Where have you been?"

"We had a homicide," Rob whispered.

"Bad?"

"Yeah. I asked Neil Caldera for his input. He'll be consulting on the case. I'm going to take a shower."

Take your shower, Mr. Indifference. Wash off her scent while you're at it.

The gap in their lives widened soon after she told him the doctor diagnosed her with leukemia. They once shared adventures all over the world while in the Navy. He served as a Chief Warrant Officer Five. She performed the duties of Lieutenant Junior Grade. Now, three years later, she sat alone most evenings in their humble abode while Rob tended to the job or whatever else prioritized his agenda. His efforts certainly weren't directed toward her.

Eight months ago, her thoughts turned to how she might convince Neil Caldera to be with her. Unlike Rob, Neil expressed genuine concern after she declared the leukemia diagnosis.

Water sprayed in the shower. She imagined Neil in there, her joining him and him getting in bed with her afterward. She glided her right hand between her thighs. In her mind, Neil's body merged with hers.

She determined to make it happen.

****

A segment of yellow crime-scene ribbon remained

tied to the corner fence post. The two-foot piece extended from the knot whished in the breeze. How had the police conducted their investigation out here and inside the barn in four hours? Were they thorough in their task? Did they collect every possible thread of evidence? He guessed not.

As Neil neared the barn doors, a breeze brought with it the smells of age and dampness mingled with the acridness of blood. He paused to inspect the depression in the vegetation between the structure and the street where Vanessa's body had been and to make certain no one noticed him before going inside. Flies and yellow jackets converged on soil and blades of grass dampened by blood.

He stepped into the barn. The eeriness of the blue luminescence crept around him from the section of wall bearing the portrait. He turned his head to face the wall. What he saw filled him with aversion. The chemical reagent used to detect blood, unseen when he first saw the likeness, now made the portrayal appear demon-like.

And alive.

A swish-swish of fabric broke the silence. Neil stilled and listened. Noise-induced hearing loss in his left ear hampered his ability to hear compared to fifteen years ago when he could pick up on the slightest sounds. A groan confirmed his suspicion. Somebody lurked outside the barn.

He tiptoed to the front of the barn and peered out between slats in the wall. A person meandered from the post with a remnant of police ribbon on it to where the body had lain. Lack of sufficient light prohibited Neil from identifying the visitor. Features and gait suggested a young adult male.

Every time he reached the spot in the grass where Vanessa Flack's body had lain, he held his right hand out in front of him, fingers clutched in a fist. He opened the hand and ogled at whatever lay in his palm. After five to ten seconds, he closed his fingers over the object, about-faced, and trudged again to the pole.

At the pole, the male swatted the loose end of the ribbon, turned his back to it, and dropped to the ground. He pulled his feet under crossed legs and hunched forward.

Neil exited the barn through the rear door and skulked behind the male. His knees popped as he squatted next to the post.

Chad Stoltz craned his neck but did not make eye contact. "I told you. They think I killed her. The police believe I killed Vanessa."

"How did you know I was here?"

"I saw you when you came out of your house."

"Why were you there?"

"I needed to talk to somebody."

"You followed me?"

"No. I hung around your house thinking maybe you had gone to the store and would be back in a few minutes. Then we could chat. When you didn't come back home, I went to the store and asked the woman if you'd been there. She told me she hadn't seen you. I bought a cola and came here."

"Where is your car?"

"I parked it over on the next street in a buddy-of-mine's yard." Chad lifted his head and looked at Neil. "I had to come back, Mr. Caldera. The police think *I'm* involved in Vanessa's death."

Chad might have answered truthfully to *Are you?* but Neil let wisdom and experience guide him in a more suitable approach. "Have they questioned you?"

"I saw the way the chief and that detective looked at me. They kept watching me. They kept whispering to each other and nodding toward me."

"Do you think they were directing their conversation toward you?"

"I'm sure of it. Why else would they act that way? They will try to pin this on me. I just know it."

"Not necessarily, Chad. You have to know the mindset of law enforcement officers to have any idea what their thinking is. They're not out to get people the way many people think they are. Of course, you might run into one now and then that is gung-ho and acts like he's God's gift to law enforcement. Strut around with an attitude because they pin on a badge and strap on a gun every day. But those are the exceptions. The best advice I can offer is stay out of their way and if you get involved with one, keep a cool head and your mouth shut."

Chad rolled over onto his knees, pulled his right leg from under him, planted the foot, and leaned forward. "I need to go."

Chapter 6

The pendulum clock on the mantel displayed five fifteen when Neil closed and locked the front door. He went to the refrigerator and took out a bottle of cranberry juice. He chose a package of ham, cheddar, mayo, and mustard and made a sandwich. He changed into lounge wear while he ate and then dropped in the worn chair, shifted to get comfortable on the lumps and reached for his laptop.

Once the computer booted, he typed his password and inserted the USB drive. He opened the folder Sloane copied the photos to and pulled up nine photos of the onlookers. He enlarged them and scrolled from image to image. The fifth picture showed the stranger off to the left.

Neil clicked the pad and zoomed in on the stranger's face until it filled the thirteen-inch screen. He enhanced the photo for clarity. Something about the man's features looked somewhat familiar, but he could not pinpoint which part. Was it the eyes or the nose and lips? Perhaps it was a combination of eyes and nose or lips and shape of face. The longer he studied them the more the features blended and blurred.

A snort startled him awake. He jerked and focused on his surroundings. The computer screen showed sleep mode. The hands on the clock pointed to one and seven. Neil removed the flash drive and shut down the computer. It was time for him to shower and dress for church. He wanted to look his best for his lunch date after the service.

****

Sloane Azevedo waited for Neil on the brick steps in front of the church. This morning was the first time he had seen her in a dress and heels. Her hair streamed below her shoulders and melted into her black sheath dress accented with a string of pearls and skinny whipstitch black leather and chain belt. Her presence and smile boosted his spirit.

"You look amazing. All this for me?"

"I just put on a dress and heels."

"It's more than the dress, Sloane. I sense envy from here. Where shall we go?"

"Chophouse Grille. Town 220 closes on Sunday or I would have taken you there. I've reserved a table for us."

Sloane hooked her right arm around his left when the last of the attendees drove away. "Shall we?" She held out her left hand. A ring of keys lay in her palm.

Neil took the keys and walked her to a black Jaguar F-Type coupe. She kept her arm around his and led him to the passenger side where she waited for him to open the door. He rounded to the driver's side, got in, and fired up the engine. The 296 horse-power, two-liter-turbo engine droned under the hood until Neil shifted and pressed the accelerator. The Jaguar lurched forward. The G-forces pressed him to the seat back. He steered out the exit onto Bethany in two seconds.

"The power reminds me of a police interceptor."

"Wait 'til you get it on the interstate."

They followed East Washington, took a left on

Hancock, right at Burnett, and left into the parking lot. Sloane waited for Neil to get out before she opened her door. He tracked around the back and took her hand held up to him. She swung her legs out and tugged upward.

"You know people will talk," she said. "Almost everybody here knows one or both of us."

He glanced at the vehicles in the lot. Three of them belonged to attendees of the church. "We'll sit across from each other. Let them make assumptions. I will not let potential gossip stop me from getting what I want."

"What do you want, Neil?"

"A confession. Straight-forward truth out of the heart."

She smiled. "Where's the confessional?"

"Wherever we want it to be when we find the deviant responsible for Vanessa's death."

"I'm in."

The Madison Chophouse Grille on South Main Street ranked among the top eateries in Madison. Neil trailed Sloane who followed a twenty-one-year-old server to his section along a bank of windows. Diners at five tables acknowledged Sloane. Two stared at Neil. She sat where she could see the entrance. They knew what they wanted; the Hawaiian chicken for her while he selected the meatloaf. The server hurried away to the kitchen.

"That was a livid stare that woman gave you. Wonder what's up with that?" she said.

"Who knows? I've never seen her before."

The fortyish woman twisted her torso and glared from the middle section as though she read their minds and disapproved of their thoughts. Sloane waved to her.

The woman huffed. Her red hair whipped right-to-left on her back when she unwound to face the party with her. Her fingers signed nonstop for the next ten seconds. The woman on the other side shrugged.

Neil ignored her. The esprit de corps he found in Sloan bested any in his thirteen years on and off the job in New York. Prudish aura posed no threat to him or Sloane beyond any gossip the woman might utter.

Sloane said, "That's Nadine Thorne. She works at City Hall. I'll handle any potential fallout."

"You have my endorsement. We'll all be better off if I stay out of it. I'd torque her frame of mind with a few to-the-point comments."

The redhead craned her neck and peered over her shoulder. Sloan repeated her wave. The woman seated at the table with Nadine waved.

"The brunette is a sweetheart of a lady who clerks at the courthouse. Did you look at the pictures?"

"I fell asleep."

The server set two glasses of water and napkin-wrapped silverware on the table. "Your entrees will be ready shortly," he said and whisked to another table.

"I should sit next to you. It's too loud in here to discuss anything across the table."

Neil tilted his head to the other table. "You'd miss all the action."

"My action is here." She grinned and swapped chairs to one on his left. "I'll give her something to talk about." She laid her right hand, palm up, on the table. He followed her lead, took her hand, and kissed Sloane's cheek.

They smiled when the redhead spouted, "Did you see that?"

"It worked." Sloane sipped her water.

"Maybe now she'll keep her prying eyes to herself."

"That's not what I meant."

"I couldn't resist the appeal."

The server arrived with their entrées. Neil let go of her hand and the server set the two plates on the table. The merger of chicken and pineapple wafted a sweet-grilled aroma. Neil looked at the meatloaf in contrast. "I should have gotten the chicken. It even smells delicious."

"That's no problem." Sloan forked one side of the breast and sliced through the middle. She separated the two halves on her plate. She picked up his knife, cut off a third of the meatloaf, transferred it to her plate, and put half of the chicken on his. "Now we're even."

"I like the way you seem to think of everything. Do you explore all your options that way?"

"Pretty much. I'll let you know when I decide."

The buzz in the dining room diminished to a hum by the time they finished their meal. Latecomers filled five available tables.

Neil dabbed his lips with the napkin and dropped it on his plate. He ordered two cups of coffee and after the server walked away, said, "Tell me your thoughts on the photos. We can stay here and talk or somewhere else."

"I have a place picked out. I will have to change into more appropriate clothes before we go. I'd advise you do the same. Anything you don't mind getting dirty."

"Dirty?"

"We might encounter a little grime."

Chapter 7

Neil followed a long driveway off Doster Road to an antebellum manor painted white with black shutters. Azaleas, gardenias and an array of wildflowers accented an immaculate St. Augustine sod.

"Nice place." He pushed out of the car and scanned 360 degrees at the forest of long-needle pines and mixed hardwoods surrounding the mansion.

"It belongs to my aunt. She lives in West Palm Beach most of the year. For now, I have it all to myself. The house, a barn, and a hundred eighty acres to roam around on whenever I want. Come on in. I'll be ready in five minutes."

That explained the car. No way could anyone afford the Jaguar she drove on a small-town police officer's salary. They strode side by side along a four-foot-wide stone walkway and up the ten-foot-wide steps to a massive twelve-by-fifty porch and walnut entry door. Neil waited in the parlor while Sloan went upstairs.

Five minutes later she skipped down the stairs outfitted in a long-sleeve denim shirt with Skylark Ranch embroidered above the left breast pocket, a pair of faded jeans and cordovan western boots.

"How do I look?"

"Like you stepped out of *Elle* onto the cover of *Cowboys and Indians*, sans the hat."

"I have some of those, too."

"Some?"

"Three. Black, white, and brown. Stetsons." She picked up a laptop case and handed it off to him. "We'll need this."

Neil stopped by his three-bedroom cottage on Maxeys and changed into jeans, a charcoal long-sleeve T-shirt, and hiking boots.

Back in the Jaguar, he said, "Where to?"

"I-20 West to the Rutledge exit."

Neil took the Jag up to ninety for the first five miles they were on the highway. Much better than his Acura, which, he thought, could climb to eighty-five without blowing its engine. Within fifteen minutes they reached Hard Labor Creek State Park where 5,408 acres and twenty-four miles of trails for hikers and horse riders intertwined beauty and history.

Neil parked the Jaguar at the stables marked with the number eleven. A park employee brought out two brown and white horses, saddled and awaiting riders.

"You can ride," she said, not a question.

"The American Paint Horse. You bet I can ride." He broke his stare over the hood long enough to look at her. "Your aunt's?"

"They belong to a friend. I buy a bucket of feed for each of them once a month and I ride whenever I want. We'll have plenty of privacy from prying eyes out here and no eavesdroppers."

She hooked the strap to her laptop case over the saddle horn, inserted her left foot in the stirrup, and heaved herself onto the saddle.

"Okay. Show me how you do it," she said.

He repeated her action and settled on the saddle.

He tugged the right strap. The horse rotated and stopped alongside her, facing the opposite direction. He pulled on the reins and nudged the horse with his heels. The steed backed, swung leftward and forward to the mare's right side.

"Six months on mounted patrol," he said.

"Then I guess you're ready."

The horses trotted toward the trail head. Once there, they slowed to a side-by-side amble. Sloane rode to his left and headed up the path amidst birds' chirps and flutters in the canopy of massive hardwood trees.

"I enjoy the outdoors," she said. "Every time I need to get away I either come here or wander around on my aunt's property. Sometimes I'll take a quilt and lie out there for hours listening to quietness unavailable to those in the city. I've seen various species of birds at different times of the year and even watched whitetail bucks grow massive antlers from April through August. It's one of those experiences everybody should enjoy, including you."

"I'd like that."

"We'll stop up ahead and look at the photos."

Neil looped the horses' reins around a tree limb and sat down next to Sloane on a fallen tree. Sloane booted the computer open on her lap, entered her password, and selected the file. She browsed through the thumbnails and clicked on the portrait. The .jpg image came up in a new window.

"This one shows the best details."

"May I?" Neil held out his hands. She slid the laptop to where it rested on her right thigh and his left.

Neil zoomed in the image and examined its brush marks. His knowledge of fine art provided an advantage over a non-trained eye. One way to spot amateur from professional technique was by the consistency of long or short brush strokes, the structural signature. He hunched and studied the painting. He found it difficult to concentrate. The screen reflected her features. The breeze flicked her hair across his cheek and he inhaled her unique scent every time he took a breath.

"Deductions? Opinions?" she asked.

"Nothing yet." *Yeah. Your proximity is not conducive to progress.*

He closed his eyes and opened them after five seconds. Studied for fifteen seconds, motioned to the left side of the portrait, and said, "These brush strokes along here arc downward and have a right-to-left origin. That signifies the artist is right-handed. Did anybody take measurements of this?"

"Not that I'm aware of. I'll check to be sure."

"Measurements will help but we can make it work without them if we can measure the barn wall. When we know its height, we can use photogrammetry to figure out the killer's height."

"I've heard of photogrammetry, but mainly for crash reconstruction. How will it apply to this?"

"It's similar in principle to blood spatter analysis where an investigator examines patterns to determine directionality and height of the assailant and length of instrument used as a weapon. If the upper part of the portrait extended higher than the artist's height, you will notice a difference in the brush strokes—"

"Unless he used something to stand on."

"Yes, considering that caveat. The lower section will exhibit a mirrored difference, given he or she stooped and did not kneel or sit."

Sloane crooked her neck to face him. "You seem to know your stuff pretty well." He turned his head to answer. The limbal ring enhanced her blue-green eyes. "Do you have the wherewithal to restrain yourself with me this close to you?" She leaned to within two inches and closed her eyes.

The answer came when Neil put his left hand on her back an inch above her jeans. She opened her eyes, touched his face, and drew his lips to hers. Her kiss was soft. Warm. Dewy. The forest stilled the moment he ran his fingers through her hair after she rested her head on his shoulder. No breeze. No chirps. Silence except for the whisk of fabric and breaths inhaled and exhaled. One horse whinnied and tossed its head.

Their lips parted, but only long enough for Sloane to swing her legs on the other side of the log and him to set aside the laptop. They embraced, closer than before. The second kiss firm and long. She moaned, slid her lips across his cheek, and nuzzled his neck.

"I've waited on this for a long time," she said.

"It sounded like the horse approved."

She straightened. "What about you?"

"Me, too."

****

The fresh air in the Piedmont region of Georgia included one major downside for Neil. Pollen and dander from the area's flora and fauna stormed him. Never had he encountered anything like it in New York. His eyes itched. Hot tears glazed them. The mucous membranes in his nasal passages swelled and made it difficult to breathe through his nose. Transition from shadow to sunlight made it noticeable.

When Sloane rounded the door to get in the car,

she saw him rub his eyes. His cheeks were damp. She waited until they were in the car before she asked him about it.

"Allergies," he said. "It started last spring."

"It's the pollen. I have some allergy medicine at home if you want to come over. It helps me."

"It's mostly itchy, watery eyes. I have some eye drops."

She looked at him. "You're welcome to come. I have no plans to do anything the rest of the day."

A tone signified a text message received on his phone. He pulled the phone from its holster on his belt and handed it to Sloane. "Will you read this for me so I don't have to pull over?" He gave the code to her and turned east on Atlanta Highway headed back to Madison.

She put in the four-digit code and read,

—*Need to see you. Seven thirty tonight. Camp Rut.*—

"Who's it from?"

"It shows a number, no name."

"Text back and ask. What is camp rut?"

"Camp Rutledge," she said while she typed a response. "Where we just left."

The sender replied. "It's Chad," she said.

"Tell him I'll be there."

She handed the phone to him. He said, "Fleishman ordered me to stay away from Chad. He was adamant about it. I believe he wants me to think Chad committed the murder."

"And you don't believe he did."

"No. There's always the possibility. It's too early to rule out anyone. You've been on the job long enough to know anything's possible. Nothing I've seen points to Chad as being involved. A skilled artist painted that image. It wasn't Chad."

Sloane said nothing.

Road noise off the tires and the occasional whoosh of a vehicle passing by them from the opposite direction remained the only sounds until Neil slowed to turn right onto Crawford Street to cut through to East Washington.

"I agree about the artist. What I'd like to know is why the chief said that to you about Chad. If he suspects him, it's news to me. Nobody mentioned Chad's name while I was at the scene and I saw nothing in the paperwork afterward."

"Off the record?"

"Okay. Off the record."

"Chad was at the barn before they knew of the murder."

"How do you know?"

"He called me."

"What did he say?"

"He stammered his words, said somebody had to be dead, that there was blood everywhere. He told me he needed me to come there."

"What did you tell him?"

"I told him I would and did. He was outside the barn waiting on me. He trembled so he could barely stand. He pointed to the barn, said 'In there' and refused to go in with me."

"You went inside."

"Yes. I saw blood in one stall. A lot. And the image painted on the wall near the back. When I got back out there with Chad, he told me the painting looked like me. Then he said he knew what I had done; about me killing that girl."

"The one in New York?"

"Yes."

"And?"

"I asked him not to mention it to anyone until we discussed it later. I also told him to not tell anyone he was at the barn. He agreed to both."

"You believe him?"

"I haven't decided. I guess we'll find out soon enough."

"We?"

"I trust you to have my back."

"I'll agree on my terms."

"What?"

"I go with you to meet with Chad after you spend the rest of today with me."

"First, we're going to the barn."

****

Chad Stoltz crisscrossed the garage for the umpteenth time, hands pressed to his head, elbows out. Neil Caldera's answer brought little relief to his anxiety. The head-high sketch drawn on the rear wall above the work bench stared back at him as if he were standing in front of a mirror. It looked like his face with blood smeared on it. He dared not touch this one.

The camera on his cellphone captured the image and displayed it on the screen with creepy lifelike portrayal. The phone quavered in his hands. He snapped seven more at different angles; had to reshoot three because they were out of focus.

When he finished, Chad pocketed the camera and looked for something to cover the sketch. He found an old section of corkboard his dad cut from the piece he attached to the wall to hold tools. The board covered all but a one-inch loop at the chin. Two boxes of motor oil stacked one on top of the other covered it to his satisfaction.

He sat on the concrete floor just inside the shadow line. The mid-afternoon sun inched the edge closer to his crossed ankles. He leaned rearward and rested on his hands, arms used as support angled from shoulders to garage floor. He stared out the open front, down the river-rock driveway, across the asphalt road to nothing in particular.

Sunlight crept up the soles of his tennis shoes. The contrast of light and shadow held his stare. The heat crawled up to his toes and spilled over onto his shins. Hot shackles clamped his legs. His scalp tingled. Face flushed. Jitters snapped him out of the trance when the uneasiness drained into his chest and pooled in his stomach. He jerked around. Nobody loomed behind him. The corkboard and boxes remained in place over the portrait. The sight had branded the image in his mind. No way to erase it. The face faded in and overtook everything in sight.

The painting in the barn along with fear of potential blame for Vanessa's murder brought on insomnia. He was young enough to handle loss of sleep for a few nights. The possibility of jail and his likeness painted on the garage wall smeared more stress on his heart, mind, and soul.

A pain management physician prescribed meds to ease pain for injuries, but what about the torment on his psyche?

Chapter 8

Two massive oak trees shaded the barn from the rear. At heights greater than a hundred feet, their limbs extended outward and scraped the roof near its peak. Moss covered the ground under them out to the drip line.

Neil stood at the front corner while Sloane got a measuring tape out of a kit she maintained in the trunk of her Jaguar. He studied the ground around where the killer dumped Vanessa's body. He walked the thirty-four feet out from the corner of the barn, turned and surveyed lines of sight from there to the road; there to the barn door; and there to where Chad waited outside the barn on the night of the murder.

"She wasn't here," he said to Sloane when she walked over.

"What are you talking about? This is where they found her body. It's not like the killer tried to hide her. She was right there in plain sight."

"That's not what I'm saying. Vanessa's body wasn't there when I got here that evening to meet with Chad."

"It was dark, Neil. There are no streetlights. Maybe you just didn't notice it."

"No. Somebody dumped her body after I left here."

"Could be Chad. He was here. He could have killed her, hid the body, called you, and moved her after you left. There, clean as you could have it. Suspect on scene. The chief told us Chad stated he discovered the body in the barn. There's opportunity, and he possessed ability."

Neil shook his head. "Doesn't fit. He had no blood anywhere on his clothes or person."

"Maybe he wore coveralls and gloves and trashed them somewhere."

"I thought of that. His demeanor suggested otherwise. Killers possess a uniqueness unseen in any other criminal faction. You know that. You saw Vanessa's body. Chad doesn't have a killer's inimitability. Look. There, there and there." He showed the three line-of-sight points by his outstretched arm. "Three angles. Three points of view. From each angle, the probability of a body seen lying right there has to be near one hundred percent, even under a moon in its last quarter as we had that evening. I was much closer to this spot than the corner there. I'm certain the body was not present."

"That makes sense. We know someone moved her from inside the barn to out here. The evidence is consistent with her being attacked in the barn stall where we have all the blood and brought out here and dumped."

"True, but I believe there's more. The consistency of the blood observed in the stall exhibits too much dissimilarity to the ground out here."

"I agree," she said. "The blood in the stall had congealed more so than the blood out here."

"A drastic variance. If the body had been moved from in there to here, the blood in both places would show consistency in clotting."

"How long do you think?"

"Coagulation typically occurs in fifteen minutes. A single drop of blood will dry in sixty minutes at a temperature of sixty-eight degrees Fahrenheit. That varies depending on humidity and other factors. The blood in the stall most probably originated two to three hours before the body was found based on the liquidity of the blood out here."

"The killer took time to paint the face on the wall."

"A master could complete one that size in a matter of minutes."

Sloane shook her head. "Unbelievable. The ME said she had been dead two to four hours. If she wasn't in the barn and not out here, where was she?"

"Exactly."

"We have to broaden our search. It should be somewhere near this barn."

"Or the trunk of a car or truck bed," he said.

"Come on. Let's get those measurements and figure out how we need to do this."

Neil shoved his fingers between the vertical plank on the eight-foot door and the fixed board in the frame and tugged. The door gave way two inches and would not open any farther. "Something's holding it." He looked down at the bottom. No clump of vegetation or soil hampered outward movement. He tugged higher on the door. Same result. No binding at the top.

He took out his phone and pressed the app for the flashlight. He aimed the light through the opening between the door and the wall.

"We have to find another way in. It's locked from the inside."

"Can you see how?"

He shook his head, backed away, tilted his head back, and looked at the loft;, looked right and left and at Sloane. "I guess it's a good thing we changed clothes, huh?"

"Seems silly to bolt a door when all anybody has to do is yank off a few side boards to get in."

Neil agreed and three minutes later followed Sloane in through the side where the best option from potential onlookers provided cover.

He set two bales of hay side by side and stood on them. He put the tape up against the nine-foot wall. He measured twenty-seven inches from the upper end of the board to the crown of the portrait. At six-one and standing on the hay bale, the top of the painting was eye level. The angle, direction and the arc of the brush strokes confirmed his suspicion. The artist stood on the ground while he painted. Neil stepped off the bales, measured out from each side. The lowermost edge to the ground was thirty-eight inches. Then he measured the image at six points. The height was forty-three inches; width, thirty-three-and-three-quarter inches.

Sloane wrote the dimensions on a spiral-bound pad as he called them out to her.

She said, "It doesn't appear as pernicious as it did the other night. I'll admit it looks somewhat like you."

"Are you suggesting I have a harmful aura?"

She closed the tablet and touched his arm. "Not at all, Neil. It's just...well...that's what you might look like if you were the devil."

****

Sloane unlocked the front door of her home and pushed inside. Neil stepped in behind her and looked at himself in an antique mirror hung on the wall to the right.

"Do you believe that bloody façade is imagery of me or just a fluke?"

She closed the door and stepped to his side. Five seconds ticked by. She fluffed her hair. "We'd make a nice picture, don't you think?"

He stared at her mirrored image. "I'm serious, Sloane."

"So am I. Look at us." She cuddled up to him. "People will say we make a nice-looking couple."

"People will opine you're out of my league and have lost your mind."

He put his arm around her. He cherished their bond. In reality, he cared little about others' views of him, especially anything having to do with his and Sloan's budding relationship. No reason existed to sway any of them to his way of thinking beyond the church. That was his sense of duty to God and humanity. His philosophy favored action to words based on kindness shown to him and deeds he could do for others with one exception. No mercy for anyone who, by design, took the life of another.

"Something clicked in me when I met you. You can call it what you want, but it certainly wasn't a loss of mind. If anything, I became fully aware of life and its purpose."

"And what is that?"

"Right now, it is to get something to drink. I'm thirsty. Come on."

Sloane took two bottles of water out of the refrigerator, offered one to Neil, uncapped the other, and sipped.

He twisted off the cap, downed a third and set it on

the table.

"Hungry?" she asked.

"I could eat something."

She looked at the clock on the range; 6:02 displayed in green on a black background. "It's already after six. I'd cook if we had enough time."

"Another time. That will be a good reason for me to come back."

"You need me to cook for you to come see me?"

"Nope. I'd be here if you never did. I can pretty much eat anybody's meals. None have a personal connection with me."

"Good answer."

She reached into the refrigerator and came out with deli ham, turkey, Swiss cheese, a jar of mayonnaise and mustard.

"Will this suffice?"

"Perfect."

Sloane pulled a loaf of multi-grain bread out of a drawer under the microwave oven.

"Toasted?"

"Light."

She dropped four slices in the toaster, set the dial lighter on one side.

"Do you have any siblings?" Neil asked.

"I have a sister and two brothers. She is the oldest, and the smartest. She's an analyst for the FBI. My younger brothers broker real estate in Tennessee. You?"

"Three sisters."

"Ah, a house full of females."

"Diverse females: Norwegian, Indian and Japanese. Imagine growing up in our house."

"Wow. How often do you get to see them?"

"I've only seen them three times since I moved down here. They're in New York."

"What are their names?"

"Brita, Leya, and Shina. Brita is two years older than me. Leya is thirty-two and Shina's thirty."

"I'd like to meet them."

"Brita and her daughter will be here tomorrow or Tuesday. I'll take you to dinner with them."

"They won't mind?"

"They'll love you."

Toast aroma filled the kitchen. Two slices popped up.

"Those are yours. Mayo or mustard?"

"Both."

Neil put two slices of ham and a slice of turkey on the toast after she smeared mayonnaise and mustard on them. She dressed hers and he added a slice each of ham and turkey. With two bottles of apple juice in hand, he followed her to a fourteen-by-twenty glassed-in porch where he sat across from her at a round glass-top table. A ceiling fan whipped the air overhead.

"Why did you choose Madison, Georgia?" Sloane asked between bites. "A lot of places offer more suitable climates though none I believe display as much beauty in April and May."

"I received a phone call from Rob Fleishman within a month of my suspension. He told me someone here in town recommended me for the pastorate. I never learned who and Rob never said. To this day, I still don't know. My limited qualification never seemed in question. I flew down, met with Rob and the church committee. They took me on a tour of the town. When I saw the antebellum homes and immaculate landscape, I understood the importance of the visit. They wanted to hook me with scenery. It worked."

"Psychology of persuasion."

"I prefer to think of myself as a less amenable person."

Sloane pushed back her chair, circled behind him, and glided her hands over his shoulders and onto his chest. She bent forward, pressed her cheek to his, and whispered, "How inclined are you now?"

"Shall we dub it irresistible?"

She spun and sat on his lap. "How about fulfill and gratify?"

Chapter 9

At seven o'clock, Sloane and Neil took the right split at US Highways 278 and 441 in the Jaguar. He flicked down the visor and put on his sunglasses. He glanced at the rear-view mirror. A vehicle pulled crossways on the road at the split. Because of a rise in the landscape, he could see only the side windows and roof.

They followed 278 east for two miles when Neil observed an older model Toyota pickup in his rear-view mirror. The truck closed the distance between them even though Neil kept his speed steady at five miles an hour above the limit.

Sloane had her laptop open and her head tilted forward. She had no knowledge anyone tailed them until Neil stomped on the accelerator. The engine snarled. The Jaguar surged forward. The increased Gs forced Sloane into her seat back.

"What's that about?"

The Toyota stayed with them, closed to within three feet of the Jag's rear. "There's a pickup on our tail."

"Just slow down and let him pass."

"That's not his intent."

"How do you know?"

"Something to do with the pipe he's flailing out his window."

Sloane glanced at the side mirror and then craned her neck and looked over the seatback. "How long?"

"Three miles. He pulled out of a side street a half mile this side of the split."

"Maybe we should pull over."

"We have no choice. Look."

Two pickups angled across the highway, their right-and-left-front fenders spaced a foot apart at the yellow centerline. The sun loomed between their windshields. A slide-back tow truck tilted rightward on the shoulder. Its amber lights flashed.

"That's no crash," Sloane said. "There's no damage to either truck."

Neil slowed to thirty; twenty. The top of the truck in his lane blocked the sun and allowed them to get a better look at the vehicles. A red Ford F-250 blocked the westbound lane. A black F-150 jacked on oversize tires blocked the other.

Three men emerged from behind the F-250, hands at their sides. Empty. All three were shorter than the top of the F-250, scrawny and wearing jeans and faded blue, orange and green tees, left to right.

Neil said, "Recognize the vehicles?"

Sloane shook her head.

"I'm pulling over here," he said and nosed onto the shoulder forty yards short of the roadblock. "If they want us, they'll have to come to us and that will give us plenty of time to get a good look at them."

The driver of the silver Toyota Tundra four-wheel drive parked in the middle of the highway. A large man around thirty-five in a flannel shirt, sleeves pushed to the elbows leaned on the hood. Sandy hair in dire need of a wash stuck out from under a grime-stained

Farmer's Edge cap.

"Out of the car." His voice boomed.

Sloane said, "They have no clue who we are beyond conjecture. They might believe we're the same people they've seen around town, but won't they be surprised if they opt to tangle with us? Him first." She indicated the Tundra driver.

Neil got out and left the car door open. "May I help you, sir?

"Yeah. You can start by handing over the keys to your car."

Neil shuffled his left foot forward and crossed his arms. "First, it's not my car. Second, you want the keys, you'll have to take them *if* you believe you possess the wherewithal to do so."

"What in the heck are you talking about, 'wherewithal'?" He slapped his thigh with the pipe.

"Oh, sorry. If you think you can."

The man's face reddened. He snorted, huffed, and rounded the front of the Tundra. "Ain't no think about it, you idiot. Hand over the keys."

The other three men had covered half the distance. That allowed time enough to implement his plan. The Tundra driver cocked the arm and hand holding the pipe. Neil pivoted on his left foot and smashed the man's right knee. The man bowed to his right, which exposed the left side of his neck to Neil's upward moving right elbow. Neil followed the elbow-to-neck impact with a shove of the man's face down onto the Tundra's front bumper. Blood sprayed from the busted nose. The man dropped spread eagle on the asphalt.

Six seconds. The other three widened their line twenty feet away.

"You're going to pay for that," said the one on the left. His voice bellowed.

"You go for the one on the right," Sloane said loud enough for them to hear her. "I'll take loudmouth and the one in the middle."

Loudmouth held out his hands, palms up, and curled his fingers. "Bring it on, lady. We can get all close and personal."

Sloane sprinted at him. A second before she reached loudmouth she veered right and her right fist slammed into the middle man's trachea. The man crashed to the pavement, hands to his throat. She snatched loudmouth's left wrist as she went by, tugged him off balance, spun, and piggybacked him. She clamped her right arm around his neck and squeezed the choke hold. The man clawed at her arm for eight seconds. The arms flopped to his sides. When she released him, he spilled forward on his face.

Neil crossed behind her toward the man on the right in the "Watch This" tee. He faked high, slammed the heel of his left hand to the man's xiphoid at the base of his sternum. The man woofed a breath and staggered forward. Neil followed with a right elbow to the left side of the man's head at ear level. The man dropped, crawled to the ditch where he collapsed, face turned away from the road.

Neil looked at Sloane. She shrugged. Neither knew the reason for the attack.

"Now that's the way to dispose of thugs in Chicago and New York," she said.

"What do you think? Shall we leave them or call it in?"

"Leave them. We can pull them off the road, move

their trucks to the shoulder and be on our way. We have an important appointment to get to."

They found keys in the ignition in all four vehicles. Easy to assume it was to assist in a swift getaway if one became necessary. Or perhaps the thugs made it a habit of leaving their keys in their vehicles. They agreed to check consoles and glove boxes for proof of identity and take photos of whatever they found.

Sloan parked the Tundra behind the tow truck, ransacked the storage compartments and photographed three documents. She took the keys with her and locked the truck. She shut off the tow truck's amber lights and removed the ignition key.

Neil moved the two roadblock trucks well off the edge of the pavement, searched their consoles, photographed his findings, locked each, and took their keys.

Sloan photographed each truck and the license plates. She said, "We should stuff a set of keys each in one of their pockets and let them sort out which is which."

One of the four remained conscious. He still had his hands to his throat. Neal squatted next to him and stuck a ring of keys in the front left pocket of the man's jeans. "Hurts, don't it?" The man uttered nothing. "Think about that next time you accost someone you've never met."

He photographed the man's face and strode to the Tundra driver. The man's left leg below the knee turned outward at an angle inconsistent with that of a healthy lower limb. He stuffed a Ford key fob and key in the man's shirt pocket, took his picture and met Sloane at the Jaguar, the driver's door still open.

Neil looked to the east and turned westward. The sun stretched a charcoal sheet across the sky and dipped below its cover. The ribbon of asphalt half-a-mile west resembled a flashlight beam moments before its batteries drained of power.

"Are you thinking what I'm thinking?" he said.

Sloane looked at him across the top of the car. "They set us up. I also noticed the lack of traffic." She looked at her watch. "Major highway. Traffic nonexistent for twelve minutes. I would expect at least one a minute during that span, even for a Sunday evening."

They settled in the seats and sped by the parked trucks and their disabled drivers.

"That was the most fun I've had in a while. Exhilarating," Sloane said.

He looked at her. "You were amazing. Where did you learn to fight?"

"My mother was black ops."

"I hope you never get mad enough to pounce on me. I'll concede now."

She laughed. "I saw how you put that first guy down. You're no slacker yourself."

"I just relied on instinct."

"That's a refined instinct you have."

Neil said nothing.

"Want to tell me?"

"Someday…maybe."

"I respect that."

They remained silent until a set of blue lights came into view ahead. A Morgan County Sheriff's cruiser idled in the eastbound lane. Its left tires were on the centerline. Neil slowed and rolled down his window.

The deputy's window was open. A Hispanic female sat in the driver's seat. She waved them onward.

"Stop." Sloane said. "I know her." Neil braked, backed eight feet. "Hey, Felicia."

"I thought that looked like your car."

"What's going on? We're headed to the park. I hope there's no trouble there."

The deputy waved a hand. "It's all good. Some traffic crash has the roadway blocked. They asked us to hold all eastbound traffic until cleared."

"It's clear, Felicia. We just drove through."

Felicia shook her head. "They cleared it and neglected to let us know. Thanks, Sloane. I think I'll go grab supper." She jerked the gear-shift lever and U-turned.

Neil turned right at the intersection toward the park's main gate. The deputy stayed on the highway.

"Thanks for letting me come along," Sloane said.

"I'm glad you did. I would've been late if forced to deal with those four hooligans on my own."

"Admit it. You need me."

He bobbed his head. "I hope to always need you, Sloane Azevedo."

****

Loudmouth man roused and stumbled to the tow truck. He tugged himself up to the driver's seat and reached for the ignition. No key. He patted his pockets and felt a set of keys. He pulled them out, saw they were not his, and clamped his fingers around them. He held onto the steering wheel and slid to the ground.

He took a flashlight from a box behind the seat and flicked it on. The search to locate his keys took him first to the three pickups. His buddies were not in any of them. He crossed back to the north side of the road and slogged along the fog line toward Madison until he found them. They were in the grass thirty yards behind his wrecker. Loudmouth searched their pockets, located his keys in the shirt pocket of his best pal and removed the phone from the pouch on his belt.

The man moaned and grabbed Loudmouth's wrist. "Hey," he babbled, and sprayed blood onto his friend's arm.

"It's me. Take it easy man. Your leg is broken. We need to get you to the hospital. Let me use your phone. I can't find mine."

The screen lit when he pressed a button on the cellphone. He called his contact, who answered on the second ring.

"I hope you have good news for me," she said.

"We ran into a little trouble. He got away."

"You stupid idiot. How could you let a preacher of all people get away from the four of you?"

"He had help."

"Help?"

"Yeah. A woman. They were in a red Jag."

"Forget it. I'll handle it myself."

"What about the money?"

"You'll get your money when I get results, knucklehead. I want another car tonight. Leave the key where I can find it."

Chapter 10

Chad perched on a picnic table on the north side of the campground dressed in baggy jeans, black pullover, and athletic shoes. He pushed off and ambled through the headlamp beams when the Jaguar rolled to a stop. He hesitated when Sloane got out on the passenger's side.

"I thought you were coming alone."

"Have you met Sergeant Azevedo?" Neil said.

"Not officially. I've seen her around town."

Sloane waited at the front of the car. Neil laid his left hand of Chad's right shoulder. "She's my friend, Chad. She is not here in an official capacity."

He stared into the forest. "She's still a cop."

"Sloane is a person just like you and me. She has feelings the same as us. She eats, sleeps, laughs and cries just as would anybody else."

"Do you trust her?"

Neil looked at Sloane and smiled. "I trust her more than anybody I know."

"Okay. Introduce me."

After official introductions, Chad sat at the picnic table. Sloane and Neil took a seat on the opposite side. Crickets squeaked around them.

Chad clasped his hands, wrung his fingers for twenty seconds in silence. "My intention was to discuss something with you about Vanessa and then something else came up."

His hands trembled. He lowered his arms, straightened them, and leaned on the table's edge. Sloane and Neil looked at each other. They looked at Chad and waited for him to continue.

He said, "There's…there's another picture like the one in the barn."

They again looked at one another. Sloane slipped her hand in Neil's.

"Where?" Neil said.

Tears trickled down Chad's face. "Our garage." He rested his forehead on the table. "I'm scared. I might be next."

"Where is your dad?" Sloan asked.

"Out of town."

Neil said, "Has anyone else seen it?"

"No. Just me. I put a panel and some boxes up there to hide it so nobody can see it."

"When is he due home?"

"Not until Saturday. He is on the west coast."

"You're staying there alone?"

"I was."

Sloane looked at Neil. He nodded. "Come on," she said. "You're coming with us."

Chad lifted his head. "Where?"

Neil said, "To see the painting."

"Then you can stay at my place where you'll be safe."

"You mean that? You would do that for me?"

Sloane smiled. "Why not? You need a place to sleep and I have plenty of room. We'll wait on you to pack whatever you need for the next few days."

"What about my car?"

"I'll drive it," Neil said. "You can ride with Sloane.

Chad looked at the Jaguar. "I've never been in a Jag before."

"Okay then. Let's go," Sloane said. To Chad, "We'll take the interstate. It'll be faster." She looked at Neil. "Much faster if you know what I mean."

Chad handed the key to his Honda Civic to Neil. "I guess we should wait awhile for you to get there since her car is a lot faster than mine."

"And nobody dares write a ticket to another officer," Sloane added.

"Then I'd best be on my way. I wouldn't want you two to get bored waiting on me."

****

The driver's seat positioned full rear in Chad's Honda suited Neil with no adjustment. At six-one, he and Chad were close to the same height, but although not overweight, eight-to-ten percent additional adipose tissue over the linebacker's stated nine percent body fat. He drove the eleven miles in silence. Windows up. Air conditional fan set to its lowest setting. No radio. He needed the time to think.

Someone in this town of four thousand possessed the means to abduct, kill, wash, and display Vanessa Flack without discovery. Neil figured it must be a person familiar with the town and its citizens. A local had to proceed with caution or risk contact with someone who could identify them either by name or by sight.

His fifteen months in Madison limited him. Sloane's four years limited her. Neither knew the townspeople enough to rule out anyone. That benefited them in one aspect. No relative or close ties to influence them. It limited them otherwise. Some people hide behind a façade in public.

The Honda's headlights swept across the front yard of the Stoltz's residence and fixed on the garage and the Jaguar nosed in the open front. He, the Jaguar and its two occupants, and the garage plunged into darkness when he shut off the lights.

The dome light in the Jaguar came on when the driver's door opened.

"What took you so long?" Sloane said and grinned. "We've been here four minutes."

"First time driving his Honda. I thought it best not to strain it." He motioned to the garage. "Have you looked?"

"Chad refused to get out of the car until you got here. He acted fine during the ride over. I got up to a hundred and stayed there for more than three miles. He laughed and chatted most of the way. Then something in him changed. He quieted as soon as the headlights hit the garage. He's terrified."

Neil rounded the front of the car so Chad would see it was him. Chad opened the door but stayed seated. "Will you show us?"

"I'd like to stay here if that's okay. It's behind those two boxes right there on the workbench. Straight to the back wall on the right side behind the piece of a corkboard. You'll see it."

Sloane leaned in and switched on the headlights and pushed the trunk release. Chad hid his face in his hands. She stepped to the rear of the car.

Neil said, "Chad, why don't you pack the items you need for your stay and we'll get you out of here."

"Okay." He got out and jogged to the front door

and let himself in. A light shone through the window between the door and the near corner of the house. Lights came on in progression in second story rooms.

"What's your stance now on his culpability?" Neil asked. Their shadows darkened upon their approach to the workbench.

"Same as yours." She flipped on a Maglite and directed its stream above the workspace while he moved the boxes and took down the board. "No wonder he's frightened. It's a spitting image. Hold this."

She handed the flashlight to him and captured twenty-six photos of the portrait with the department's camera. He held the tape ruler in place for her to take additional photos. When she finished, he leaned over the bench for a closer look and shined the beam from different angles to grasp the greatest detail. Although of a different subject and smaller in scale compared to the painting in the barn, the brush stroke patterns along the top, bottom, and each side matched beyond a reasonable doubt.

An expert could better quantify detail.

Sloane strode to the rear of her car where she stowed the camera. She returned to the garage with a blood sample kit. She dipped the swab in a bottle of saline, swiped the damp end across the painted surface and placed it in a clear tube with a screw cap. She repeated the procedure three times; each swab secured in separate tubes. The samples labeled, initialed, and marked with time, date and location.

They were standing at the trunk when Chad shut and locked the front door. He had changed into a pair of knit shorts and a Morgan High School pullover. He opened the door of his Honda and slung an overnight bag across to the passenger seat. His hair was wet, and he smelled of shampoo and bath soap.

"That was quick," Sloane said.

He gave a terse bob of his head. "Ready to get out of here." He ducked into the seat and started the car. "Y'all coming?"

****

The midnight blue Toyota Avalon blended with the darkness under a century-old oak tree fifty yards off the street. Nothing blocked the line of sight to the Stoltz's residence eighty yards away.

The person in the driver's seat peered through a pair of night-vision binoculars when a dark-colored sports car wheeled into the driveway. The lights shut off. The occupants stayed in the car. The person in the passenger's seat rotated his head and looked parallel to the street.

Chad.

A second vehicle pulled into the driveway four minutes later. Chad Stoltz's Honda nosed to the open garage alongside the sports car. Neil got out and rounded the front and chatted with Sloane Azevedo, who exited the first car.

Chad darted to the front door and went inside the house.

Sloane and Neil ambled into the garage.

"This just keeps getting better and better. Count your blessings while you can, Neil Caldera."

The two vehicles backed into the street twenty minutes later and headed west. This time Chad drove his own car. No reason to follow them. They were going to either Caldera's house or Azevedo's.

She pulled out a cellphone and called her second

target.

****

Sloane and Chad bade goodnight to Neil and watched the intermittent glow of the Acura's taillights amidst the trees until they died out from view. Chad sat down on the steps and hung his head. Arms rested on knees. His hands dangled.

Sloane lowered herself one step below him, propped on an elbow, tilted her head back and gazed at the night. She waited for him to speak if they were to engage in any conversation before going inside. A cool breeze fanned them out of the northeast. Sloane waggled her head to fling the hair off her neck.

Chad said, "You like being a cop?"

"I do."

"You don't act like any others I know and you don't look like one."

She kept her gaze on the sky, focused on his comment. "How do I not act like others?"

"You're nice, not mean or condescending. I feel like I can talk to you and you won't judge me just because I'm a teenager and a jock. Not all jocks are dumb, you know. I should graduate with a three-point-six GPA. I got a scholarship to play football at UGA and plan to major in journalism."

"I imagine your dad is proud of you. I would be."

Chad lifted his head. "He seems to be. He travels a lot with his job. He attends my games. They've not missed a one since I began playing in sixth grade. Do you believe Vanessa's murder will ever be solved?"

He switched from talking about himself to express concern for Vanessa. Good.

"Everybody's working on it."

"Why do they think I did it? Vanessa was my friend. I wouldn't do anything to hurt her."

"The chief said you claimed to have seen the body inside the barn before the discovery of her body outside."

"That's not what I told him. I told him I saw the stall where it looked like somebody had to have been killed. I never saw her body in there. That's the truth. The chief even warned Preacher Caldera to stay away from me."

Sloane leaned away from the buzz of a mosquito near her left ear and swatted at it. "How do you know that?"

"Word gets around."

She waited for him to continue.

"He killed a girl."

Sloane whipped her head around.

Chad stared straight ahead. He jerked and slapped his right forearm. "It was in New York. He shot and killed the girl right there on a busy street. Dozens of people witnessed it. He doesn't seem like anyone who'd do something like that. Wham. Bam. She's down. That's it. Too late. You can't un-shoot a gun."

"Why are you telling me this?"

"Because I feel like you should know. You like him and he likes you. That's obvious. He may not be what you think he is. I'm just saying."

"He's exactly who I think he is, Chad. I trust him and so should you."

"Even though he killed somebody?"

"Because he did."

"You already knew?"

"Yes."

Chad tugged his bag onto his lap and clutched it close to him. He batted the air in front of his face.

"Come on, let's go inside before these tiny vampires suck more blood out of us," Sloane said.

Chapter 11

The clock on the mantel displayed a time of eleven thirteen. Neil went straight to the bureau in his bedroom where he kept his eye drops. The bottle was on its side next to a rectangular tray where he stored his keys, loose change, and wallet. He uncapped the bottle and tilted back his head. The clear liquid burned on contact.

He shoved off his shoes, undressed and showered. The bathroom steamed to a dense fog. He shut off the water. The towel rack seemed farther away than he remembered. He reached for the towel and missed; he braced on the shower's frame. Another miss. He succeeded on his third attempt. His tug dislodged the near-end of the rack.

With the towel pressed to his face, he propped against the tiled wall and stilled to clear his head. After fifteen seconds, he dried off and pulled on boxers and lounge pants. Furnishings in the bedroom hazed. He jammed his legs on the foot of the bed. He righted himself and felt his way out of the room. The hall tunneled down to the size of a golf ball. His tongue swelled and clung to the roof of his mouth. Eyes burned from a thousand stings. Gravity tugged him over the back of the sofa. The room faded to black.

****

The side door into the kitchen opened with a suck-of-air sound. A gloved hand pressed the door until it seated in the frame. A person dressed in charcoal head-to-foot crossed the living room, unlocked the front door, and stepped behind the sofa. The clock on the mantel emitted three chimes.

The intruder gazed at Neil lying flaccid on one end, torso twisted and head canted rightward on the armrest. The only movements were the discernable rise and fall of his chest. The poly-cotton ripstop left pant leg brushed against the russet leather on the sofa's arm when the man rounded that end and stepped over Neil's legs.

"Hello, Neil." The tone sounded bitter. "Can good also be evil? You are the proclaimed sin-fighter. You should know if any such contrast exists. What do you say?"

A twitch jerked the first finger on Neil's right hand. No verbal response.

"What do you intend to do when you wake up? Will you proclaim the truth or continue to hide behind your façade? I assure you of one thing, Mister Clergyman. You will not find answers for what you are looking for here in Madison. Decide. Think of your parishioners. Keep your secret locked away. No one will ever know the true Neil Caldera. But be warned. The wrong move will ruin your future in the church and in this town. You don't want that, now do you?"

The intruder caressed Neil's face, trailed his chest, and explored his manhood, buttocks, and legs.

"Stop the pretense, Caldera. People have their own ideas about things and it scares a large majority of them to voice their opinions. They're afraid somebody will disagree with them or challenge their beliefs. Then what? Look around you. Is freedom really possible?

Choose the right option and find out what waits for you on the other side. Good and evil have no bearing on what's beyond. They're all within the spectrum of life. All you have to do is pick one."

The intruder pulled a knife from a sheath on a nylon riggers belt. The blade clicked when it locked.

"Truth holds the key to freedom." The voice came from the kitchen.

****

The stranger sported dark slacks and a shirt similar to those worn at the crime scene. He stepped toward the sofa. His arms relaxed at his sides. Hands empty.

"Who are you?" the intruder said.

"Your death angel if you make any aggressive move with that knife." His voice projected passion.

The intruder chuckled, waved the knife. Light glinted off the four-inch blade. The manner in which the intruder held it and the fluid motion suggested someone with skill. "You think you can stop me from that distance?"

"You have it all wrong. Perception-reaction time for the average human is one-and-a-half seconds. Response times shorten by as much as twenty percent for certain athletes and persons with improved motor skills."

"How does that apply to our circumstances?"

"I *know* my limitations," he said.

The intruder flaunted the knife in a crisscross pattern. "You can try to save him or come after me. It's your choice."

"And you can run or fight. Your choice."

The stranger smirked to impart fear into the intruder who sidled leftward to the far end of the couch.

He countered two angled strides and saw the blaze in the intruder's eyes fade to uncertainty. The shift positioned both nearer to the front door. The sofa remained between them.

He continued, "Six feet to the door, pause long enough to twist the knob and pull open the door. That's three seconds tops. I'll give you that head start." He said it as if he planned to pursue.

The intruder swapped the knife from right hand to left, dashed to the door, jerked it open, and fled into the darkness.

The stranger rounded the sofa and shut and locked the door. He straightened Neil's legs and rotated him supine on the sofa. He dropped to a knee and checked Neil's pulse and eyes. Neil's pulse was strong, but the eyes exhibited inflamed conjunctivae.

Neil stirred. Eyelids fluttered. He started to sit up and hesitated when he saw the stranger. "Where am I? Who are you?" He looked around. "What are you doing in my house?" He pressed the balls of his hands to his eyelids. "What did you do to me?"

"How do you feel?"

"Why are you in my house?"

"Someone dressed in tactical gear and balaclava broke into your house. The person was standing over you with an Emerson CQC-6 knife. You were slumped over the back of this sofa. What is the last thing you remember?"

Neil grabbed the back of the sofa and stuck out his left hand. "Help me sit up." The stranger took the hand and pulled. Neil swung his legs to the floor. "I remember coming in, showered and everything blurred. That's it."

"Did you eat or drink anything?"

He shook his head. Glanced at the clock. Looked down the hall.

"The eye drops. I got home, looked at the clock on the mantel, and went straight to my bedroom. I put drops in my eyes before I got in the shower."

"Have them tested."

"Do I know you? You look familiar, like I've seen you recently."

"I must go. I have somewhere to be."

With that, the stranger walked out and shut the front door.

****

Neil leaped to his feet and braced a hand on the arm of the couch. He pressed his left palm to the center of his forehead. Streaks of pain shot behind his eyes. He waited for the cataclysm to settle and eased to the front window nearest the door. He swiped aside the drapes and looked out. The stranger was gone. No vehicle. No one loitered in the yard or street. The glitter of stars spattered a velvet sky.

He let the drape fall back over the window frame and locked the front and side doors. Silence ruled the house. He ran a glass of tap water and gulped it. Refilled it, drank half and set the glass in the sink and hobbled to the bedroom.

The bottle of eye drops stood upright on the bureau where he'd placed it. He knew what he should do, but doing it was another matter because of constraints. Time worked against him if he followed procedure, secured the bottle and turned it over to the police. Who knows how long it would sit in an evidence locker before an officer transported it to the crime lab. Once there, the eye drops would again be secured in evidence and await analysis for six to eight weeks or longer because of work overload and priorities.

No. That was unacceptable. Nor fair for him if forced to wait for the truth. He refused to wait. Other options existed. One of them would offer the desired results when he wanted them.

Chapter 12

Neil woke at seven, showered, dressed, and called in a favor to a friend who supervised a private laboratory in New York City. The contact on the other end of the line assured a turnaround time of forty-eight hours following delivery. He addressed the envelope containing the bottle of eye drops and slipped it into his shirt pocket.

He drove to Perk Avenue on West Jefferson, a restaurant he frequented for breakfast a minimum of one morning a week. This morning he sat at the last table and faced the length of the dining room instead of taking his usual table for four near the front windows.

He deviated from a breakfast of grits, cheese-laden eggs and biscuits. He'd become fond of the Southern dish, but his mood prompted him to select the "Cinn & Tell" latte and French toast. A super-quick energizer followed by a sugar spiral plunge. He would offset the lack of energy when the time came by alternative means.

A fiftyish man entered the restaurant and cast an eye over the room as if having a difficult time choosing where to sit. He said something to a woman at the counter and pointed. She nodded. The man loped to a table two up from Neil. He nudged a chair back with a foot and sat angled forty-five degrees left of front-to-back.

The man's shirt exhibited sweat stains around the collar and arm pits and the thighs of his jeans soiled from repeated hand wipes. Wrinkles in both garments suggested the man slept in them. The guy's unwashed hair clung to his scalp. Typical of a grunge, Neil opined to himself.

The waitress delivered Neil's breakfast, and a large OJ and toast for the grunge.

Halfway through his meal, a five-year-old girl scuttled by on her way to the restroom. Her brown curls bounced like springs on her shoulders. Two minutes later the bathroom door opened. The girl wandered up to Neil's table, curled her damp fingers over the edge, and rested her chin on the table between her hands.

"I know you," she said.

Neil flashed a wide smile. "I know you, too, Birdie."

Birdie slid out the chair to his left, crawled up onto it, shifted to sit, and crossed her arms on the table. "I heard my daddy tell Mommy somebody painted your picture on a barn. He said the police are going to imbestigate you."

"He did?"

She bobbed her head. "He said you looked like the devil. Are you the devil?"

The grunge sprayed a mist of orange juice. A coughing spell seized his body. He neither covered his mouth nor cleaned the mess once the coughs subsided.

"That's something you should ask your mom," Neil said.

"Okay."

As Birdie bounded off, she paused at the grunge's table. "You'd better go get that cough seen about,

mister."

"Scram kid."

Birdie ran to her mother and locked her arms around the woman's arm. "I don't like that man. He was mean to me."

The grunge crammed a half slice of toast in his mouth, chomped open-mouthed and tipped the glass of orange juice to his lips. Juice trickled from the corner of his mouth and dripped on his shirt.

Neil slid the plate with his unfinished French toast to the middle of the table.

He waited for the grunge to set his glass on the table. Neil scooted his chair away from the table and strode toward the front. When he got even with the grunge, he put his hand on the table and said, "Next time be discreet when you spy on somebody."

The grunge shrank back, shook his head. "I have no idea what you're talking about."

"I suggest you keep it that way."

****

The busyness in and around the offices at the church resembled a disturbed wasp nest. Men and women hauled boxes along a hallway and out one of the side doors to a utility trailer attached to a year-old black Ford Super Duty truck. None acknowledged Neil's presence. Each one passed by as if he wasn't there. He rounded a corner and observed the origin of their treks.

He waited outside his office. Members of his congregation, people to whom he offered comfort, guidance, and leadership for fifteen months had unified against him. From where he stood, he could see bare walls, open desk drawers emptied of their contents and three boxes stacked against the wall to the right of the desk.

When they finished, no evidence would exist of his presence. At the rate they hustled, they would clean out the office by eight forty-five. In fifteen minutes.

Why? What brought on the suddenness?

"Neil?" The voice was female. Not Reverend Caldera. No Mr. Caldera. Neil. It conveyed a message. He needed not ask for any translation when he whirled and saw the church's secretary, Nan Wilkerson. "The chairman of deacons wants to speak to you in the sanctuary."

That cinched it. This was no office remodeling party. No thank-you-for-your-service upgrade. He was out.

He headed up the hall to the nave, head held high and eyes focused ahead. No regrets haunted him. He'd served every day with dignity, followed his uncle's advice to stay true to God because "you never know when a congregation will turn on you or why."

Rob Fleishman sat off the steps which led up to the lectern dressed in his uniform. The fourteen members of the deacon board perched on the first two center pews, seven on each pew.

Every head turned when Neil entered.

Rob cleared his throat. "I'd ask you to have a seat but we won't be here that long so I'll get right to it. The board discussed this matter and decided unanimously your services here are no longer required. Any questions?"

"No."

"Just like that? No?"

Neil tightened his lips.

Rob pushed off the steps. "You want to know

why?"

"No."

Neil turned around and trailed back through the door.

"Seriously, you're going to just walk away without getting an explanation?" Rob's voice reverberated on the other side of the door.

Neil continued on to the parking lot and got in his car and drove away. After he turned right on Brooks Pennington a silver four-door sedan pulled out of a driveway south of Bethany a hundred yards behind him.

The car paced him to Buckhead Road where Neil veered right into the turn lane. He slowed to a stop and waited for the vehicle to overtake him. The car, a 2002 Chevrolet Impala, rolled by on the outside lane and continued through the intersection well below the posted fifty-five-MPH limit. The private detective sat at the wheel.

Neil whipped over and followed the Impala north until they passed behind the high school and reached the stretch of highway bordered by trees on both sides. He pulled out to pass, cut off the Impala and forced the driver to the shoulder. He left his Acura nosed to the shoulder, got out, rounded the front of his car and marched to the passenger's side of the Impala where he jerked open the door.

The driver had twisted in his seat, head back to the window, hands up in front of his chest, palms out.

Neil leaned into the car. "It ends here. Now. Do you understand?"

The gumshoe gave a short nod.

"Are you sure or shall I convince you?"

The man opened his mouth. Nothing came out.

He startled when Neil's fist hit the dash. "Hey. I'm talking to you."

"Okay. I got it."

Neil backed out of the car. "Get out of here. I don't want to see your face again, ever." He slammed the door, backed away and stood there until the Impala was out of sight.

The whoop of a siren alerted him to a police cruiser's approach. The car braked to a stop in the traffic lane and the passenger-side window lowered.

"We have another body," Sloane said. "Follow me."

Chapter 13

At eight forty, Neil trooped alongside Sloane to where the killer had posed the nude body of a female on the grass. Someone had spread the legs, propped her back on the bleachers at the north corner of the football field. Arms angled inward below the breast. Fingers laced at the bellybutton.

The body exhibited mutilation similar to that sustained by Vanessa Flack: torso sliced in diagonal ribbons; thighs split midline to the knees; ankles dislocated and rotated outward. Peri-mortem bruises around the armpits. No injury above the shoulders. A minimal amount of blood pooled along the perimeter of the buttocks and thighs. Dry hair.

Detective Huber hunkered on the field side of the remains, notepad in his right hand. "Thanks for coming, Caldera." His voice came out hoarse.

"Your request or Rob's?"

"Mine." He cleared his throat. "The chief is en route. No mention of you when I talked to him twenty minutes ago. The word is you're consulting on the Flack murder. I could use the help on this one if you have the time."

Time no constraint. Services no longer required elsewhere as of this morning. Rob Fleishman and the deacon board severed those ties without apology.

"I'll be happy to assist you if I can, Detective."

"Any first impression?"

"The killer's taunting you. I'm alluding to the Department." Neil said. "Have you located the crime scene?"

"I have two officers searching the buildings and grounds. So far they have located no other blood."

"What can you tell me about her?"

"Katie Moore. Eighteen years old. Five-nine. One-thirty. She was a senior here at the school. Played third base on the girls' softball team. Member of ROTC and scheduled to start Air Force Academy in the fall. No steady boyfriend. Two brothers in college. Dad flew an F-15 in the Gulf War. Mom's an ER nurse."

Neil pulled on sterile gloves, squatted opposite Huber and checked the girl's fingers and jaw for signs of rigor mortis. The muscles in the fingers resisted somewhat; the jaw muscles held the mouth closed. The buttocks and back of the right thigh didn't blanch when he pressed the skin.

"Lividity is fixed. That occurs in about six hours after death. She's been here most of that time otherwise the body would show a different pattern. Rigor exhibits the early stages. Based on that, the window you're looking for is probably seven to nine hours."

They backed away when Sloane brought out her camera.

Huber said, "It's almost nine now. If the body was put here, let's say, three or thereabouts, then Katie must have met the killer wherever at no later than midnight to one. That sound right?"

"Yes."

"But where?"

"Where did Katie live?"

"Somewhere off Doster. About three miles from here."

Doster. The name sounded familiar. He tried to remember why. "Expand the scope to include a three-mile radius to include her home. I doubt Katie would have gone out any farther than that considering the time of night and her having to be at school this morning. The killer had to come in contact with her somewhere. Check the likely locations first and go from there."

"I agree and will. Hopefully, we'll get a break soon."

"What about her clothes?"

"There's no sign of them anywhere."

Neil turned in a three-sixty and studied the school grounds and parking lots.

"Has anyone discovered a sketch similar to the one found in the barn?"

"Not that I'm aware of."

"Any word from the ME on Vanessa?" Neil said.

"Last I heard they are to release her body to the funeral home this afternoon. The family keeps calling our office. They want to have her funeral tomorrow."

Rob Fleishman nosed his department-issued Dodge to the edge of the grass and got out. He threw up his right hand to Neil as though they hadn't seen one another for days.

Huber huddled on the driver's side with Fleishman and the two officers who completed their search. Huber looked over the hood at Neil and shook his head. The officers' search turned up nothing.

"Neil?" It was Sloane. "Would you mind?" He moseyed to her. She motioned to the body, but whispered, "There's no painting."

He waved his hand in an up-and-down manner toward Katie's body. "My guess is it's at the scene or origin. Just like the barn. Inside versus outside where the killer left Vanessa."

"That could be just about anywhere."

"Huber told me Katie lived off Doster."

Sloane stilled. "That's near my house."

He remembered. Then, "No."

"Yes," she said.

"No. I mean…Is it possible?"

"What?"

"Chad. He stayed at your place last night."

"Oh, God." Sloane slapped a hand over her mouth. Fleishman, Huber and the two uniform officers stared at them. She lowered her hand and whispered, "It has to be a coincidence. I know for a fact he didn't leave the house. Dew covered the windshield of his car this morning. At least I believe it did. I can't remember."

Neil would not commit. He exhaled a long sigh. "I don't know. Have you heard of any association Katie and Chad may have had outside of school?"

"No, but I probably wouldn't. Huber might know. I'll have to wait and ask him when Fleishman's not around."

"Ask me what?" Huber said.

The two uniforms crossed the parking lot, with Fleishman headed toward the administration offices.

"About any links between Katie and Vanessa," Sloane said.

"What's that have to do with Fleishman?"

"Neil and I were just discussing Chad Stoltz. The chief seems determined to nail him for Vanessa's murder. I, we, wondered if he expressed the same mindset about this one."

Huber frowned. "That's why he's going to see the principal. Chad's car was spotted on Doster near Crawley last night. He wants me to look into it." He shook his head. "Chief ordered me to concentrate on Stoltz as the prime suspect in both cases. That's all good if he did it, but where's the evidence? Nothing puts Stoltz with either of them at the time of their deaths or anytime earlier."

"Did Katie live with her parents?" Neil asked.

Huber said, "She did. Their place is on Crawley. That's a passel of evidence against Stoltz right there for sure. Seen on a road near where Katie lived the night she was killed. I think I'll go see the judge, get a warrant for Stoltz's arrest, and wrap these cases up in time for a celebratory lunch at Huddle House. You two care to join me?"

"When the crime-scene techs get here have them meet me in the student parking lot." The chief's voice on Huber's talkie drenched the aura of amusement gained by the disdain before either Sloane or Neil answered him.

Huber acknowledged and looked at Neil, to Sloane and shook his head. "Unbelievable. He's going to have Stoltz's car searched."

Sloane said, "He has no authority to search the vehicle without his father's consent."

"You know that and I know that, but obviously, he doesn't care. Fruits of the poisonous tree and all that implies," Huber said. "No judge will allow it."

Neil's eyes met Sloane's.

"Um, that presents another problem," she said.

"Like what?"

Neil said, "My fingerprints are in there."

Huber shifted his eyes from Neil to Sloane to Neil and back to Sloane. He crossed his arms. "Either of you care to let me in on what's going on here?"

Silence.

"I'm waiting." Huber's hazel eyes blazed under his furrowed forehead. The onus fell on Neil and Sloane and he expected one, or both, to be forthcoming.

"It's on me," Neil said. "Chad called me Saturday night and asked me to meet him at Fletcher's barn. That's how this conundrum began. I saw the sketch in the barn before Vanessa's body was discovered."

He paused.

"Okay, I'm aware of all that." Huber uncrossed his arms and planted his hands on his hips.

"Chad contacted me again yesterday and asked to meet. Sloane and I were together when the text came in on my phone. We met him at Hard Labor Creek. He told us he found another drawing similar to the one in the barn."

Huber threw up his left hand. "Stop right there. Why am I just now hearing about this?" He turned to Sloane. "With all due respect, Sergeant, why didn't you notify me of this last night?"

"I documented everything and collected samples, Detective. Let him finish."

Neil continued, "The second portrait seemed to have brought on greater anxiety for him than had the one in the barn. He expressed his fear and told us his father is out of town. We told him we wanted him to show us so I drove his car to his house while he rode with Sloane. The portrait was on the garage wall."

"Okay, I get that. Tell me about the sketch. What

were the similarities?"

"There's no doubt the same artist painted both. Smaller, but the likeness was striking. We understood why Chad wished to stay someplace other than home. The image looked like him."

"I guess you will now tell me he stayed at your place. That you're his alibi for Katie's murder."

"No. I saw him last around eleven."

"And where was that if he didn't stay home?"

"At my house," Sloane said.

Huber jutted his head forward, jerked his arms up and stilled as if ready to conduct an orchestra. "Are you crazy? What were you thinking?" He lowered his hands to his hips for her answer.

A white Georgia Bureau of Investigation crime-scene truck rolled to a stop forty feet away. Two Crime Scene Specialists based out of Region Six office in Milledgeville hopped out wearing navy pullover shirts.

"We'll get back to this subject later," Huber told Sloane and strolled to the rear of the truck where the agents already had the doors open. He said something to the women and motioned back the way they had come. The specialists climbed back into the truck, U-turned and drove out of sight.

****

The deputy coroner arrived on the scene to work up his part of the investigation. A forensic pathologist at the state medical examiner's headquarters would autopsy Katie Moore's body. Huber walked him through the scene and identified his findings while Sloane and Neal took refuge from the mid-morning sun behind the bleachers.

Neil said, "You said you knew Chad did not leave

the house. Is it possible he might have sneaked out of the house without you knowing it?"

"Not in the timeframe necessary to have committed murder."

"How would you know if you were asleep?"

"I wasn't. After you left, we sat out on the steps until the mosquitoes forced us inside. He dawdled around like someone lost in a vast wilderness. He closed the drapes, paced room-to-room and repeatedly checked the exterior door locks. That continued for well over an hour, during which I tried guiding him to safety by answering his persistent questions."

"If someone saw his car on Doster last night, it must have been on the way to your place, and whoever saw it perhaps assumed he was going to meet Katie Moore."

"Unless they were mistaken."

Neil peered over Sloane's shoulder at Huber and the deputy coroner as they placed Katie's body into a body bag spread open on a gurney. The deputy zipped up the bag and secured it to the stretcher. Huber moved to the head. The deputy coroner pulled a lever at the foot and when they raised the gurney, the wheels dropped and locked.

He said, "It's an attempt to frame him. He lives near the barn where Vanessa was murdered. Last night he stayed within minutes of Katie's house. He knew them. Who knows what the GBI techs will find in his car. That's a chunk of circumstantial evidence if someone wishes to make a compelling case."

"Forget whatever's in the car. That's inadmissible. Entry must be lawful."

"What is Fleishman's basis for entry? Two murders

occur in his city in one weekend. The families of the victims and citizens pressure him to make an arrest. The media wants an update. But he has no evidence to link anyone to either crime except Chad's statement that he saw Vanessa's body in the barn. What does he do? Without probable cause, the option is the plain-sight rule or lie to gain access. To what level would he go?"

"Chad told me he did not see her body in the barn. He insisted he told Fleishman he saw a place in the barn where it looked as though someone was killed."

"Fleishman heard what he wanted to hear?"

"Seems that way."

"He's got tunnel vision. He's focused on Chad and no one else."

Sloane's eyes shifted to Neil's chest. He supposed she wondered about the package in his shirt pocket. The eye drops he needed to ship next-day delivery to the lab in New York once the post office opened for business.

He patted the pocket. "I had two visitors after I got home last night, or so the second one claimed."

"You didn't see the first?"

"No."

"Then how do you know anybody was even there?"

He recounted the sequence of what he remembered between his return home at eleven thirteen up to the stranger's departure somewhere around three fifteen.

"Are you sure he was the same person you talked to at the scene Saturday evening?"

"It was him."

"Do you believe his story?"

"I don't know. The fact is, somebody entered my house before I got home last night and put something in my eye drops. It has to be the drops. I ate nothing and drank nothing except tap water. It could have been the stranger or if he's telling the truth, the person wearing tactical gear he ran off. That's why I'm shipping this to the lab."

"If it is the truth, the person in TG returned to make sure they incapacitated you."

"Or intended to kill me."

Sloane put her hand on his arm. "Maybe you should stay at my place until we catch him."

"It's obvious this TG person wants me. I have to stay visible."

"That's not the only way to do this, Neil. Please, let me help you."

Chapter 14

The clerk at the post office assured delivery of Neil's package before noon the following day. It was one step closer to the result, whatever that might be. Caution raised its flag. The smart choice would be to heed its message.

Neil parked his Acura halfway up his driveway and studied the house and yard. Forensic evidence from the two men existed somewhere on the property. You always take something with you. You always leave something there. No matter how miniscule. Trace evidence. Fibers. Hair. Soil. Pollen. The list contained multiple potentials.

Blades of fescue danced in the breeze. Dust kicked up off the driveway in a miniature dust devil. Five days without rain left the soil sunbaked.

He got out of the car and circled the house at a distance of fifty feet. Nothing stood out to him. The second time he closed in to twenty-five feet. Ten. Five. Nothing visible to the naked eye stood out to him. No crushed grass. No impressions of footwear in the yard or on the asphalt driveway. No slashed screens or tool marks on window frames. No witness marks on the front door.

The last area he checked was the side entry door. He took out his keys and was about to insert the key in the lock when he saw it. A brownish-red smudge extended from the knob's stem onto the base cap oriented from one to three o'clock. He leaned in and examined the stain from various angles. The appearance exhibited consistency with transfer in a right-hand grip and rotation of the knob.

Neil took out his phone and shot a dozen photos at different views and distances. He sat on the second step and scrolled through them. Enlarged one and examined it. Detail suggested a gloved hand gripped and turned the knob. Blood most likely transferred from a forefinger or middle finger. He zoomed in on another picture and came to the same conclusion.

He called Sloane. She answered on the first ring.

"That was fast."

"I had the phone in my hand to call you. Huber and I just left Katie's parents. They both denied knowing she wasn't in the house when they went to bed at eleven. They described the clothes she had on. We found nothing in Katie's room to indicate when or why she went out."

"Did Katie have a car?"

"A yellow Honda Fit. It's not at their house. Huber called in a lookout for it. I got to thinking and I might know where the sketch might be. I discussed it with Huber and he agrees it is worth a look. Are you free to meet us at the barn?"

"Yes, if you will stop by my house first. There's something here you need to see. Huber, too."

"Did you have another break-in?"

"No. Tell Huber radio silence. I prefer Fleishman not know I found blood on my doorknob."

****

Sloane and Huber arrived in Huber's unmarked

detective's car at five minutes before eleven. Seventeen minutes after Neil called her. He waited on the steps of his front porch in the shade of a red maple tree.

Sloane was the first to open her door and hop out. The camera hung around her neck by its strap and sprang breast to breast left-right and right-left while she walked. A blood-test kit filled her left hand.

Neil pushed off the step and met her halfway to the corner of the house.

Huber dragged himself out of the Ford. Two days of little or no sleep and lack of progress made in the two murder cases gave him a haggard appearance. Dark circles under his eyes. Hair drenched with sweat clung to his head.

"He looks worn out," Neil said to Sloane.

"He'll be fine. We'll get a break soon. I sense it. There's nothing like that shot of adrenalin you get when a solid lead pans out and leads to an arrest. You know that feeling."

"I do. We never know which tidbit gleaned along the path will lead to an indictment."

"That's why we're going back to the barn. It's more theory than anything else."

"We meet again. Why not confess and save us the trouble we'd get into by beating a confession out of you? If not, I'm sure I could locate a water hose around here somewhere I could cut to a satisfactory length."

It's weird how lack of sleep turns people into comedians and everything that comes out of their mouths seems funny to them. Neil experienced many such times in his career.

He said, "Come around this side."

Detective Huber inspected the door and knob.

"When did you first notice it?"

"I found it, took photos, and called Sloane."

"I didn't see any signs of forced entry. Did you go inside to check the house?"

"I already know someone was in there because I talked to one of them."

Huber looked puzzled. "One of them? How many were there?"

"Allegedly two." Neil told Huber about the eye drops, his passing out, and the stranger's visit. "The same man was in the crowd outside the barn Saturday evening. I'm certain of it."

Huber looked at Sloane.

She said, "It's the man I showed you in the photos."

"And you never saw the first man?" He asked Neil. "No."

Huber tightened his lips. The dimples in his cheeks deepened. A blank gaze eked from dim eyes.

Neil discerned Huber's air of skepticism. Some things automatically raise suspicion in an investigator's mind when people utter unsupported statements. He'd offered no proof of the first man's existence. The stranger could have transferred the blood found on the knob. He needed proof.

Huber shifted his intent look over Neil's shoulder.

"Is this stranger's word all you have?" he said after several seconds.

"For now."

"We have a lookout for him already out there," Sloane said. "He may be the type that doesn't want to be found."

"That's not good enough." Huber said. "I want this

man found. He could be our killer."

"It's not him," said Neil.

"How do you know? You can't state that with any certainty. The killer could be anybody."

"No. It's not just anybody. You're looking for someone with links to Vanessa and Katie. These murders are not random acts. They're deliberate actions on specific targets. Look, I know you're frustrated. You're tired. You're stressed. You're pressured to find this madman. I understand that, believe me. I've been there. Forget this stranger. I'll find him. As of this morning, I have nothing else I need to do."

"He's right, Detective," Sloane said. "I'll collect a sample of this blood for DNA analysis. My bet is the blood is Katie's."

Neil said, "If the blood is hers, which I believe it must be, it narrows your suspect pool to one of three options: the stranger; the unidentified man based on the stranger's statement; and me. I have no alibi. You have evidence on my door and possibly inside the house to link this location to Katie. What you do with that is up to you. You only have my word related to the stranger and the alleged unknown man."

"Photograph and collect a sample," he said to Sloane. "I'm going inside."

"We need a warrant or consent," Sloane said.

"No problem," Neil said. "I'll let you in through the front door."

Neil unlocked and pushed open the door and allowed Huber to go ahead of him. He flipped a switch and the overhead light on the ceiling fan came on. He stayed near the door while Huber conducted his walk-through of the house.

The oak-colored hardwood floor creaked in places under Huber's footfalls. He circled the sofa, strode into the open kitchen and ambled along the hall to the other end of the house.

Shuffles of feet indicated his return five minutes later. He held a writing pad in his left hand and an ink pen in his right.

"Okay. Walk me through the sequence from the time you got home up to the time the stranger left here. You know the drill. Show me and don't touch anything."

Neil crossed to the back door. "I came in here, glanced at the clock there on the mantel, and walked straight back to my bedroom." He stepped forward and motioned to the hallway. "I put drops in my eyes because of allergies, showered, and got woozy. I made it to the sofa and the next thing I remember is seeing the stranger's face hovering above me."

"Tell me what he said to you."

"He told me someone dressed in tactical gear and balaclava broke in here. TG was standing over me with a knife. He told me I slumped over the back of the sofa. He asked about the last thing I remembered and I told him what I just told you. He suggested I have the drops tested."

Huber scribbled on the pad.

"Anything else?"

Sloane stepped in.

Neil said, "I thought he looked familiar and told him so. I asked him about it and he told me he had somewhere to be and he had to hurry. That was it. He left through the front door, which was standing open. The door was closed and locked when I got home. I have no idea how he or the other one got in. I can only assume it was the side door based on the stain."

"What was he wearing?"

"Nice clean shirt and slacks. Expensive duds. Similar to what he was wearing Saturday evening."

Huber penned more notes.

"I'll wait out on the porch for you to finish in here if you wish."

"No, you're okay." Huber crossed to the windows. "How dark can you make it in here?"

"Dark enough if you plan to use UV light."

"I do. I have a new flashlight designed to track blood. They marketed it for hunters, but it works as good as Luminal without the bothersome spray."

Neil stuck his hand behind the drapes at the top of the window nearest him and pulled down a room-darkening shade. He repeated the action at the second window on the front wall. Sloane pulled down the ones in the kitchen and dining room.

"Perfect." Huber pulled a Gerber flashlight out of his hip pocket and pressed the button. "Glow baby glow." He aimed the stream of light first at the side door, frame, and floor. No positive results. He waved the light in a sweeping motion over the surface of the floor, along the rear of the sofa, rounded the arm, down the back and seat cushions and front. He rounded the right-side arm and paused.

"I've got something. Right here." He narrowed the beam and squatted. He craned his neck and looked up at Sloane and Neil who had moved behind his right shoulder. "It's blood. No doubt about it." He turned back and angled the light. "It's smeared on the outside here. Looks like there's a fabric pattern in it."

"Mid-thigh to a grown man," Neil said.

"What were you wearing last night?"

"Jeans. After I showered, I put on lounge pants."

"I can confirm the jeans," Sloane said. "He was wearing them when I last saw him at eleven o'clock."

"Where are they?"

"Hamper. Bathroom. They're both in there."

"I'll get them," Sloane said. She marched out of the room and returned, the hamper in hand. She dug out the garments and held them up while Huber scoured them with light.

"They're clean. The pattern doesn't match what I'm seeing in the smear, anyway."

Neil said, "You wouldn't expect it to be if the person was in tactical pants."

"Supports the man's statement," Sloan added.

"You're both right. Maybe the stranger was telling the truth."

Sloane photographed the smear and included a measuring device, while Huber resumed his search of the living room and the other five rooms. The two swabs she used soaked up the blood even out of the crevasses in the leather.

"What if it's one of the men who accosted us yesterday?" Sloane whispered. "You know they will want revenge after what we did to them."

She placed the swabs in tubes, sealed and labeled them.

"I've considered that a possibility, but no, I just remembered something the stranger said. The one in tactical gear had an Emerson CQC-6 knife."

Sloane nodded. "Military. Special Forces get issued those."

"Your mother."

She again nodded.

"That means we should consider our suspect ex-military or someone with ties to them. The thing I want to know is how he got in here to begin with. The door was locked."

"And old," she added. "The lock has too many scratches around the keyhole to define old from new if somebody used a lock pick to gain entry."

Huber returned to the living room. "It's clean." His tone sounded neither relieved nor disappointed. He plopped down on the couch. "I'd like to relax a minute before we head to the barn. Do you have any bottled water?"

"What's your strategy?" Neil asked on his way to the refrigerator.

"Whatever it takes."

Once Neil touched the chilled bottle, he grabbed two more. He handed one to Sloane and the second to Huber. Huber thanked him, twisted off the cap and guzzled half.

"How far are you willing to push this?" Neil took a sip of water.

Sloane pressed her bottle to the side of her neck.

"Like I said, whatever it takes within the boundaries of the law."

"I need a favor."

"What?"

"Fleishman's cellphone records. And get me a link to track his phone." He said it to test him. He needed to learn to whom and what Huber showed his loyalty.

Huber smiled. "That's two favors."

"One more. Track the GPS in his city-issued car."

A voice on the portable talkie blared, "We found the car."

"Ten-four," Huber said. "I'm en route."

Chapter 15

The yellow Honda Fit filled a spot covered with gravel on the Confederate Road side of the Quick Shop. A Morgan County deputy greeted Huber and Sloane outside his cruiser.

"The car is registered to Lance and Beth Moore on Doster Road," the deputy said. "The store owner said dew covered it when she got here this morning at eight. That suggests it's been here overnight. The doors are unlocked and the inside looks clean."

"We'll take over from here," Sloane said to the deputy. She looked at Huber. "I'm going to check for surveillance. Don't touch the car until Neil gets here. I want him to have the first look inside."

A woman of thirty-five with coal hair and smooth honey features called to Sloane from the far end of the store. "I'll be right with you." Her umber eyes widened when Sloane turned into the aisle. "Sloane."

They hugged.

"I need a favor, Jeya. I need to see your surveillance from last night."

The woman hurried to the cubicle. Sloane followed and waited while the woman faced what looked like a new digital video recorder and flat-screen monitor. The device purred while a series of windows appeared on the screen.

"Does it have anything to do with that yellow car?"

"Yes. Was it there when you closed?"

"No. I left here at ten twenty. I had parked my car in that same spot."

The screen displayed an image of Jeya leaving the store at 10:20:31. It showed her cross the front and pull onto the highway headed east.

"I started it there because in this mode it will skip to the next time it detected motion."

The next prompt captured a police car cruise through the lot at 11:18:07.

Fourteen minutes later, the yellow Honda wheeled into the driveway and parked. The car sat there for ninety seconds before a dark sedan approached from the east on Confederate Road and nosed at an angle to the back of the Honda. The driver's door opened and Katie pushed out wearing a white pullover, jeans, and pink sneakers. She closed and locked the door and opened the front passenger door of the second vehicle. No interior light came on. Katie stood there for eight seconds based on the time displayed on the screen before she nodded and got into the sedan.

The car backed onto Confederate and headed west.

"Will you copy this for me?"

"I'll do better than that. I'll link you to my system and you can watch it anytime you want."

A chime signaled the front door opened. Neil stepped through.

"Over here," Sloane said. "We have her on camera at eleven thirty-two. She got into what looks like a black or navy sedan at eleven thirty-four."

He rounded the counter and stepped to her right side. "Are you able to determine make and model?"

Sloane looked at Jeya who typed in the time,

brought the vehicle in view and enlarged the image.

Neil leaned closer. "That looks like a Lexus."

"Look there." Sloane touched the emblem shown in the center of the car's front end. "It's a Toyota."

"Did this video ever show the rear of the car?"

"No. The driver backed out onto the road and drove west."

"Run it from the first view," he said. "I want to see it again from the start."

Jeya set the timer and touched the screen to play in enhanced mode. Sloane watched Jeya assist a man in a pair of coveralls and a straw hat. The familiar-looking man pointed to the fuel pumps and handed off two twenties. The man glanced at Sloane and rubbed the front of his neck before he pushed out the door to a white panel truck parked on the far side of the pumps.

Sloane's face flushed remembering the four men at the roadblock. She clasped Neil's hand and redirected her focus on the video.

When the car on screen drove beyond the camera's coverage, Neil said, "If that's a Toyota it has to be an Avalon. At least now we know what vehicle she used."

"If it's the same one as the night she murdered Katie Moore."

Neil frowned. "The killer had to know about surveillance. This doesn't feel right. It's too easy."

Sloane studied Katie's image. "We never found either girl's clothes."

****

Huber waited for them outside the Quick Shop, pad and pen in hand. The paper grated when he ripped it off the pad. "The chief has set a press conference for three o'clock at City Hall." He handed the note to Neil. "He asked you to be there."

Neil read the message. "Be ready to discuss forensics aspect of two murders. Meet chief fifteen minutes prior to the conference."

The paper crackled in his hand when he wadded it. He stuffed the wad in his left front pocket and turned his attention to Katie's car.

A citrus scent filled the car. The fragrance came from an air freshener clipped to the air-flow louver in the dash. A white canvas bag lay on the front passenger seat. The bag bore an ROTC insignia centered on the side in gold and black.

A strand of dark hair eight or nine inches long adhered to the driver's headrest. The color was consistent with Katie's. Sloane collected the hair.

"There's nothing here," Neil said. "Looks like someone detailed it within the last few days. No dust on the instrument panel. There's very little grime on her floor mat. The inside's clean."

Huber said, "I'll meet you at the barn after I have a look at the video. I'll call Katie's parents and tell them when they can come get her car."

****

A chain and lock secured Fletcher's barn's front doors. Sloane led Huber around the side and tugged off the loosened boards where she and Neil gained entry to measure the painting.

Sloane slinked between the boards and pinched her nose while she waited for Huber and Neil to squeeze through. The humidity intensified the muskiness of animal scent mixed with the pungent stench of decayed blood.

"This is even worse than yesterday," she said.

Huber clicked on his Gerber flashlight. He swatted at the sudden swarm of flies, which rose off the oval glow of blood to his left on the dirt floor.

"There's your reason right there," Neil said.

"I guess we now know where Katie died," Huber said. "The same place as Vanessa Flack. He's bold, whoever he is."

Sloane said, "And must have a key to the lock."

They stepped to the center of the barn to avoid the flies.

In any major investigation, headway surged and ebbed comparable to ocean waves. Timing of leads depended on what floated to shore with high tide or out with low tide. The latter often required a deep-sea dive. Both required expertise and luck for success. Sloane, Neil, and Huber possessed a plethora of skills. They would welcome some good fortune.

Neil said, "The killer returned to this location not because of boldness. It's a comfort thing. Who would ever believe a killer would carry his prey to the same place unless a specific reason exists for it? I could understand it happening in a major city where too many places to hide exist. A vehicle parked on a curb or at a warehouse might go unnoticed by hundreds of casual observers. Not here in Madison. Not in a small town where people notice deviances from the norm."

"You said that like you believe the killer might not be a male. We haven't established gender yet." Huber said.

"Going on percentages, males make up around eighty-five percent of serial killers and are more prone to use a hand-wielded weapon versus a female's refined methods. Consider the injury pattern and ask yourself:

Who spares a female victim's face and genitalia in a mutilation-type murder and what is their reason behind it?"

"Someone who exhibits restraint for personal reasons; not an outright hatred of women. The killer wants the victims to look whole, not a faceless representative. In addition, these are not lust-murders. Otherwise he or she would desecrate their sexuality," Sloane said.

"So, who does that rule out?"

"Madison's population is 4,300. Eighteen thousand live in the county. If you dismiss ninety-nine-point-nine percent of the populace based on age and other criteria that leaves four within the city limits or twenty-two potential suspects county wide. If fifty percent of those are female, the number drops to eleven countywide and two in the city."

"She's pretty good."

"That's one theory," Huber said, not sounding convinced. "I saw the video. Nothing there indicated gender to me. Anyhow, we need to get started. Looks like we will be here a while." He crisscrossed the six stalls, shined the light first down, around, and worked his way up the sideboards.

Sloane and Neil stayed on the rearward side of the last stall on the right where the army of flies defended their newfound territory. Neil searched for something he could use as a fan and located a cardboard box in a storage cubby. He ripped off one side of the top and folded the corners on one end inward to make a handgrip. The makeshift fan cleared away enough flies for Sloane to photograph and collect samples of the blood.

The air movement did nothing to combat the stench, especially for Sloane. Her nose remained within arm's length of the source until she finished her task.

"Y'all better come see this," Huber said from the front of the barn.

They looked at where Huber directed the light. An exposé drawn with blood half the size of the first one stained the left door.

Sloane let out a gasp. "That looks more like you than the other."

"What's this maniac have against you, Caldera?" Huber said. "Something is definitely going on here."

"I wish I knew, Detective."

"Maybe I should revisit a confession, but on another front. What big secret are you hiding that would cause somebody to keep on coming at you like this?"

Huber flicked the beam to Neil's face. Neil batted it away.

"Nothing related to any of this."

"Why did you even pick Madison, Georgia to come to? That's what I'd like to know. You should've stayed wherever it is you came from. You're out of your element down here and if all this is because of you, then you can pack your bags and leave."

Sloane's face flushed. "Darren Huber you should be ashamed of yourself." Her suave voice echoed relentless and loud within the confined space. She stiffened her arm and pointed. "He's the best shot we've got at nabbing this butcher and if you can't see that then I'm sure we can find one of our patrol officers who'd love to fill your position."

"Okay, I got it, Sergeant. I got it." He turned to Neil and gave a terse bob.

Neil nodded.

Sloane said, "All right then. It's settled. Let's get this done. It's hot and stinks in here."

****

The odor from the barn overpowered the fabric softener's scent in Neil's shirt and pants. He shoved off his shoes and put them in a used grocery bag to clean later. Shed the clothes in the laundry room, tossed them in the washer, added extra detergent and started the machine. Shampoo and body wash took care of his hair and skin, but the smell lingered in his nostrils.

The murders of Vanessa Flack and Katie Moore consumed Neil's thoughts. Eight hours remained in the first forty-eight since Vanessa's death. Katie's murder occurred approximately thirty hours after Vanessa's. The dilemma became visible to him in an entangled wad. An outsider with lack of access to the files handicapped him to a degree. He wondered if Huber used the scientific method; the best practice to follow for making informed decisions.

Observe. Inquire. Hypothesize. Analyze.

Neil began with the killer's choice of victims: Vanessa and Katie. He wrote their names in blue ink at the top of a page in a spiral-bound notebook. Why them? What did the killer expect to achieve by selecting those two? He dropped two lines and wrote, *Reason*.

He allowed room for an answer to come later and penned, *Location*. Initial contact remained a mystery. No one knew where the initial encounter occurred for either victim. Neil filled in the address for the property where they received their fatal injuries and each discovery.

At mid-page he put *Weapon & Injury Patterns*. The

injury patterns meant something, but what? The killer's choice of sharp-force instrument made the act personal. The pattern showed control. Each slice remained precise one after the other while being inflicted.

Why did Vanessa and Katie not fight their attacker? Neither girl exhibited defense wounds to their hands and arms. No bruises on their face or head from being struck by a fist or blunt implement. No injury to lips or gums to suggest a hand pressed over their mouths. How did he subdue them?

He scribbled, *How Subdued* at the top of the second page and left enough open space to fill in the answers.

Neil jotted *Means of Transport* midway down the page. *One; transport from abduction sites to the barn. Two; transport from barn to location of discovery.* Difficulty of the second proved greatest due to the body's condition. By what means could the killer remove their bodies from the barn and leave no obvious trail? Lack of blood and trace evidence on or near the bodies indicated someone packaged them for transport. That further required a wash-and-re-package site between the barn and place of discovery. Not an easy task.

He wrote, *Intermediate site within reasonable proximity to the barn. A place that is accessible and suitable to his need.*

Not enough answers to too many questions. Neil tossed the notebook to the chair-side table and leaned back in the chair. He stared at the stippled ceiling. The faded surface resembled a satellite image of Death Valley or the surface of the moon—mottled features, yet unidentified specifics. Like the murders. A broad range of answers spread out before them, but no certain path through the maze of questions led there.

A knock on the door roused him from his half-trance.

Chapter 16

A nineteen-year-old girl dressed in jeans, brown leather sandals, and a New York Jets jersey leaned on the balustrade. Her flaxen hair pulled back in a ponytail. The smile on Brita's only child lifted Neil's frame of mind eight levels from the doldrums of the day. He never figured out why she claimed him as her favorite uncle when her father's brothers prospered on Wall Street. They had far more to offer her.

"Hi, Uncle Neil."

"Sharnee. What a nice surprise." He backed out of the doorway. "Come in. How do you like MIT?"

Sharnee crossed to the sofa, spun and leaned on the arm. A rivulet of coconut oil in the air followed her. "I love it. I've decided to major in Brain and Cognitive Sciences. I stopped by earlier but you weren't here."

Neil closed the door, crossed to his chair, but remained on his feet. "It's been an unusual weekend. Maybe you can help me with the neuroscience of morality and tell me why people act maniacal."

"They have morons here, too? I thought people in Georgia have laid-back attitudes. Mom worried about you all the time in your old job."

"Your mother is a good woman. Where is she?"

"She's at The Ritz on Lake Oconee." Sharnee threw her right leg over the arm of the sofa and perched there on her right hip. "You shocked her with the change."

"They left me no choice. I refused to sit behind a desk."

"Do you miss it?"

"More than I ever believed I would."

How could he not miss his former job? Enthusiasm drove him to work, if for nothing more than whatever thrill crossed his path. A TV news correspondent once told him he strived to find the gruesome stories because people love to hear them. Well, Neil thrived on the challenge to solve them.

"You think you'll ever go back?"

A question he often asked himself. The streets beckoned him in dreams. They prodded his return.

"I don't know. Maybe."

"Why the ministry? This religious stuff can't pay much."

"Money's not the reason, Sharnee. A servant's treasure awaits him or her in Heaven."

"A moot point from my perspective. Don't do you much good down here."

"I got satisfaction."

"You got satisfaction in the other job based on what Mom told me…wait a minute. Got? As in past tense? Have you quit the church?"

He harrumphed. "More like they quit me. The deacons called me in this morning and told me they no longer required my services. I'm not sure if I feel bad, good, or indifferent about it."

"Just like that? They didn't even give a reason?"

"No reason. That's it. Done."

Sharnee leaned forward, planted her hands on the armrest. "That's tommyrot. I guess all that talk about deacons' hauteur must be true. Why would they dismiss you without a reason? That sounds messed up."

"I have no idea. Everything seemed to go well around here until Saturday evening. We had a murder—"

She straightened. Her cerulean eyes widened. "Murder? Who?"

The leather cushion squeaked when Neil sat on the chair. He rested his elbows on his knees. "We had two murders this weekend. Girls. They were seniors at the high school. Contrary to what you may believe, there are people here who confirm their disregard for human lives. The chief of police asked me to help."

She slid off the arm onto the cushion. "Did you go to the scenes? Were they gruesome?"

Neil dipped his head.

"Do you have pictures?"

"I have those from the first scene."

"May I see them?"

"I'll make a deal with you. I'll let you if you promise to not tell your mother."

"Deal."

Sharnee bounded off the sofa. She grabbed the laptop and set it on the kitchen table. The computer purred when she pressed the power button. The screen brightened blue and a prompt asked for a password. She typed what Neil told her. He inserted a USB drive into the port. When prompted, Sharnee opened the file. A picture of Fletcher's barn filled a window on the screen.

"What was her name?"

"Vanessa Flack."

"Was Vanessa's body discovered in this barn?"

"Off to the right there." He touched the screen.

He waited for Sharnee to form her initial assessment before he offered more information. She viewed eight photos of Vanessa and her surroundings. She leaned back in the chair.

"She died somewhere else."

"Yes."

Sharnee studied the photos taken inside the barn. "He's smart. The blood's confined to a small space. No trail."

Neil tensed when the next photo showed the sketch painted in blood on the barn's wall.

Sharnee shrieked and jumped out of the chair. The chair tilted rearward and banged to the floor. She pressed her left hand to her chest.

"That's you."

"That's the consensus."

"Why you?"

He set the chair upright. "I wish I knew."

"Tell me the police know who did this."

Neil stared at the screen.

Sharnee said, "I'll find the guilty party, Uncle Neil. I will solve this case for them, and you. Does anybody on the force know what happened in New York?"

"I know of one."

"What does he know?"

"She. She knows everything."

"Ah. You've found somebody to confide in. Tell me. What's her name? Is she pretty?"

"Sloane Azevedo, and yes. She's alluring in looks and personality."

"Is she working on the case?"

"Sloane's a uniform sergeant. She collected the evidence and took photos at the crime scenes. The department has a detective working the cases."

"Only one? How does that work if they get overwhelmed with felonious offenses?"

"They have two detectives. The entire county averages two homicides per year. If you consider domestic cases, stranger-to-stranger murders seldom occur in Madison."

"Is that why this Chief Fleishman person asked you to assist them?"

"He asked me because he refused to turn the case over to the GBI. He exudes pride. A person in his position wants to maintain control. They relinquish control if another agency gets called in to work it."

"How well does he know you that he asked you for a consult?"

"He's chairman of deacons at the church."

"He enforces the law and governs the church? No wonder he's prideful. I don't trust him. Neither should you."

"I don't."

Chapter 17

The second step leading to the Fleishmans' front porch wobbled beneath Neil's foot. He glanced at the loose plank, weathered and cracked from exposure. The porch floor showed a similar appearance. The boards buckled and stained in places from feet, and where petals from hanging baskets landed and dried.

A voice responded to his knock on the door, "Hold on a minute." Her words came out strained.

Tess Fleishman's face lightened the moment she opened the door and saw him. "Come in. It's so nice to see you. Rob's not home if you're looking for him." Mrs. Rob Fleishman looked as though she suffered a fate worse than the floor on which he stood. Skin paled. Brown eyes matched the surrounding circles. Sweat matted her chestnut hair. The pink cotton shirt and navy capri pants she wore fit loosely on her body.

"I came by to visit you, Tess. I hope you don't mind."

"You are always welcome, Neil. You should know that by now."

Tess's arms trembled when she lifted her walker and set it forward five inches. Her feet shuffled in black slip-on house shoes. She took seven steps to clear the foyer. Neil closed the door. He put his hand on the rail next to her left hand and supported her mid-back with the other.

"May I?" He motioned to the walker with a tilt of his head while he tugged on the handrail.

She released her hold.

Neil set aside the walker. He stooped, and in one smooth motion cradled his left arm behind her knees and lifted her off her feet. The left shoe flicked off and sailed across the room. He expected flaccid tissue under her garments. Instead, the muscles in her back and thighs felt firm and fit. He carried her to a brown suede recliner angled at forty-five degrees from the wall. There she had a view of the flat-screen TV mounted on the wall above a sofa table, and her garden through a side window. A green, tan, and brown couch backed to the wall on the far side of the window.

"You know how long it's been since a man held me in his arms?" she said. Her body shivered.

A plaid afghan draped the arm of the sofa. "Is this what you use for cover?"

"A long time," said Tess. "I'd almost forgotten how good it felt."

Neil lifted and unfolded the afghan and draped it over her legs to her waist. He grabbed the shoe and slid it onto her foot. A purple bruise discolored her left leg above the ankle, another sign of the disease.

"Anything I can get for you?"

"It's sweet of you to ask. I have a cola in the fridge, if you don't mind."

"Not at all. Anything else?"

"I could use a kiss."

Neil smiled. "I'll be right back with the soda."

The kitchen looked as though it had gone unused for weeks. The stainless double-sink shined. No crumbs or dust visible on the granite counters. He pulled open the refrigerator door. The top shelf held milk in a half-gallon carton, a jug filled with sweet tea, and bottles of orange and pineapple juices. The soda stood on the second shelf. He removed a twelve-ounce can and returned to the living room.

He popped the tab and handed the drink to Tess. She took a sip and set the can on the table to her right between the chair and a window overlooking her flower garden. She extended her arms, licked her pink lips.

"I'll have that kiss now, please."

Neil leaned forward and kissed her forehead. She brushed his cheek with her lips and embraced his shoulders. Her hands slid off as if powerless to squeeze and pull him to her. He caught her arms as they dropped, folded her hands into his. She held onto his hands. "I adore you, Neil. You blessed this town by your presence. I'm blessed that you're here. I needed this. Thank you." She released her grip and let her hands drop to her lap.

"My pleasure, Tess. Are you comfortable?"

"As much as I can be. You're a strong man, Neil. I never figured a padre would have such strength."

"It's one of the good traits I inherited."

He backed onto the edge of the sofa, turned toward her, and rested his elbows on his knees. He studied her slender face, her eyes, and read despair in both.

"You don't have a bad fiber in your body, Neil. I knew it the moment I saw you in the supermarket the day we met. Remember? It was the Saturday before your first day at our church."

"As long as I live."

"Rob told me we were getting a new pastor. I knew who you were the second I laid eyes on you even though you looked nothing like a minister. You showed magnetism I'd never experienced. It became an instant trust for me."

"What if I told you I have a marred past?"

"Who doesn't? God knows I have. I focus on the present, and plan for whatever future I may be blessed with. Whatever happened in your past hasn't affected the person you are today."

"You may change your mind before I leave."

"Why? Are you planning to have your way with me? Take advantage of my weakened thirty-six-year-old body?"

"Somebody please, save me in this moment of temptation."

Tess laughed. "You did kiss me, you know. If you had taken me to the bedroom instead of this chair, this visit could have become reminiscent of better days. My body still works even if it's not as fit as it once was. I'm not fragile. I won't break if I'm squeezed."

"And make Rob jealous."

She sighed. "Rob Fleishman has paid no attention to me in weeks…make that months. I get a peck on the cheek before he leaves most mornings, and I'm usually out when he comes home in the evenings. I have no idea what time he even gets in. The long days drain what little strength I wake up with by suppertime."

"We'll pray for a miracle."

"For me or for Rob?"

"Let's start with you."

Tess looked toward the window. She lifted her right hand and wiped a tear from her right eye. "Look at me, Neil. Leukemia wrecked my life. I have no strength to plant new flowers. My meals consist of frozen dinners or nutritional drinks. I have needs and no one to satisfy them. Rob wants nothing to do with me. I think he may be having an affair. A wife knows. What reason do I have to live?"

"Tess?" He softened his voice.

She looked at him. Eyes wet. Her lips twitched.

"How did the sound of your name make you feel?"

Tess opened her mouth to speak, closed it, and swallowed. She covered her mouth and coughed. "The way you said it made me feel good. It's the next best thing to hearing, 'I love you.' "

She shifted her eyes toward the hallway and stared for several seconds. "I want to show you something. Go to the second door on your right and look in the guest bedroom. There's a painting on the wall to the right of the door above the bureau. Bring it to me."

Neil strolled along the hall. He pushed the door open and stepped in the room. A child's portrait filled an eleven-by-fourteen frame. Lines distinctive to the artist curved and shaped the face and made her appear alive. The watercolor image dated eight years earlier. The artist signed the lower right corner, Rob Fleishman. He stared at the signature. No signature existed on the blood portraits. He gazed at the brush strokes. The watercolor lacked enough clarity for comparison to the brush strokes on the killer's portraits.

Neil lifted the print off the nail in the sheetrock wall and carried it to Tess.

She propped the frame at arms' length on her thighs. "This is me on my tenth birthday. Rob sketched it from a picture my mother took that day."

"There's no doubt it's you."

"One day I'll have to show you his most recent

works. He's a genuine artist by anybody's standards."

Neil wondered if Rob's recent projects included the two in the barn, and the one in the Stoltz's garage. The one Tess held in her hand showed minute similarities to them. Not enough for evidentiary value and this one proved circumstantial.

"Is he an Artist Registry member?"

"He is. He became a premium member ten years ago. Premium members must have nine original paintings or more in their portfolio. Rob has twenty-two, I believe. It may be more by now. I don't know. He shares none of his work or hobbies with me. He never has."

"Has he mentioned the homicides?"

"Nothing. But like I said, he gets home late and I'm either in bed or getting ready for bed. The difference I've noticed is his attitude. I hear him grumble and talk to himself. He never used to do that."

"When did you first notice this change?"

"Last week."

"Anything else?"

Her gaze averted to her lap. She sucked in her lower lip raked her teeth across it. Her chest jerked when she inhaled. Shoulders sagged when she exhaled a sigh.

"Talk to me, Tess."

"I stumbled across some of his clothes that had blood on them. Something didn't seem right about the way they were soiled, and wet."

"Wet?"

"Soaked. The front of the shirt and pants were drenched but the seat of the pants and backs of the legs were dry.

"When was this?"

"Sunday morning."

Neil thought of the scene at the barn. Rob was there in his official capacity. Perhaps he tried to wash off the blood.

She continued. "I don't concern myself with anything Rob does nowadays. I just wish he would take some time to talk to me. We haven't carried on a conversation longer than a sentence or two in weeks. He acts like he's too busy to even be here. And when he is here, he stays elsewhere in the house or out at the shed. It's like he can't be in the same room with me anymore." She sniffed the air. "Do I reek of body odor?"

"Quite the opposite."

"I should hope so. I bathe the best I can as my plight allows. I used to mist my body with an after-shower spray, but I no longer have a reason for that."

"Maybe you should. Where do you keep it and I'll get it for you?"

"Are you serious?"

"Why not?"

Tess's face brightened with a smile. She unbuttoned the top button of her shirt and reached for the next. "I might need some help to get out of this shirt."

"It's best you leave it on, Tess. I might not be able to control myself."

Her cheeks blushed. "Look on the shelf inside the walk-in closet. There's a red box behind a lavender pouch."

Neil retrieved the bottle and returned to the living room. Tess's open shirt revealed her cleavage. She smiled when she sprayed her neck, and spread the cloth first left and then right, to spray the swell of her breast. She pushed aside the afghan, rotated the bottle, and sprayed the air above her. The mist descended to her clothes and chair.

"Okay. When Rob gets close enough to smell me, he may wonder if I'm having an affair. If you don't mind, put this back and bring me the lavender pouch. I'll put on some make-up. Make him suspicious."

"And jealous?"

"I'll not expect that. Mystified will be enough."

Chapter 18

Heat shrouded Neil when he opened the door of his Acura. He'd forgotten to crack the windows before his visit with Tess. He started the engine, turned the climate-control fan on full blast, and directed the air-flow louvers to blow on his face and chest. The clock in the instrument panel showed two thirty-three. The outside temperature readout showed seventy-seven degrees.

Dust and pollen clung to Tess's gray Traverse nosed in under a boxed eave metal carport. The space next to it was empty.

Neil pulled out his phone and called Sloane.

"I just had an enlightening visit with Tess Fleishman. She told me she found some wet clothes with blood on them."

"What's that noise? It sounds like a tornado."

"It's the air conditioner." He lowered the fan speed and flipped the louver. "Is that better?"

"Did you say wet?"

"She used the word *drenched*. In the front. She said the backs of the shirt and pants were dry."

"Rob stayed at the scene awhile after you left and helped load the body in the ambulance. That might account for the blood."

"That's not all. I saw a watercolor sketch he signed. Tess said he is a member of Artist Registry with

138

several projects to his credit."

"That'll be easy enough to confirm. I'll check their website."

"There is one more thing. She tried to seduce me."

"How?"

He told her how Tess seemed to struggle on the walker, how he carried her to the chair. "She bared her cleavage and remarked how her body still worked despite her appearance. She told me Rob no longer paid any attention to her, and she thinks he is having an affair."

"What did you say?"

"That we'd pray for a miracle."

Sloane laughed. "I bet that withered her spirit."

"She changed the subject. One thing though, her muscle tone felt taut for a person supposedly inactive for six months."

"Maybe you took her breath away and she tensed when you picked her up. What woman wouldn't?"

"Personal experience?"

"Not yet."

Neil imagined Sloane's smile.

"Tess showed difficulty walking. If she experienced spasticity, that could explain the difficulty and the tenseness. That's when she showed me the watercolor and told me about the bloody clothes."

"I'd like to see them."

"She's steamed about something and has plenty of time to simmer. Anyways, Brita and Sharnee arrived this morning. I'd like to take you to dinner with them if you're free. Six o'clock with my sister and niece. Gaby's on Oconee."

"I love that place. I'll be ready. Come by at five

thirty. I have a lead on the case I want to run by you."

"I'll see you in a few minutes. I'm on my way to the station to meet with Rob."

****

Feet shuffled in the corridor outside Sloane's office. Huber appeared in the doorway. He leaned on the jamb. The knot on his tie was off centered and loose around his neck. His light blue shirt wrinkled and darkened where sweat soaked the collar and down the front.

"How are things in Hell?" Sloane said.

Huber chuckled. "That bad, huh?"

"I smell the sulfur from here."

"One of the guys just farted."

Huber lumbered over and dropped a packet on the desk. Sloane opened the bottom drawer in her credenza, took out a can of air freshener and sprayed two bursts beyond the edge of the desk. Set the can on the corner.

"Right. Blame it one somebody else. After the press conference, go home. Get some rest. That's an order."

"It's all there. Everything Caldera asked for."

She removed the stapled documents and Huber's notes. An itemized cover page listed Rob Fleishman's phone records, cell tower pings, and GPS link to the city vehicle issued to the chief. She stuffed the papers in the envelope.

"Good work. Did you see anything of interest?"

"He's spending a lot of time on Four Lakes Drive."

****

Chief Fleishman looked up from the notes spread on his desk when Neil knocked on the jamb. He wore a white shirt and red tie. Two three-ring binders and a three-inch stack of folders filled the right side of the desk. Inside those and pushed toward the front sat a black multi-line desk phone.

"Come on in and close the door. Anything in the Moore girl's car?"

Neil tugged one of two cloth-covered chairs in front of the desk back two feet and sat. The cushion cooled his back through his shirt where the air conditioner had blown on it.

"A single hair on her seat. Otherwise, the car's clean."

Rob leaned back in his chair. The chair legs groaned. "That's too bad. I was hoping to have something to give to the press. They've hounded the office all day. I've received nothing but preliminary findings from the autopsy and the crime lab's analyses."

The pride heard in Rob's words at the church that morning ebbed to reticence.

"What do you need from me?" Neil offered as though their previous meeting never happened.

"Keep the eggs off our faces. I'm sure they will throw quite a few at me and the Department for keeping the cases in-house instead of turning them over to the GBI. Who knew we'd have a second homicide so soon? I may have made a mistake."

Neil waved. "Hold off on inferences, Rob. Detective Huber and Sergeant Azevedo possess ability and resolve to crack these cases. They require freedom to perform without interference from you or anyone else."

Rob propped his arms on the desk, jutted his head. "By else you're insinuating the mayor and city council?"

"I'm not insinuating anyone. I'm including everyone."

"If you're peeved about this morning, get over it. The deacon board did what we thought best for the church and the community. You had your chance to speak, and you refused. This is my department, Neil." Rob glowered at him. Eyes askance. "I'll run it my way."

"I have no qualms about the board's decision. I'll remain silent on that topic. This subject is different. You have the right to run this place as you please, but you assigned the cases to Huber and Azevedo. You asked for my input so here it is. Let them do their jobs." He wanted to add, *you do yours.*

Chief Fleishman tilted his head upward and tightened his lips. He stared at Neil five seconds and then said, "Fair enough." He reached for a file atop his inbox on the end of a credenza. "I received this report ten minutes ago." He opened the folder and showed the contents to Neil. "It's the autopsy report on Vanessa Flack. I figured you'd like to see it before we talk to the press."

Neil flipped to the second page to the Findings and read the pathologist documented summary and conclusions. Page three summarized biographical information and visible external characteristics. The pathologist focused on and described Vanessa's external injuries in great detail. She measured length and depth of the crisscrossed incised wounds on the chest and abdomen before she opened the body with the standard Y-incision.

The pathologist reported no injury to the internal

organs, which she first examined in situ—in their anatomical positions—and subsequently each organ one by one after she removed and weighed them.

The Medical Examiner ruled the cause of death as exsanguination due to sharp force injuries.

Toxicology listed as Pending.

Neil looked up from the report. "Her narrative and findings are in line with what I observed at the scene and death by exsanguination is what I suspected happened to Vanessa. I agree with her opinion related to depth and angle of the incised wounds. They suggest the killer may be ambidextrous. There's no tissue bridging along any of the slashes. The blade used has a keen edge but an unusual profile. She opined it might be sharpened on only one edge. I agree."

"Should we be looking for a straight razor?"

Neil shook his head.

"What then?"

Neil wanted to tell the chief he should key on an Emerson CQC-6 knife used by military personnel. That was the knife the intruder brandished according to the stranger. "Some type of tactical knife."

"Anything else?"

"I believe we'll learn similar results once we receive the findings on Katie Moore."

"What can you give the press?"

Neil rose to head over to City Hall. "The basics. That's all they'll ever get from me."

****

Basic information apart from important facts in evidence found its way to the forefront of Neil's thoughts in his short walk to City Hall. News vans and trucks filled many of the spaces on High Street at the

Bank of Madison across North Main. He walked alone unlike that evening in New York. Then, reporters swarmed him, blitzed him with questions sounding more accusatory than inquisitive. They demanded more than basic information and in return received no comment. Today, no reporter ran up to him or blindsided him with their presence. To them, Neil blended with the throng.

That changed five minutes into the news conference when Chief Fleishman introduced him.

"I'm handing over the reins to the department's consultant, Neil Caldera."

The six steps to the podium felt like he slogged halfway up Everest. By their attendance, the officious reporters settled for first-hand knowledge in lieu of an exclusive unavailable to them outside the room. Neil planned to leave them hungry. He aimed to walk away from the same discontented looks he witnessed two years earlier when guilt began its scourge on his soul.

Reporters from the major networks and two cable news stations identified by their press credentials and the bundle of microphones on the front of the lectern filled the first few rows of metal chairs. Other attendees represented newspapers and large and small market radio stations.

Cameras clicked. Eyes focused on him.

"Two evenings ago, I witnessed the work of a killer's depraved indifference to life outside a barn on East Washington Street here in Madison. Chief Fleishman requested my response to the scene and asked me to consult on Vanessa Flack's murder and render opinions. Katie Moore suffered the same fate between ten thirty last evening and one o'clock this morning. The killer posed her body on the grounds of Morgan County High School. Injury patterns to Vanessa and Katie display the consistency of a skilled, well-trained individual capable of incapacitating the victim in a matter of seconds. Once the killer robbed Vanessa and Katie of life, the assailant washed the bodies and assured their discovery by an act of public spectacle.

"The person responsible for these murders dared hide behind a thin façade of superficiality. The assailant deviates from the spectacle of normality to appease a personal desire. We will expose this concealment and the person beneath."

"How soon do you plan to accomplish that?" one reported blurted.

"I'll not give specifics."

"Do you think the killer will strike again and what are you doing to prevent another murder?" said another.

"To answer your first part, anything is possible. I'll leave the prevention aspect to the law enforcement authorities."

"How were they killed?"

"Although Vanessa and Katie sustained sharp force trauma, I defer the cause of death to the medical examiner."

"What about the weapon used to inflict the injuries?"

"We're looking into the possibility that it might be a tactical-type weapon."

"Can you be more specific?"

"That's as far as I'm willing to commit at this time."

"Do you have any reason to believe a female

committed these murders? Is it not true most serial killers are male?"

"Statistics show males commit eighty-five percent of serial murders. Given Morgan County's population of 18,000 and omitting the majority based on age and other criteria, potential suspect numbers are few."

He motioned to a reporter he recognized from WSBTV. She asked, "What are your qualifications and how do you plan to catch this killer?"

"Too much emphasis on credentials skews focus. We strive for results. The Scientific Method provides a means to that success. We're assured the evidence collected will lead to the perpetrator and secure a conviction at the appointed time."

A male in his forties stood and identified himself as a representative of the Atlanta Journal and Constitution. "Do you care to elaborate on the evidence and do you have a suspect?"

"I have no comment on the evidence or suspects."

Neil strode to and out the nearest door.

Chapter 19

Sloane's Jaguar rolled to a stop in front of her detached garage. She killed the engine and sat there with her head on the headrest. The sun warmed the car's interior. The warmth relaxed her. It made her drowsy. She lowered the two front windows. A breeze fanned her face from the passenger's side. She closed her eyes.

The wind shifted. That's when Sloane smelled the distinctive odor a person secretes when under emotional stress. An ammonia smell brought on by a high-protein, low-carbohydrate diet. She opened her eyes a second before a shadow blocked the sun and the muzzle of a pistol pressed her left temple. Nothing other than black fabric reflected in the side mirror. The rear-view mirror reflected an empty driveway.

The person opened the door and motioned her out of the car. The one standing wore tactical gear and a balaclava. Sloane remembered what Neil had told her and guessed this must be the same person. The one she dubbed TG. She complied, hands out in front of her. When she stood, TG thrust her back against the side of the Jaguar. Sunlight in her eyes prevented her from getting a good look at the face. The eyes suggested a female. TG snatched Sloane's pistol out of its holster on her right hip in a cross-handed grip, ejected the magazine, and tossed the pistol onto the back seat beyond her reach. The magazine struck the asphalt and bounced near the left rear tire.

TG whistled.

A man came into view from behind the garage. A camouflage facemask hid most of his face but did nothing to hide his identity from Sloane. The same build. Same faded blue tee shirt. Grease swipe on the lower left two inches above a frayed hem. Brown work boots.

Loudmouth.

A second man rounded the far corner of the house wearing his green "Watch This" tee and a ski mask.

TG waited until the man in the blue shirt got to the car, backed ten feet, whirled and jogged into the woods.

Loudmouth said, "Well, well, well. If it ain't the lady Sergeant come home for supper. We're going to eat well tonight, honey. You bring the sweet and I got the meat."

"You ain't fooling," the second man said and laughed.

Sloane sidled leftward away from the car door. The two men countered her movement. Fifteen feet apart. Twenty feet away from her. "Two on one? Can't either of you handle me alone?" She faced the man in the "Watch This" tee. "Can you, Billy Ray? Davis might even let you go first."

Billy Ray backed a step. "She knows our names, Davis."

"Shut up and take care of business," Davis said. "The broad won't say a word when I get through with her. I guarantee you."

"I guess yesterday wasn't enough to convince you." Sloane sprang a step toward Billy Ray to taunt him. He flinched. She laughed at him. Get your opponent angry. An angry foe makes mistakes.

Davis pulled a fixed-blade hunting knife from behind his back. He waved it in front of his face. "Time for supper. Think I'll have tenderloin tonight."

"You're right. The tender loin you'll have tonight will be yours, Davis Leggett."

Sloane sprinted toward Davis, dropped into a straight-leg baseball slide and drove her right heel midway between his privates and his belly button. Davis slashed at her with the knife. The blade nicked the leg of her uniform before he lost his grip. She scooped the knife mid-air and sliced his right forearm in a backhand stroke. She ended the slide-scoop-slash motion on her feet.

Davis tumbled to his back and scrunched forward. The crotch of his jeans darkened, followed by a urine scent. Blood dripped off his arm.

Sloane glared at Billy Ray. "Take off the trash, Billy Ray." She leaned into the Jaguar for her pistol, grabbed her keys and the packet of documents and closed the car door. She picked up the magazine and jammed it home.

The click broke Billy Ray's mouth-open trance. "Yes, ma'am."

"And you can forget where I live." She said it with the tenacity of a bear determined to protect her cubs. Her focus stayed on him while he hurried to Davis, hauled the larger man on his shoulder in an awkward fireman's carry, and tottered toward the road.

Sloane waited until Billy Ray struggled out of sight before she examined her posterolateral thigh where the knife blade cut through the cloth. The fibers snapped when she tugged apart the slit. The four-inch cut underneath amounted to little more than a scratch. It stung when she touched it. Her first encounter with barbed wire resulted in more damage than this.

A vehicle door slammed in the distance. She listened. An engine revved. Exhaust spewed its rumble. It lessened as the vehicle moved farther away.

Nothing appeared disturbed or out-of-place in and around the garage. Sloane circled the house, checked the windows and the back door on her way to the front. Secure. She entered and locked the door.

Sloane set her keys and the envelope on a mahogany table in the hall, shrugged out of her uniform shirt on her way to the bedroom. She laid the shirt on the bed. The Velcro screeched when she tugged the straps on her body armor. She hung the vest on the back of a chair in the corner. The damp undershirt clung to her chest and back. She slipped off her shoes, unbuckled her gun belt, coiled it, and placed it on the chair with the vest. She stepped out of her pants and kicked them to the side of the bureau. After removing her undergarments, she stepped into the shower.

Her breath hitched when the cold water sprayed her skin. Adrenaline surged through her body. Cold showers invigorated her, along with their added benefits. Cold water softened her hair and smoothed her skin. She washed and rinsed her hair. The body wash filled the shower with scents of caju fruit, lime, and spearmint.

After ten minutes, she toweled off, brushed and dried her hair and put on a silk robe that came to her upper thighs. She sat on the bed and stared at the clothes hanging in the closet. Her clothes lined the rod from one end to the other. They screamed aloneness. Living alone suited her for years after she graduated from Notre Dame. Now, her aunt's colossal antebellum intensified the void in her life.

It wasn't the house. She loved the house and every piece of furniture in it. She enjoyed the privacy and quietness the land surrounding the house provided her. The place satisfied every need except one.

****

Neil ascended the steps to Sloane's porch two at a time. He pressed the doorbell at four fifty-eight. He ran his fingers through his hair. Checked his shirt and slacks. Feet pattered toward the door. His heart rate increased. It surged when Sloane opened the door dressed in a loose-fitting cream button-up top and navy pants.

"You look nice," he said. *Smell nice, too.*

Her smile grew wider. "So do you. I just have to slip on my shoes and I'll be ready." She turned and glided toward the back of the house.

He watched every step. The fluidness of her stride in bare feet on the hardwood floor captivated him. The way her hair bounced and waved on her shoulders beckoned him. He wanted to follow her, take her in his arms and again experience her kiss. The passions that kiss conveyed lingered in his mind. He yearned for another, and another. Every moment spent with Sloane fueled his desire for her love.

The click-clack of shoes replaced the patter of feet. Sloane came into view five seconds later. She strolled to him. A small clutch bag hung from her left shoulder by its thin strap. A manila envelope flapped in her left hand. This time she didn't pause at arm's length. She slid her hands around his sides and gazed into his face.

"I missed you today," she said.

Neil leaned to within three inches of her face. "How shall I make it up to you?"

She closed the distance. Their lips touched. The same soft and dewy kiss of yesterday feasted on his heart. He embraced her, tilted his head. Sloane's kiss seared through his being.

When their lips parted, she said, "That might get me through dinner."

"What if it doesn't?"

"Then we'll sneak off to find a private cove on the lake where no one will bother us."

Neil backed across the threshold onto the porch. He waited for her to lock the deadbolt and let the storm door swing closed. He looked out at the countryside. Birds with black, white, and yellow feathers flitted tree to tree. They chirped, craned their necks before taking off to another limb on another tree. One dipped to a bird feeder at the edge of the yard. A cardinal fluttered by and perched on a limb above the feeder.

"The yellow ones are goldfinch," Sloane said. "They visit the feeders in late afternoons and evenings. They'll soon migrate back northward."

They descended the steps and crossed to Neil's Acura. Sloane stuffed the envelope between her seat and the console. Once they buckled their seat belts, Neil peered at the disturbed sod between the Jaguar and the house.

"What happened there?"

"Where?" She pushed up in her seat and looked where he pointed. "Hmm, I'll have to check that out tomorrow. It looks like something dragged across there."

Neil performed a Y-turn and drove to the road and turned east. When they passed through town, he said, "What lead do you have on the case?"

"Before I get to that…" She tugged the packet up and showed it to him. "The records you asked Huber to get for you. They're all in here." She stuck it back in place, opened her purse, and pulled out a slip of paper. "I ran the license plates for the vehicles. Davis Leggett is the loudmouth. The one in the "Watch This" tee is Billy Ray Haney. The other two are James Elmore and Thomas Wiggins. Elmore drove the Tundra. He's out of commission a few days in the hospital. Leggett owns the tow truck."

Neil guided the Acura down the entrance ramp and merged onto I-20 behind a semi blowing black exhaust that smelled of diesel fuel. He sped up around the tractor-trailer and maintained his speed at seventy-two.

"They'll want revenge for what we did to them," he said. "Somebody hired them. It's somebody with connections; otherwise, how could they get law enforcement to block the highway? You heard what your deputy friend told us. Somebody asked the Sheriff's Office for help. I dare believe an officer perpetrated this, but who if not someone in law enforcement?"

"I hate to think of it. Corruption exists everywhere, not just in places like Chicago and New York."

"It only takes one."

She nodded. "And one to fight it."

"In our case, two. We're in this together, Sloane. They will come for both of us, not just me. I imagine they want me gone from here. If that's the case, I've got

153

news for them. I'm not leaving."

Sloane looked at him. "You mean that?"

"Yes. My reason outweighs their threats. I grew up on Long Island. These rednecks lack resilience for the war I'll declare on them."

"You are unemployed as of this morning. Why stay here in Madison?"

He reached for her hand. "Because you're here."

Chapter 20

Brita greeted Neil with a kiss on his cheek and a hug outside Gaby's. "I've missed you. These fifteen months have seemed more like fifteen years. Leya and Shina send their love."

"I've missed you, too." He put his hand on Sloane's back and introduced them.

Neil studied his sister's oval face, thin cheeks, and brown eyes. She stood three inches taller than the average five-six Scandinavian women. Her brunette hair curled to her shoulders, pulled back on the left side. The weariness he'd observed the last time they were together no longer presented itself. She looked happy and her smile showed it.

Brita said, "I called ahead. They have our table ready."

The hostess showed them to a table for four overlooking the water. Sloane sat to Neil's left, Sharnee on his right. Brita sat across from him. "Kyle will be your server. He will be with you in a moment."

Kyle came out of the back dressed in a white shirt and khakis. His straw-colored hair tucked under a black cap. "May I interest you in a bottle of Chardonnay or cocktail and one of our appetizers?"

Sharnee chose the blue raspberry lemonade and Brita ordered a bottle of Sauvignon Blanc for the table. She ordered the calamari appetizer after everyone agreed.

While Brita and Sloane engaged in a get-acquainted chat, Sharnee leaned in to Neil. "You were right. She's pretty."

Sloane paused mid-sentence, swiveled her head and smiled at Sharnee. "Thank you. I was just telling your mother how proud she must be of you. MIT is a great school. What are your plans afterward?"

"When Uncle Neil starts his own business, I hope he'll let me work with him. Every investigative firm could benefit with a neuropsychologist on staff."

Sloane looked at Neil with scrunched brow. "When is this new business supposed to open, Uncle Neil?" She said it in jest.

"Well, now that the church no longer requires my services...If I started a business, I'd need a good partner."

"About this partner of yours," Sloane said. "Would she be an equal?"

Sharnee's foot nudged his leg.

"Fifty-fifty," he said. "If I found the right partner."

"Sixty-forty works for me," Sloane said.

"Hey, what about me?" Sharnee said.

"You may have half of my sixty," said Sloane.

The server returned with their drinks and appetizer and took their dinner order—Sharnee selected the lobster while Sloane, Brita, and Neil chose the grilled arctic char.

Sloane sipped her wine, said, "So, Brita, tell me what Neil was like growing up in a house full of females?"

"Mother taught him how to be a gentleman. Our parents adopted me when they thought Mother could not conceive. I was fourteen months old. Two months afterward, she found out she was pregnant with Neil. Complications at birth resulted in a hysterectomy. They wanted more children and adopted Leya, an Indian, and Shina, from Japan. Differences in ancestry never mattered to him. He showed his respect and defended us when necessary. Nobody ever teased him about his family more than once."

"What would he do?"

Brita glanced at Neil and back to her. She grinned. "The same thing if anyone attacked you. Teach them a lesson in etiquette."

Steam rose off the entrées when the server set their plates on the table. The aroma of the char and lemon butter sauce won over their focus and restricted conversation to between bites and frequent laughter.

Brita dabbed her lips with her napkin and laid it on her plate. "Is she the one?"

"Is she the one what?" Neil said it aware of her inference.

"You know darn well what, little brother."

Sloane clutched his left hand. "I entice him every chance I get, Brita."

"Entice him all you want, Sloane. I assure you he's worth every moment of your efforts."

****

"I have a surprise for you," Sloane said.

"What kind of surprise?"

"You'll see when we get there."

Her directions led them west on Linger Longer Road, north on Lake Oconee Parkway to I-20, west one exit where they got off and a few miles later reached Blue Springs Marina. The sun sank below the treetops by the time they strolled to the dock where an Avalon pontoon floated in the third slip from the end.

"What do you think?" Sloane said, motioning to the boat.

"That's the nicest pontoon I've ever seen."

She smiled, took his hand, and stepped ahead of him on the boat. "We have it for as long as we wish."

"Sounds good to me."

Sloane started the boat, accelerated out of the slip. The boat glided on top of the smooth water powered by its Mercury 135hp engine. After they passed Blue Springs Road, Sloane slowed and pulled into a cove, shut off the engine and lowered the anchor. Bosky banks on three sides shielded them from potential prying eyes. The wake smoothed behind the boat.

Clouds to the west transformed to pink and lavender pillows edged in silver on the dying day's cyanotic sky.

"Isn't it gorgeous?" Sloane said, pulled off her shoes, squatted, and set them on the deck at the head of one lounger. She turned to look at him. He sat on the lounger watching her cloaked in the twilight.

"Yes, it is."

"You're not even looking."

"Oh yes I am."

She touched his left cheek as he reclined on the lounger. He took her hand in his. Crickets chirped in the nearby landscape. Moonlight filtered through the treetops behind them and painted the pontoon in splashes of silver.

Sloane squeezed his hand. "Relaxed?"

"Yes. I needed this. Do you come here often?"

"Once a week on average. You're the first person

I've brought here."

"I'm honored."

He swung his legs off the side and sat up. He maintained his hold on her hand. Firm, yet tender. His thumb caressed the back of her hand. Her eyes met his. They emitted the honesty and the goodness she believed hallmarked his heart. Attributes she sought after in a mate. She took a deep breath and held it a few seconds before she let it ease out.

Sloane tugged his arm. When he stood, she embraced him a moment and backed away.

"Excuse me a second." She turned her back to him. She slid her hands up under her blouse, unhooked and removed her bra. She dropped it next to her shoes. "Okay, now. Where were we?" She pressed her body against his, arms around his waist. "Better?"

Her softness and warmth filled the space between his chest and his arms when he squeezed her. Contact with his muscular chest sent tingles through her body. She imagined how much her sensitivity might intensify without layers of cloth between them.

"You are taking Brita's advice seriously," he said.

"I'll take the chance on a worthwhile investment."

She leaned into his palm when he brushed her lips with his thumb and his hand caressed her left cheek. A sailboat glided southward on its way to the marina. Its captain was perhaps trying to reach the marina before twilight's end. The pontoon swayed on the ripples after it floated by. When she steadied her feet, the shift across his chest teased her delicate points. Her tight depths ached for fulfillment. Sloane squeezed her thighs together the minute Neil kissed her lips and cheeks and worked his way to her neck. Her willpower faded when her leg pressed the side of the lounger. She lowered herself onto the pad and scooted to her left.

"Sit with me."

Neil sat on the lounger at the level of her waist. Sloane laid her hand on his right thigh. He said nothing when her hand glided up the thigh and the tips of her fingers touched him. His breath hitched. She waited five seconds for him to stop her. He laid his hand on her abdomen.

The ringtone on Neil's phone pealed. He answered the call. The voice on the other end wailed into the phone. Sloane sensed bad news based on Neil's downward glance and scrunched brow.

He said, "I'll call you back in five minutes." He ended the call. "Sharnee's missing."

****

Sloane stuffed her feet into her shoes. The engine rumbled to life. The boat swayed when she backed out of the cove, whipped around at her spin of the steering wheel and surged forward. Neil covered his ear while he talked to Brita on his phone. In five minutes, they docked the pontoon in the slip. Sloane snatched her bra off the deck and sprinted alongside Neil to his car.

Neil sped along the unfamiliar road focused on keeping the car between fog lines while he listened to Brita.

Sloane stripped off her shirt, fought the car's jostle while she put her bra and shirt back on, and secured the seat belt across her. "What did she say happened?" she asked when he lowered the phone.

"Brita and Sharnee stayed at Gaby's chatting with the staff after we left there. Sharnee told her mom she was going to sit at one of the outside tables with Kyle while he took his break to watch the sun set. Brita walked to their room. When Sharnee didn't return after thirty minutes, Brita went back to Gaby's and Sharnee was gone. She asked Kyle, and he told her Sharnee was still sitting at the table looking out over the lake when he had to go back to work."

"She might still be close by if she decided to explore the grounds near the resort."

He shook his head. "They found her phone between the patio and the water."

"They're in Greene County. Has she notified the sheriff's department?"

"She called me first. The manager at Gaby's told her she would call them."

The tires on the Acura screeched in the right turn onto the ramp to I-20 West at mile marker 121. Neil's knuckles whitened on the steering wheel. He stomped the gas pedal. The engine snarled as the car zoomed down the ramp and merged onto the interstate headed in the opposite direction.

Sloane said, "Where are we going?"

He looked at the clock in the dash—9:02. "The barn. If this is the work of our killer, I want to get there before it's too late. We'd waste our time at the restaurant other than comforting Brita. I know she wants me out here trying to find Sharnee, and that's what I intend to do."

"It's the right choice, Neil. You're right. We would do nothing but twiddle our thumbs and wring our hands if we went to the resort."

"Any news on the Avalon in the video?"

"Huber told me he's waiting on a response from the tag office. I'll call and tell him to get over there to watch the barn."

Fifteen seconds into the call Sloane yelled, "Why not?" into her cellphone and flung her left arm upward. She waited and said, "Never mind. I'll take care of it." She touched the screen and put the phone to her ear. "This is Sergeant Azevedo. I need a car for stakeout on Elm, 10-40—quickly, no lights and siren—with a line of sight to Fletcher's barn on East Washington. Document every vehicle. No contact…How long?…Okay. Call me ASAP." She ended the call and turned to Neil. "Huber's out on an assault call. One officer has the perpetrator in custody on his way to the jail. The other is out on a burglary. Looks like it's up to us."

Neil shook his head. They passed by mile marker 117. He figured on seven more minutes from their location. Two minutes to exit 114 and another five to reach the barn. Traffic slowed ahead upon their approach to mile marker 116. A passel of blue and red strobes flashed near the Bethany Road Bridge.

"No! No! No!" Neil struck the steering wheel with the heel of his right hand. "This can't be happening."

A tractor-trailer in the right lane blocked any hope of a lane change. He stopped behind a black SUV. Sloane rolled down her window, unbuckled her seat belt, stretched, and stuck her head out the window. She dropped back onto the seat and shook her head.

He eased the car's left side tires onto the shoulder. He pondered their options. One option led across the median to the eastbound side and drive the two miles to the exit against the flow of traffic. That involved too much risk with traffic flow at speeds greater than the 70 mile-per-hour limit. They could sit there and wait on the police to clear the roadway. That delay might cost Sharnee her life if she wasn't dead already.

Blue and red lights flashing on the pillar supports showed the source of the strobes beyond the overpass.

"We're going around."

Neil shut off the headlights and nosed the Acura into the median. He guessed the responders focused on their task and they would not notice the Acura when it crept by with no lights. He angled to the far side and followed the edge of the eastbound shoulder a hundred yards to the bridge. Emergency vehicles blocked the two traffic lanes, emergency lane, and the shoulders on the westbound side west of the Bethany Road overpass. The Acura angled rightward fifty yards beyond the mass of vehicles and returned to the open roadway.

No one came after them. Neil switched on the headlamps and ninety seconds later got off the interstate. He jammed the brakes and stopped at the intersection. He looked at Sloane.

"What if they were stuck in that traffic?"

Chapter 21

Motion jostled Sharnee out of her stupor and slammed her into the cargo bulkhead. Paralysis restricted her ability to move her arms. No. Not her arms, her hands. They tingled. She rolled to her back. A zip tie dug into her wrist. Her fingers touched metal above her. Exhaust rumbled below. Red light glowed at her head and feet on the left side.

Memory of the dead girls' pictures on Uncle Neil's laptop tightened her throat. The red lights dimmed. The car rolled a few feet. The lights brightened. The car stopped. She envisioned the dead girls and Neil looking for her.

Although fear seized her body, a link between her and the vehicle would prove she was there. She drew her legs upward. Warm urine soaked her panties, her pants, and the carpet.

She patted along the metal enclosure until she located the emergency release lever. She curled her fingers around the T-shaped handle and tugged until she heard the thump. The deck lid sprang upward. She scrambled over the lip of the trunk and tumbled to the asphalt. Headlights shined in the distance. Vehicles approached from a distance of two hundred yards.

Light filled the trunk's interior. Sharnee launched toward the darkness. She skirted the end of a guardrail and crossed the up-slope of the shoulder. A car door slammed. The grass-covered ground changed to bare soil a few feet before vegetation thickened beneath a canopy of hardwood trees and scattered pines. She plunged into the darkness.

Bramble slowed her progress. The thorns pricked her skin through her pants and shirt and her exposed arms and hands and face. Streaks of red flesh appeared while she forced through them and distanced herself from her attacker's vehicle. Fifty feet into the woods the undergrowth thinned. She regained the speed lost in the thicket. Low hanging hardwood branches swatted her face. She flailed her restrained arms and swiped at her hair when she ran through a spider web.

She wiped her face and glanced over her shoulder. Headlights and taillights lined the highway as far as she could see through the trees. No flashlight beam flitted toward her.

The woodland made it impossible to run in a straight line. She ran deeper, unsure of her bearing or when she might find civilization. Headlights ahead to the right preceded a drumming of tires on the pavement. The truck stopped. Sharnee altered her course toward the truck and screamed. Fifteen seconds later she pitched forward as if someone grabbed her ankle and threw her to the ground.

****

"What are the odds?" Neil looked at Sloane. "Do we take a chance and go back to have the troopers search every vehicle? Look for the Avalon or head to the barn? She could be in one of those cars. What if she is? We were right there." He pushed his hair back and kept his hand pressed to his nape.

"Go on to the barn, Neil. It's our best option. If we

don't, we might be too late. I'll call GSP and have dispatch alert the troopers on scene for the car. We have no guarantee the traffic will still be blocked by the time we get back there. We can get their dash cam videos."

Neil stared the length of the on-ramp opposite them while Sloane relayed their message to the Georgia State Patrol. No traffic flowed west on I-20. The thought of Sharnee bound, trapped inside a killer's vehicle off in Wherever Land made him feel helpless. The fact she might be among those vehicles blocked by the crash, and they drove right by her, made him sick. No matter how much he questioned the choice to detour around the traffic jam, Sloane was the clear-headed one in this. He turned right toward town.

Sloane ended her call and said, "Message delivered."

Neil stared through the windshield. "I guess we can forget Fleishman's records. They are useless to us, now."

"I know this is difficult for you, Neil. Sharnee's your family. Trust your instinct, not your heart. Think of Vanessa and Katie. What are the similarities? What were the differences? The killer's comfort level dictates her actions. She follows a set strategy. That's her weakness. You know this. I don't have to tell you. She will make a mistake and when she does, we'll catch her."

"This time it's personal."

"It's been personal, Neil. Why do you think she painted your face on the barn wall? Think. You know her. Who is she?"

"I don't know."

"Yes, you do. Have you been with anyone since

you moved to Madison?"

"No."

"Look at it from my perspective. A lot of circumstantial evidence points to you, not as a suspect, but as an involved party. The killer painted your portrait on the barn not once, but twice. Blood transferred on your doorknob outside your house and on your sofa inside your house. Happenstance did not leave it there. You could have hired those thugs to attack us yesterday and confront me at my house earlier today."

"They were at your house today and you didn't think to mention it? Why would you not tell me?"

"I planned to until you got the call from Brita."

"What happened?"

"A person dressed in tactical gear and balaclava accosted me after I pulled up the driveway and parked. I rolled down the windows and sat there enjoying the breeze with my eyes closed when I smelled the distinct odor of ammonia sweat and felt the muzzle of a pistol press my left temple. Though she never uttered a sound other than a whistle, the eyes were female. She took my gun and tossed it onto the back seat after she ejected the magazine. She then backed away, whistled and loped into the woods. Davis Leggett strutted from behind the garage. Billy Ray Haney came at me from the far corner of the house. Davis pulled a knife, and long story short, I took care of him with extreme prejudice. He fared far worse than me. I'm sure he required medical treatment and should be out of commission for a while."

"And you?"

"The blade nicked my thigh. It's nothing more than a superficial injury."

"What about Billy Ray?"

Sloane grinned. "He just stood and watched, dumbfounded. I told him to haul off the trash. He's their weak link."

Neil turned right onto East Washington. "Tomorrow we ought to exploit that weakness. If he knows anything, we'll break him."

"Davis Leggett may talk after the round-two knockout today."

The Acura wheeled onto Elm. After fifty yards, Neil U-turned, pulled to the shoulder and shut off the headlights. The moon lit the barnyard and the strip of asphalt seventy-five yards east and west of the barn.

They sat in silence for the first five minutes.

Neil said, "I'm sorry for snapping at you. I had no right to ask. And no, I did not hire those thugs. You should know that."

Sloane removed the seat belt, tucked her left leg and rotated toward him in the seat. "I know. I was just making a point. We're in this together. I want you to know everything about me."

He laid his hand on the console. Sloane took it and pressed it to her chest. Her warmth seeped into the back of his hand and wrist. He gazed out the window opening at the stars and thanked God for Sloane's friendship and support above and beyond the call of duty related to the job. He trusted her and believed she trusted him.

****

The wreckage of an SUV and a pickup truck with utility trailer blocked the two westbound traffic lanes and the emergency lane at Bethany Road Bridge. No emergency vehicles on scene. Tess Fleishman jammed on the brakes and stopped behind a white sports car seventy yards from the crash.

A few seconds later Tess jerked her head at the pop of the trunk and looked at the rear-view mirror. The Ford Fusion's rear deck lid blocked her view beyond the rear window. She whipped her head rightward when the car recoiled after the girl leaped from the trunk. The killer swore at the shadow racing toward the tree line. She shifted to Park, shoved open the door and jumped out. By the time she reached the back of the car her prey had disappeared into the forest. Two sets of headlights closed upon her a hundred yards east.

She slammed the trunk, got back into the car, shifted to reverse and whipped over to the emergency lane before the oncoming vehicles overtook her. The two right side tires dropped off the asphalt onto the grass shoulder ten feet from the guardrail. The two vehicles slowed to a stop; one car filled each traffic lane. Three more jammed behind them. Too many eyes loomed nearby for her to leave the vehicle to pursue the girl.

Tess shrugged out of her black taclite shirt and removed the body armor. The cold air out of the vents struck her damp undershirt. A shiver jolted her body. She crossed her arms and heaved a sigh. Her fingernails dug into her palms.

A tractor-trailer, a panel truck and two SUVs added to the jam. A vehicle equipped with blue strobe lights crossed the median beyond the overpass. Thirty seconds later a blue Georgia State Patrol vehicle squeezed between her and the sedan in the outside lane. The trooper stared ahead.

She waited, confident her anonymity remained

intact. Nothing connected her to the girl other than the vehicle and then only until she returned it to the impound lot. She had Davis to thank for her access to the repossessed vehicles.

Emergency vehicles lit the night sky with red and blue flashes within four minutes of the crash. That presented no threat to her. They focused on their tasks, not her or the many others forced to wait in line. Fire Rescue would free the injured from the wreckage. Ambulances would transport their patients to the hospital. Police would perform their on-scene inquiries and open the roadway after wreckers towed the involved vehicles.

No time constraint. No one expected her. Wait for clearance. Return the car. Drive home.

She waited.

A sedan angled across the median, no headlights or taillights, paralleled the eastbound lanes and out of sight on the west side of the bridge supports.

Smart person. I should have thought of that.

Two state police cars and a sheriff's unit funneled traffic into the outside lane of I-20 under Bethany Bridge. Tess watched two troopers work the roadblock. They shined light into the occupant compartments, held something in their hands she assumed were driver's licenses, and looked in the trunks of three cars.

She saw her chance when a tractor-trailer slowed and stopped in line. It blocked her view of the officers. If she could not see them, they would not notice her. Tess steered the Fusion across the two traffic lanes and into the median. She angled away toward the eastbound side, careful not to touch the brake pedal. No alert to her avenue to freedom.

The car bounced in the dip and surged up the far side of the median onto the shoulder. The ride smoothed on the asphalt. Tess followed the broken white lines lit by the moon for fifty yards, switched on the headlights and sped east.

****

The screen on Sloane's cellphone lit with an incoming call. "It's GSP," she said, keeping Neil's hand pressed to her chest. "Nothing? You searched them all?…How soon will they be available?…I'll pick them up first thing in the morning, thanks." She lowered the phone to her lap. "A trooper and three deputies set up a spot check before they released traffic. They documented every license plate and even captured video of the drivers on their body cams. Otherwise, they found nothing. No Avalon. With any luck, the videos will show us something." She squeezed his hand.

"We've focused on the barn and yet have no clue to where the killer took Vanessa and Katie afterward to wash their bodies. Time constraints suggest it must be nearby."

Sloane said, "I agree. It's a place where she could work unchecked."

"And quickly."

"That eliminates a bathtub due to its confined space. The cleanliness of the bodies rules out lakes, ponds, or creeks. That leaves swimming pools."

Neil shook his head. "It's not a swimming pool. No chlorine odor on their bodies."

"She might have access to a non-chlorinated pool." Sloane lowered her hand holding his to her thigh. "You don't think…Oh, my God. It makes perfect sense."

"What?"

"The baptismal pool at the church. It's only a mile from the barn. It's secluded. Who would ever think to look at a church? The baptistery there fits her scope of circumstantial evidence against you."

"It gets better. The church installed a handicap lift for the baptistery." Neil stared at the barn. "If she was coming, she should be there by now."

A Harley thundered by. Their world again hushed to the chirps and trills of crickets and katydids. That lasted two minutes. Tires screeched at the intersection when a Madison Police car whipped onto Elm and stopped alongside the Acura. The officer extended her arm and head out the open window.

"A Jane Doe was just brought into the ER with a head injury. They told me her wrists were bound together with a zip tie."

Chapter 22

Sloane leaped from the Acura and ran ahead of Neil through the doors into Morgan Memorial Hospital Emergency Department. Two nurses, one in burgundy scrubs, the other in green scrubs, sat behind the partition. An analog clock on the wall displayed 9:43. A physician looked up from the chart she held.

Sloane said, "I'm here to see the Jane Doe brought in this evening."

"Her name is Sharnee Tetreau," Neil added.

The doctor looked first to Sloane and then to Neil. "Are you family?"

"Niece," Neil said. "Where is she?"

"She's no longer here. She sustained a closed head injury, so we transferred her to Piedmont Newton."

Sloane nudged Neil. "I'll call Brita. Let me have your phone." He entered his pass code, pressed a number, and handed the phone to her. Sloane stepped away.

"How did she get here?" Neil asked.

"Two men brought her in. One was Arlo Messana. I've never seen the other one. He carried her while Arlo told us he heard her scream and by the time he got to her she was unresponsive. This was somewhere on Baldwin Dairy Road near Bethany."

"Was she alone?"

"He didn't mention anyone else."

Skepticism swelled in Neil's mind. Sharnee vanished at Lake Oconee—a thirty-minute drive from the hospital—and within an hour of her disappearance, two men deliver her to the emergency room with a head injury? The story struck him as far-fetched except for the fact the doctor identified one of the men by name.

"How well do you know Mr. Messana?"

"I've never known him to lie, if that's what you're asking."

****

Tess got off I-20 at exit 121 where she doubled back to Madison on U.S. 278 and pulled up to the gate at Leggett's impound lot on Turner Road twenty minutes after she fled the crash site.

The Ford's headlamps sprayed light through the double cyclone gate. A lock connected a chain looped around the inside posts. Tess shut off the headlights, leaving on the parking lights and got out. The southwest wind shoved a band of thunderstorms up from the Gulf of Mexico. The increased humidity changed the air from muggy to tropical. With it came the scent of rain. Sweat soaked her hair and dripped into her eyes. Her shirt clung to her skin. She removed a key from its hiding place at the base of the gatepost on the left, opened the gate. She climbed back into the Fusion, closed the gate as a precaution, bounced along the uneven dirt drive through a stand of trees, turned left up a hill into a Y-shaped opening where she backed in next to the Impala.

The same Impala she drove when she saw and talked to Neil. She shut off the lights. A security lamp sprayed milky light from a utility pole in front of the business a hundred yards away. No chance of anyone seeing her through the surrounding trees. Tess closed her eyes and pulled her wet shirt away from her chest. Her thoughts centered on Neil while cold air blew on her face and neck and coursed beneath the shirt.

After five minutes, Tess killed the engine, grabbed her gear. She strode to her SUV on the far side of the Toyota Avalon used to transport Katie. Six additional vehicles identified by their repo status provided no reason for her to use the same vehicle a second time.

Tess pulled behind the building and went inside. She opened the flashlight app on her cellphone and opened the cabinet where the business kept the keys to the confiscated vehicles. She replaced the Ford's keys on an empty hook, stood there and studied the others while she decided which ones to take. She chose keys to the Altima, Accord, and Optima.

She returned to her SUV and secured the gate. Wind battered and rocked the Traverse on her way home. Dust and debris flew across the stream of her headlights. Her chest hitched when she turned into the driveway and saw Rob's city-issued car parked short of the open carport.

At 10:08 she parked under the shelter, grabbed one of Rob's old shirts off the rear seat, shrugged into it. The sleeves fell to her knuckles. The tail extended to mid-thigh. Tess acted weak while she tugged her walker out of the vehicle and opened it if by chance Rob was watching her. She crossed the thirty feet to the rear steps in twenty-one steps.

Rob opened the door. Light flooded the set of steps. He descended the four steps to her side and latched onto her left arm two inches above the elbow.

****

Thunder rumbled and lightning flashed over Covington. The first drops of rain pelted outside Piedmont Newton Hospital ED by the time Neil whipped into the nearest open parking space. He and Sloane raced through the downpour to the entrance. Rain hissed on impact with trees and the ground. The overhang at the entrance presented minimal shelter from the windswept downpour. The automatic doors slid open with a whirr when they triggered the sensor.

Once inside, Neil pushed back his hair with his fingers and watched Sloane do the same with hers. Water trickled down her face. Her long fingers brushed her eyes and cheeks.

They strode past a dozen people in the waiting room to a registration counter. A woman in purple scrubs wearing dark-rimmed glasses typed on a keyboard. "May I help you?" she said without looking away from the screen.

"We're here to see the girl transferred from Morgan," Neil said.

The woman's pink nails clicked the keys. "Are you family?"

"Yes."

"I need some information first." The woman's left hand hovered over the keyboard while she moved the mouse with her right. "The patient's name?"

Neil answered the woman's questions, many with "I don't know."

"Her mother is on her way here," Sloane added.

The woman averted her eyes from the screen to Neil. "Trauma room three through that door." The door swung open into the corridor.

They found Sharnee supine on an exam table, still

in her clothes, eyes closed, IV fluids running in her left arm, and a bandage taped to her forehead. A red abrasion circled her right wrist. A male wearing a white coat over a yellow shirt and dark slacks, head shaved and sporting a goatee, talked with a Hispanic female in plum scrubs between the table and a supply cabinet.

The doctor introduced himself. "Are you the police?"

"Sergeant Sloane Azevedo, Madison Police," she said. "The patient's name is Sharnee Tetreau. This is her uncle, Neil Caldera. What can you tell us?"

The doctor frowned. "I'm waiting on a callback from the neurologist, but symptoms indicate a closed head injury. The patient arrived unresponsive, with evidence of impact to her head and wrists bound together. A head CT scan showed no acute hemorrhage, which is a good sign. No other injuries. We're keeping her sedated for now. Her tox screen showed positive for ketamine. I called the EMS transport team, and they denied administering it. There's no note of it mentioned in the outside hospital record. Does she have a history of recreational drug use?"

"None," Neil said.

The doctor's eyelids popped wide open and his brows shoved upward.

"None," Neil repeated, sternness stressed.

The doctor's left brow lowered. "By whatever means she ingested it, its presence no doubt had a positive effect on the severity of her injury. Ketamine improves physiologic severity and systolic blood pressure."

Neil looked at Sloane who nodded. They were thinking the same thought of origin.

"Someone kidnapped her just after sundown. If the killer used ketamine to subdue her, would that account for the level documented in her toxicology report?" Sloane asked.

"It depends on the method of introduction but it's possible, yes."

The door opened inward. "Neurology is on the line, Doctor," a petite blonde said and walked away.

He excused himself and followed her out into the corridor.

Neil took Sharnee's hand and squeezed and kissed it. Her arm and hand remained flaccid as he lowered it to her side. Her chest rose and fell with shallow breaths. The monitor displayed updated vitals. He witnessed a drastic change in contrast to the jauntiness he'd come to identify with her. From her toddler years, Sharnee showed genuine altruism in her initiatives. She loved people, and they adored and admired her.

A much better example than the man he had become. Thirteen years hunting and thinking like criminals to capture them altered his outlook. It turned him into a machine motivated by justice. An instrument voided of mercy.

Sloane laid her hand on his upper back, rested her head on his upper arm. "Anyone watching you would think you were her father."

"I don't believe it would be possible to love a daughter more."

She patted his hand on Sharnee's. "You stay here. I'll go out and wait for Brita.

The wheels on the stool rattled when Neil rolled it next to the exam table. He straddled the stool and sat. Fraught with emotion, he cradled Sharnee's hand to his chest and laid his left hand on her shoulder. He gazed at her lying there and thought of the woman lying dead on the street in New York. He had cradled her that day in his arms. A stranger whom he never met while she lived imparted sorrow in his heart at her death. A choice he made led to her demise. The image of her lifeless body warm in his arms brought him back to Sharnee who somehow escaped assured torture and death at the hands of a killer evidenced by the aftermaths he'd witnessed the past two days.

That knowledge prompted a smile. Even though the effect of the injury was not yet known—categorized as serious and not critical—Sharnee held onto life. Neil imagined the emotional turmoil the killer sensed when Sharnee got away from her captor. The killer's scheme foiled at the brink of success. An endeavor marked by failure.

While he waited on Brita to get there, he pulled out his cellphone and connected to an app for maps. He typed in the desired location and waited for the images to load. He enlarged the section south of Madison to display I-20, adjusted the map to show Bethany Road Bridge and Baldwin Dairy Road. He switched from Standard to Satellite and enlarged the points between I-20 east of the bridge and north to Baldwin.

What he saw confirmed his conjecture, but would it support the story given by the doctor at Morgan ER?

****

"Where have you been?"

The sea water and mint fragrance of Rob's cologne inundated the air milliseconds after he half-cradled, half-seized Tess's arm. Clothed in casual shirt and slacks, his untied shoelaces suggested he had just gotten home or was on his way out. His recent application of cologne projected the latter.

Tess had an idea Rob's jaunt destined a visit to Four Lakes Drive. A secretary at City Hall caught his eye months ago. A wife notices those things. Infidelity on his part no longer mattered to her.

"I had to get out of the house for a while. The walls were closing in on me." Tess feigned instability when she lifted her left foot to the first tread. She latched onto the wooden rail, leaned over, and retched.

"In your condition? I was getting worried about you. It's after ten o'clock. You should have called me."

"Since when do you care how I feel? I sit in this house all day every day, while you focus on matters of greater importance to you. You never look at me anymore and when you do, I see pity."

"That's not true."

"It is true." Tess yanked her left arm forward. Rob tightened his grip. "Let go of me." He released his hold, but kept his palm pressed to the arm. She jerked away and faced the open door.

He pressed a hand to her back. "Please, let me help you."

She whipped her head around, glowered at him. "I no longer need your help, Rob Fleishman. Do whatever it is you planned to do this evening. I'll be fine right here at home."

Tess slid her hand up the rail, hauled upward with her arm while stepping up each tread until she crossed the threshold and slammed the door. She held her breath, listened for any sound of movement. The door to Rob's car thumped shut. The engine whined, gave way to the wind's howl. Light trespassed through the windows on the driveway side of the house while the car backed into the street. When darkness prevailed once again on that side of the house, Tess shoved the walker. It struck the wall and clanged to the floor.

Lilac light flashed the dimness. Tess filled her lungs to capacity and fisted her raised hands. She tensed and vented her rage at losing her prey. The double-lung scream melded with a rumble of thunder as if her scream detonated a secondary explosive device.

She laughed at the imposing rumble. She ran to the window and gazed at the night sky. The lilac lightning strobes preceded claps of thunder by four seconds. Tess hurried to her closet where she unlocked her olive footlocker and threw open the lid. She pulled up a panel covering the bottom and took out a black leather vest, a pair of red satin shorts and above-the-knee leather boots.

Tess stripped out of her clothes and donned the risqué outfit. She shrugged into a black slicker. The front of the coat swayed open as she bounded down the steps into the torrent. She imagined herself a high-priced call girl sauntering across a busy street up to a luxury hotel where her suitor, Neil Caldera, awaited her arrival. Or the mistress he beckoned to share an exotic evening with at their chosen hide-away.

Head tilted back, large drops splashed her face and washed locks of wet hair aside. Tess tore out of the slicker and opened the vest. Her exposed skin glistened beneath the spray of the LED security light while the cool rain trickled shivers through her body. In her mind, Tess welcomed Neil into her lair. He forgave her trespasses against him and his niece who, fortunately, escaped her captor. She never intended harm to his niece. She took her to gain Neil's attention. Her plan was to play the part of hero and return the girl to her family who would shower their gratitude on her. The indebtedness she desired most was Neil's. Failure trumped the scheme.

Tess believed she could convince Neil to forgive her as well in the real world. She felt certain of her ability to accomplish it. She planned to woo him into bed in the manner of Samson and Delilah. Pretense set aside, use instinct bred in her from birth and affirmed by her maturity and experience.

Chapter 23

The door into the restricted area of the emergency room thumped and swished open before Sloane and Brita made it halfway across the waiting room. Brita's umbrella ticked on the tiled floor when Neil stepped through. She embraced him. Her body trembled.

"How is she?" Brita said when she backed to his side.

"Stable. Her vitals are good and there's no cerebral swelling. It looks like she'll make a full recovery. They are about to move her to a room. The nurse said someone will notify us when they get her settled."

Brita dropped to the nearest chair, closed her eyes, and let out a sigh. "Thank God…Sloane said some men found Sharnee in the woods. How did she get there?"

"I think I know." Neil picked up the umbrella, pulled out his cellphone, and opened the satellite image.

"Do you think they are the ones who took her?"

"No. It wasn't them."

"How can you be sure?"

Neil sat to Brita's left, set the umbrella on the floor at his feet. Sloane took the seat on the other side. "Look at this." He held the phone centered in front of Brita so she and Sloane would have a good view of the screen. "This is a satellite view of the road and surrounding area where the witness stated he picked up Sharnee." He enlarged the picture with forefinger and thumb.

"The four-lane you see here is the interstate. A crash blocked traffic on the westbound side right there at the bridge when Sloane and I got there ten minutes or thereabouts after you called me.

"My guess is the abductor got caught up in the traffic jam. Sharnee somehow got away and ran off into the woods between the interstate and Baldwin Dairy Road, right here." He touched the location on the screen. "Within a hundred yards east of the bridge the forest widens where the roadway curves north. East of there, the stand of trees looks no deeper than thirty yards. It's feasible she ran into this area based on where traffic backed up."

"It fits the timeline from event to discovery and arrival at the hospital," Sloane said.

"So, how did this Good Samaritan find her? No houses exist along there. I need to talk to him. I want to get a first-hand account of what happened."

Neil holstered his cellphone. He flumped back in the chair and stared across the open room focused on nothing in particular while Brita and Sloane whispered back and forth. Although their undertones seeped into his aural canals, his mind centered on Sharnee and the demise she avoided by her escape.

"Neil…Neil?" Brita nudged his arm.

He stirred, craned his neck until his eyes met hers.

"We can sit here all night brooding over this or that, but there's one aspect neither of you have mentioned. I want to know how this person knew to go after Sharnee. The only person with any knowledge of our visit was you."

The words stung. Lack of caution on his part put Brita and Sharnee in harm's way. With an avalanche of circumstantial evidence planted by the killer against him, he should have expected she might follow him to Gaby's by the Lake.

"She must have tailed us."

"She?" A man at the registration desk jerked his head around to look at Brita. "What do you mean, '*she*'?"

Sloane shifted the chair to face Brita. In a hushed tone, she said, "Certain facts imply a woman killed the first two victims. Some evidence in both murders points the finger at Neil. It's part of the killer's plan, but we have no clue as to reason." She looked at Neil. "This is not your fault. No one followed us. I'm sure. She must have located us by some other means. When she saw who we were with, she waited and approached Sharnee after we left. It's the only logical explanation."

The "other means" inflamed Neil. "Other means" meant compromised cellphone or bugs planted in his home or a tracking device on his car. A cellphone topped the list of most reliable means once you have the number. Not always at home or in a vehicle, a person will have their cellphone with them at all times.

One after another, deliberate actions focused on Neil. He identified no reason. For fifteen months, he lived in harmony with the church and the community. An assault on him and his character began the past Saturday evening. Someone painted his portrait in blood on the barn wall and contrived evidence to implicate him in the murders.

Although he may never learn the killer's motive, he determined to find her.

Neil said, "She's smart, whoever she is. We need burner phones to ensure privacy and provide some misdirection if she is tracking my phone."

Sloane nodded. "Leave that to me."

"Get three. I want one for Brita."

Brita took Sloane's hand in her right, Neil's in her left. "I just need assurance that Sharnee will recover from this."

"Both of you will," Sloane said. "We all will."

A tone blared from the PA system. Then, "Code blue, Triage three. Code blue, Triage three."

Adrenalin surged through Neil at the mention of "Triage three" in the page. He leaped to his feet. Triage three was where fifteen minutes earlier he saw Sharnee. A man in slate-blue scrubs pushed into the waiting room. He looked left, ahead, and right. His eyes passed over Neil before he backed through the doors and turned away.

"What's the matter?" Brita's eyes widened. She straightened in the chair. Panic molded her face.

Neil rushed to prevent the doors from closing and held them open. "That's the room where they assessed Sharnee."

"That code was for her? Dear Jesus, no. Not my baby."

Brita ran ahead of Neil and Sloane, turned at an intersecting corridor. Neil motioned left, followed by another left after fifty feet in sight of the door to the room. They huddled at the corner and watched three people in scrubs and a woman wearing a white lab coat hustle to room three.

"Wait here."

Neil marched to the door and cracked it open enough to peek inside. The person lying on the exam station wore soiled jeans and camel work boots caked with red clay. He was shirtless. Blood gushed from a gash in the right side of the man's exposed abdomen. Neil closed the door, turned to Brita and Sloane and mouthed, "It's not her."

Brita's shoulders relaxed in a slump. She rested her head on the wall.

Sloane put her arm around Brita. "I'll find out where they took her."

"I don't know what I would've done," Brita told Neil.

He understood Brita's inference. Too many times he had witnessed families grieve in their homes or in waiting rooms at hospitals after a loss tore into them. He repressed his feelings, focused on the cause and not the effect.

Now those external stimuli elicited a response in Neil and he lacked the strength of will to fight it. Not wanting to leave Brita alone, he waited for Sloane's return. When Sloane appeared in the corridor thirty seconds later, Neil closed himself in the nearest restroom where tears gushed in a total body cleanse.

When he came out—a hint of relief inside and face washed of any evidence of his sorrow—Neil entered the room to find two deputies from Greene County Sheriff's Department huddled beside Brita and Sloane.

"We have very little to go on,"—Neil heard one deputy say—"so I don't want to leave you with any false hopes. We'll put all our efforts into finding the person responsible."

False hopes? What a copout. I know how this works.

"What is your agency's protocol on abductions?" Brita asked. "I want to know you'll not just file a report and keep your fingers crossed for someone to come in and confess to the crime."

Neil remained a spectator. He wished he could see the deputy's face. Brita had taken charge of the dialog using an effective strategy.

"Like I said, a detective will contact you tomorrow for a follow-up. There's nothing more we can do tonight." The deputy ducked away, turned on his heels, his reddened face held at a forty-five-degree angle to his path of travel as he and his sidekick skirted Neil.

After the door closed, Neil said, "What did you say to him?"

"I imparted a concerned mother's request."

"You imparted or insisted?"

Brita grinned. "No one harms family without repercussions."

****

In black silk pajamas and hair still wet from having indulged in pleasures known only to her, Tess Fleishman shut off the headlights and slowed the Traverse to make the turn onto Four Lakes Drive a few minutes past eleven. The asphalt gleamed in spots under the streetlights. Tess lowered her window to get a clearer view. This first visit to the location under cover of darkness was necessary to identify any challenges she might need to overcome when she executed her plan.

The Traverse rolled forward at idle speed into a falling mist toward her destination and points beyond. Blue light flickered beyond windows in homes where televisions played. Other homes stood in diffused light and shadows. No person roamed outside any of the storm-littered residences.

The vehicle she expected to find was angled nose first at the back corner of a taupe California Bungalow halfway down Four Lakes Drive. Dimness in the front of the house suggested light originating from a room elsewhere, perhaps a kitchen. Tess craned her neck to look when the SUV rolled beyond the far side of the house. A lit window near the rear corner rewarded her search.

Tess parked at the end of the street and crept in shadows of leaf-filled branches to the home of the City Hall secretary. Although wetness under foot soaked her slippers, her choice to wear them were twofold—stealth and lack of distinct footprints.

Rain drops pitter-pattered on the leaves in their descent to the ground. Tess sneaked along the side of the house and listened at the lit window. After a few moments a female uttered something. Tess strained to hear and above the pitter-patter of raindrops again heard it. A distinct moan uttered by the woman filtered through the double-paned window six inches away. The moans increased in number and intensity.

An opportunity existed to rush in and confront them while Rob and his paramour nestled in the heat of passion. To expose and embarrass was not the plan. Neither was right then the time.

Tess slinked from the window, rounded the rear corner and studied the rear, left side, front and right side of the house for the least challenging way inside. She paused at the same window on her second pass down the right side. The ecstasy persisted as before. Tess rounded the corner and decided on the rear door, three steps above ground level and fronted by a four-foot-by-five-foot concrete stoop. A third trek around the house with no pause at the window assured the rear door was the correct choice.

She settled on a deadline for her surprise on her way back to her Traverse. Thursday night. Finality delivered on the eve of their fourth anniversary.

Chapter 24

At five thirty the next morning, Neil roused when Sloane pushed open the door to Sharnee's hospital room holding a brown paper bag in her left hand. She wore her uniform. Brita slept facing the bed on a pull-out chair between the bed and the wall. Sloane kissed him.

"You look tired," she whispered. She caressed his cheek and lowered her hand to his shoulder.

He stood and embraced her. "This chair is not conducive to providing comfort. Not that I'm complaining. Just stating the facts as my numb behind endured it."

"I suppose this might require a massage of your keister?" A grin played on her lips.

"Is something wrong with his keister?" Brita sat on the side of her make-shift bed, smiling at them. "I couldn't help overhearing you two."

Neil said, "The chair put the wrong part of me to sleep."

Brita and Sloane chorused a laugh.

Sloane opened one phone in her hand and handed it to Brita. She gave the other one to Neil.

"They're charged. I put in our names and numbers. The chargers are in the bag. Any improvement in Sharnee during the night?"

Brita rubbed Sharnee's forearm. "Her blood

pressure normalized. Everything else remains the same as it was when they moved her to the room. They scheduled another CT scan this morning. They said someone would be here to take her around seven thirty."

"Call me when you get the results of the scan. I've got to head to the station."

"I'll walk with you." Neil followed Sloane into the hall. "What's on your agenda today?" He pressed the lowermost elevator button.

"I've got to convince Huber he should look for a female for these murders. He's so caught up in the circumstantial evidence he can't see beyond the fogged mirror he's holding."

"He saw the security video from the Quick Shop. That video shows a female behind the wheel of the car."

"I agree, but you heard him express his take on that."

Neil gave a terse nod. "Yeah. He's blinded by more than just the facts. We need to find that car."

A ding signified the elevator's arrival. The doors slid open. Sloane stepped into the elevator.

"That's my priority as soon as I get to the station. There shouldn't be many Toyota Avalons registered here in Morgan County. If I come up empty, I'll expand my search to neighboring counties."

Neil followed. "I have confidence you'll find it." He turned and punched the button for the first floor and took her hand. He wanted to be present whenever she located the vehicle and expressed his desire to inspect it.

"Rob won't allow it. He'll call in the GBI."

"We'll see." He said it and grinned.

The doors slid open. They strode out the front doors to Sloane's Jaguar parked in the first space beyond the divider. Humidity hung heavy in the air from the previous night's storm. Road noise from commuters' vehicles on I-20 rose in the distance.

"I'll think good thoughts today for Sharnee and Brita. You have my love, Neil." Sloane pressed her left hand to Neil's chest and kissed him. "I'll call you when I have something on the car."

Sloane turned to get in the car. Neil pulled her to him. He pressed his cheek to hers and whispered, "Yours is the love I want, Sloane."

He watched the Jaguar until it traveled out of sight and ambled back into the hospital. Brita looked up from her magazine when he entered the room.

"She's enamored of you, Neil. I sensed it in our chat. Her demeanor shows it. For someone to get out of bed this early just to express kindness toward someone she just met indicates more than a penchant. She did it out of pure love for you. I hope you see that."

He sat in the chair at the foot of the bed. "I do."

Brita laid the magazine on the bed. "You know I've never meddled in your personal life but you need to hear me now. Sloane's good for you. She's selfless. She's intelligent. Without a doubt one of the most gorgeous women I've ever met. Let her love for you breech that barrier of yours and reciprocate that love."

"How is it you always have relevant answers?"

"I'm your sister. Believe me, sisters know those things."

She picked up the magazine and opened it on her lap. Her head tilted forward but her eyes stayed on

Neil's.

"Are you delving into my soul again with that look?" he asked.

"Just making sure you got the message."

He got it. Since Brita approved, or more so acted as an advocate on Sloane's behalf, who was he to deny the obvious. Sloane loved him. He loved her. She wanted to be with him. His desire for her consumed him, transported him to a world of reverie.

Brita lowered her eyes to the open pages.

Neil closed his. When he opened them, the time on his wristwatch displayed 8:36.

"You were talking in your sleep," Brita said. "Who is Tess?"

Neil's eyelids fluttered. "Tess?" He rubbed his eyes, blinked twice and looked at Brita.

"Yeah, Tess. You mumbled her name three times. Who is she to you?"

"Nobody."

"It didn't sound like nobody. Tell me."

"Tess Fleishman. She's the wife of the police chief. They attended the church until she announced they diagnosed her with leukemia. I went to visit her yesterday to talk about some things and see how she was doing. She came on to me."

Brita rolled her eyes while she shook her head. "I hope you told Sloane."

"I did."

"Good. Hide nothing from the woman you love. Honesty opens the door to unfiltered love."

Sharnee emitted a moan and opened her eyes. Monitors showed no change in her vitals. Brita sat beside the hospital bed, her hand on Sharnee's. Neil perched in a chair on the opposite side at the foot of the bed where he could see her face.

"She's awake." He pushed out of the chair and took Sharnee's left hand in his. Her eyes shifted left and right before again looked left and fixed on his.

"How did I get here?"

"A man heard you scream and found you in a patch of trees near the side of a road. He took you to the hospital in Madison and they transferred you here."

Sharnee grimaced. "My head hurts."

"You have a concussion."

"The doctor said you will have a full recovery," Brita added.

She turned her glossy eyes to her mother. "Mom, I'm sorry."

"You have nothing to be sorry for, honey," Brita said. She lowered the bed rail on that side and eased onto the bed. "What do you remember?"

Sharnee squeezed her eyelids. She drew in a deep breath and let it out in a long sigh. "Everything." She opened her eyes and looked at Neil. "The person who took me was a woman. She came up to me while I sat at a table overlooking the lake. I never heard or saw her until she leaned across the table from behind and tapped my shoulder."

"What was she wearing?"

"Tactical gear. All black. Like a SWAT team wears except for the helmet. She wore a mask."

"Are you positive it was a female?"

"A hundred percent. I saw her eyes and heard her breathing. She pressed her hand to my mouth and nose. I don't remember anything else."

"Any distinct odor to whatever she held?"

"It wasn't chloroform. I know that much. I passed out in a matter of seconds."

"They found ketamine in your system. How did you get away?"

Sharnee licked her lips. "I need something to drink." Brita poured water into a Styrofoam cup and positioned the straw for her to drink. Sharnee shifted to a sitting position and took the cup.

After three long draws on the straw, she said, "A sudden stop jolted me awake. I was in the trunk of a car with my hands bound in front. I could hear traffic slowing around me and felt the vibration of the car not moving. I felt around for the release and when I found it I pulled as hard as I could. Fresh air rushed in and I could see headlights coming at me in the distance. I realized then we stopped on a four-lane highway. I threw my legs over the edge and rolled out and ran toward the trees. The last thing I remember is thrashing through low-hanging branches and screaming when my foot snagged on something out there. Even that's a blur."

Brita kissed Sharnee's head. "You're safe now. Lay back and rest."

Halfway back to the pillow she jerked upright. "What if she comes after me?"

"She won't," Neil said. "Now that you got away from her I'm sure she'll focus elsewhere. She'll cover her tracks and carry on her normal schedule so as not to draw attention to herself."

Sharnee reclined to the pillow. "This may seem gross, but...I peed in the trunk to leave my DNA in there."

Brita scrunched her nose.

Neil said, "Ingenious."

****

Neil reached for the burner phone to call Sloane with the news when his cellphone rang—Tess. Brita's enquiries flashed through his mind. *Who is Tess? You mumbled her name three times. Who is she to you?*

He answered the call.

"I hope I'm not calling too early, Neil. I just heard about your niece. Is she okay?"

"She's fine, Tess." Brita turned her head, glared at Neil with her right brow lifted. "She's awake and able to carry on a conversation. How did you hear?"

"The sheriff in Greene County called Rob this morning. Rob told me it was your niece who was kidnapped last night at Lake Oconee. It saddened me to hear that, Neil. Was she able to describe the kidnapper?"

"She's still hazy right now. When her faculties clear she'll recall a few more details."

"I hope so for all your sakes. Is there anything I can do for you or your family?"

"We have everything we need. Thanks for the offer."

"Let me know if I there's anything I can do, Neil, anything at all. My love, thoughts, and prayers will be with you today."

Neil stared at the screen once it faded to black.

"Okay, Neil." Brita said. "We need to talk."

"Not here."

Brita turned to Sharnee. "We're going to the cafeteria."

Sharnee nodded, closed her eyes.

The bustle in the hospital cafeteria forced Brita and

Neil to a corner table as far away as possible from the rattle of flatware and increased conversation level of crowded tables filled with diners.

Brita ate a cup of oatmeal topped with mixed berries. Neil consumed a breakfast sandwich of egg, tomato, and bacon.

Brita cradled her refilled cup of coffee in her palm and crossed her legs.

"All right, little brother. Tell me what's going on."

Neil sipped his coffee and set it on the table. His fingers remained clamped around the cup. He began with the call he received after the first murder, the conversation with Chief of Police Rob Fleishman including the man's request for consult, and the portrait sketched in blood on the barn wall. He told her about the stranger; the failed attack on him and Sloane by the four men; the intrusion into his home and the tainted eye drops; the second murder, subsequent discovery of blood inside his home and a second portrait of him painted in blood.

"How does the Tess woman fit into all this?"

"I met Rob and Tess Fleishman my first week in Madison. They were members at the church. He was a deacon whom the board elected chairman last year. A few months ago they announced Tess was diagnosed with leukemia. She quit the church although he remained to fulfill his duties as chairman. Deviance from normal conduct here and there led me to believe Rob might be responsible for the murders. I went to their home to talk to Tess. While there, Tess volunteered evidence supportive of my conjecture including Rob's talent for the art of painting and his increased absence evenings and nights of late. She also came on to me."

"Which you rejected," Brita said.

"Yes." Neil sipped coffee, lowered the cup to chest level.

"How did she respond?"

"Disappointment."

"No anger?"

"None obvious."

"Hmm."

"What?"

"Nothing. Just thinking." Brita took two sips of her coffee. "Does she suspect her husband's having an affair?"

"She mentioned it moments before she showed me a piece of his artwork."

"Then Tess is venting her anger elsewhere. She'll use whatever that is to get you."

"What makes you think that?"

"Intuition."

Chapter 25

The two-block walk—the length of two football fields—from the police department to the tax commissioner's office took Sloane two-and-a-half minutes. Less time for the stroll than by a car when she considered the walk to a cruiser, maneuver the parking lot, intersections, park on Hancock Street and walk around the corner of the building to the entrance on E. Washington.

Reddish-lavender clouds ducked under the morning sun on the horizon. The weather pattern brought with it low humidity and temperatures ten degrees below average. Sloane looked forward to the stroll back to the station, with a break in the cases in hand.

A slender, caramel-skinned woman in her forties greeted Sloane. "You look chipper this morning, Sergeant." Long fingernails painted fuchsia clicked the keyboard on the workstation. The color closely matched the woman's lipstick.

"Good morning, Nariah. I need a favor."

"Oh?" Her fingers hovered above the keyboard.

"Detective Huber called yesterday to request a list of vehicles for a case he's working on."

"Let me check for you."

The woman rolled back in her chair and pushed to her feet. She swayed through a doorway to the right. A second woman perused forms at a desk in the far corner. No one waited to renew license plates or for help with other transactions. The room smelled of stale air. Two minutes later the woman returned holding a white letter size envelope in her right hand. She placed it on the counter in front of Sloane. Huber's name written in blue ink identified the requestor.

"Thanks, Nariah."

"Glad to help. Tell him to ask for me next time."

Sloane waved and ambled through the building. She opened the flap and removed the single page print-out and read it on her way out. The document listed the license plate numbers, names, and addresses of four Toyota Avalon owners. Sloane re-folded the page and stuffed it in the envelope.

The second she saw the man on the sidewalk Sloane knew him to be the man in the photos at the crime scene. She tensed, alert for any advance the stranger planned for her. She matched her first step toward Hancock with one of his toward her. Five additional strides each would put them within arm's length of each other.

The stranger stilled after two more steps forward, ten feet away. He extended his left hand in which he held a slip of paper turned where she could see the handwriting.

"Sergeant Azevedo, I have a message from Arlo Messana for Neil Caldera."

"Who are you and what is the message?"

The stranger held out his right hand, palm outward. "I'm going to show my ID to you." He slid his hand inside his suit coat, came out with an ID wallet and presented it open to her.

Sloane looked at the ID, took the note from the

mystery man's hand and glanced at it.

Before she asked, the stranger said, "Mr. Messana requests Mr. Caldera's visit to discuss the young lady dropped off at the emergency room last evening. Noon at the address provided. Tell Caldera to not be late." With that, the stranger strolled past Sloane without making eye contact and crossed the street. He continued on into the parking lot of SunTrust Bank.

Sloane watched the stranger's swagger until he was out of sight. She wondered why he visited Madison and if his presence had anything to do with the events of the past three days. He let himself be photographed at the scene of Vanessa's murder. A man of his description visited Neil in the early hours of Monday morning around the time of Katie's murder. Somehow, he knew the person who transported Sharnee to the hospital.

Everything seemed too calculated in her observance to be chance occurrences.

Neil agreed when she talked to him on her way back to the station.

"Who is Arlo Messana? Do you know him?" Neil asked.

"I've heard the name but never met him. I'll run an NCIC check on him and call you with the results."

"Let me know if he's a sociopathic killer or anything similar, otherwise I prefer to hear what he has to say first."

****

The first space in the Georgia State Patrol's parking lot faced the flagpole. Huber nosed the unmarked sedan short of the clump of pampas grass at 9:03. The American and Georgia flags waved at passersby in front of the gray brick building. Sloane gazed at the American flag. The symbol of liberty atop the pole acknowledged Vanessa's and Katie's rights to pursue in life their every desire. Rights stripped by their killer.

Sloane strolled alongside Huber, ascended the steps onto the porch between two white columns and entered the front door. She hoped for a match either by vehicle or license plate number to one of the four vehicles listed on the printout.

"You must be Sergeant Azevedo and Detective Huber," said a stout woman in GSP uniform. The blue shirt gave emphasis to her curves. "I have the DVD ready." She picked up a thin jewel case and her short fingers set it on the counter.

"Is there somewhere we may view the footage? It would save us time."

"Sure. Step through that door and I'll set it up for you."

The electronic lock clicked.

They filed through the door and shadowed the woman to a computer set up on a portable workstation. She plopped onto the roller chair and inserted the DVD into the tray in the CPU. The CPU hummed.

"You looking for a particular vehicle?"

"A Toyota Avalon and any car or SUV driven by a lone female under the age of forty," Sloane said.

The woman tapped the mouse, opened the video program. "That narrows the search. I have video from two of our units. What's the woman wanted for?"

"A kidnapping in Greene County and the murders of two young women here in Madison. We believe she may have gotten caught in traffic after the crash. Security video captured our second victim Sunday night getting into a dark colored Avalon."

The dash cam footage filled the screen. Clarity was adequate for their purpose. The time stamp in the lower right corner displayed 20:54:17 at the start of the recording and showed an arrival time at the crash of 20:59:43. Huber hovered behind the woman's left shoulder. Sloane grabbed a chair and sat to her right. The woman forwarded the recording to when troopers cleared the inside lane and set up a checkpoint. The time was 21:26:08. Troopers shined light on drivers and in their vehicles and allowed them to continue on their way.

No Toyota Avalon appeared in the segment. None of the vehicles displayed a license tag even close to any of the four. The authorities detained no one between setup and shutdown at 22:10:31.

The second dash cam recorded identical results.

Huber wandered through the security door, paused at the entrance. Sloane thanked the woman, pocketed the DVD and hastened after Huber who shouldered the door open and walked toward the car.

Sloane called after him. "Perk up, Detective. This job requires absolute focus. We follow every lead. No exception. That means those we find trivial or irksome."

"I didn't say anything."

"You didn't have to. Your body language signals disinterest. We have four vehicle owners to locate and question. Are you with me?"

Huber rammed his left hand in his pants' pocket and came out with the key to the car. He slid in and started it without uttering a word. Sloane got in and held the list open on her lap. Huber backed the car around, drove forward and stopped nosed to Highway 83.

"The closest one is on Sycamore. Let's start there and work our way outward."

Sloane's mind drifted to the stranger. She created in her mind the way she'd seen him that morning. Nonchalant. Composed. No communication apprehension. For whom had this man showed up in Madison? Was it Neil? What reason did he have for coming here? The name, Declan Gadow, was printed on his ID. Were the name and credentials real or had he used an alias and faked the ID to divert attention? One way she knew to confirm, but not while with Huber. She needed to wait until she was alone before she contacted her source.

"There's the address." Huber motioned to a flattop brick mailbox and dropped his speed.

A boxwood hedge in need of pruning blocked all except the white top of a vehicle parked in the driveway outside the clapboard house. Huber swung right between the hedge and the mailbox onto an asphalt driveway.

"That's not the car," Sloane said of the white Toyota Avalon seventy-five feet away.

Huber backed the unmarked police car into the street and drove to the intersection where he stopped. "Which one next?"

"March."

A long driveway led to a two-story house—white with black shutters—a hundred twenty-five feet off the road. A vintage red Ford pickup stood beyond the left curve of the paved drive under a metal carport.

Huber and Sloane followed the walkway and

ascended the steps. He knocked on the front door. They waited thirty seconds and finally heard heavy footfalls, the click of a lock, and the suck of air on the storm door when the entrance door opened. A barefoot man in his mid-forties wearing a white tee and gray cargo pants dabbed his face with a blue bath towel. He stared down at Sloane.

Huber held out his badge, identified himself and Sloane and spoke the man's name.

"Yes, how may I help you Detective?" He rubbed his hair with one end of the towel.

"Do you own a Toyota Avalon?"

The man let the towel fall to his shoulder. "My wife's car. She left for work at nine. Is something wrong with her? Is she okay?"

"I'm sure she's fine. What color is the car?"

"Black."

"Can you two account for your whereabouts Sunday evening between ten and midnight?" Sloane asked.

"Yes." He unlocked the storm door and pushed it open. "Please come inside. We flew home Sunday evening from a weekend in Vegas," he said on his way to a room he used for a study. Huber and Sloane followed. "Our flight didn't land at Hartsfield until eleven forty. I had parked the Avalon in the daily lot." He picked up a folder on a mahogany desk, removed their boarding passes approved by TSA at McCarran International and a parking receipt stamped with a time of 12:42 AM. "We were in the Avalon. That should be easy enough to confirm."

Huber handed the documents back, thanked him for his time.

"Another dead end," Huber said when they neared the car. They got in and he started the car, sat there in the driver's seat, window down, arm on the beltline of the door.

Sloane lowered her window. A breeze blew through the interior. "This is not a dead end, Huber. Consider it a detour."

"Okay then, tell me where this detour leads us now?"

The third registered owner listed an address on Rawlings Drive in Rutledge. Hardwoods surrounded a modest cedar ranch-stained moss olive fifty yards up a dirt driveway backed by a line of tree-topped undulated terrain. Dark streaks discolored its Brownwood shingles. No vehicles under the carport.

"It doesn't look like anybody's home," Huber said.

Sloane shoved open the door. "Let's check, anyway. You never know. We might get lucky."

Chapter 26

A few minutes before noon, Neil arrived at the address on Fieldcrest Lane given to Sloane by the stranger, the home of Arlo Messana, the man who found Sharnee and took her to the hospital. Neil followed the long driveway for more than a hundred yards under massive trees to the two-story Victorian painted white with forest-green shutters. He got out and knocked on the front door. The door rattled in its frame. The rooms behind the front windows appeared subdued by the darkness in them. Neil descended the five steps to a concrete pad and ambled to the corner of the house.

A covered walkway linked the back of the house to a detached three-car garage. The breezeway and garage stood in disrepair. Paint peeled on the closed doors and the darker trim surrounding them. White smoke plumed from the back of the house and trailed the oatmeal clapboard siding toward where he stood.

The aroma of pipe tobacco suggested the owner of the house occupied the screened back porch he'd seen on his approach. He walked to the back of the house. The man he sought sat in a metal rocker, head down and tilted to his left. The retired minister wore a yellowed white shirt, brown Dockers and loafers, no socks. His left hand rested on his thigh. His fingers cradled a rustic bowl pipe. Smoke twirled upward from the bowl.

Neil watched the man through the screen thirty seconds before he circled to the steps. The treads, stringers and rails looked and smelled of new wood. They felt solid underfoot as he ascended. The man remained still, head forward. The sight of the old minister's face delayed Neil's knock on the screen door. Rumors failed to prepare him for the reality before him. Raised scars three inches long and a half-inch wide marred the otherwise smooth skin of the forehead and right cheek of the sixty-one-year-old man.

Neil tapped on the door. The man in the rocker lifted his head.

"Reverend Caldera. I'm pleased you stopped by on such a beautiful day."

"Mr. Messana?"

"It's unlocked. Step on in and have a seat. May I call you Neil? I'm not much for titles. I haven't seen many who could live up to one much, anyway."

Neil pulled open the door and crossed to a five-foot swing where he sat on a blue paisley cushion. The chains squawked due to the tension put on them.

"You don't look like any cleric I've ever seen."

"I guess it's a good thing God chooses by what's on the inside and not appearance, huh?" Neil said.

"I see exercise must be important to you, Neil. You know the Scripture says bodily exercise profits little."

"Spiritual strength in a weak vessel won't account for much the way I see it. A person should take care of the vessel God gave them to fulfill His purpose."

Arlo gave a suasive smile. "I couldn't agree more. Most bishops, pastors, reverends, whatever they prefer to call themselves nowadays are too weak to hold up their britches or too obese to get into them. You seem like a smart fellow. I gander you know my inference."

"I do. Many people disgrace the church by their sloth."

The old man leaned forward. "More than that. It's downright cruel. You see this face? It used to be handsome according to my wife. Forty-one years. She has stuck with me. One of my so-called peers did this to me sixteen years ago. A leather strap wrapped in barbed wire inflicted irreparable damage. First, he nudged me into a ditch with his car while I enjoyed an evening stroll over on Ferrell Lane. He and two of his friends dragged me into a pine thicket, told me I should mind my own business that his affairs were none of mine. The one who manhandled me sweated profusely. He was around thirty. Athletic build. I was forty-eight at the time. If I was my old self, they never would have gotten away with it. I would have exacted my revenge upon them."

"What then?"

"I crawled to the road and flagged a ride to the hospital. The staff notified the police. A lot of good that did me. The officers wasted time and taxpayer's money. They came to the Emergency Room and talked with me. No notes penned by either. A short incident report put on file. That was it. I don't even believe they interviewed the people responsible for this." He motioned to his face, leaned back and took a draw on his pipe and stared at the distance. Smoke swirled his face. "You want to talk to me about the young lady."

"She is my niece. Her name is Sharnee. Thank you for helping her."

He gave a terse nod. "I knew there had to be some connection. Hadn't been for that flat tire I never would have seen her lying there. Some would say it was luck. I believe nothing of the kind. That tire had fewer than a thousand miles on it and showed no sign of a puncture."

Neil leaned forward. "I need to know what happened."

"How is she?"

"They transferred her to Piedmont Newton. She suffered a severe concussion."

Mr. Messana shook his head, dumped the burned tobacco in a clear ashtray on a side table. The bowl looked like a thimble in his hand. It clinked three times on the glass. He laid the pipe on the table.

"I was on Baldwin Dairy Road headed toward Bethany. I felt a sway in the truck. I knew it had to be a tire, so I pulled to the shoulder and got out and saw the flat tire on the left rear. From where I was standing, I-20 runs parallel about seventy-five yards south of a patch of woods. An air horn blared, tires screeched and metal banged on I-20. The bawling tires and crunching metal continued for three or four seconds.

"I had just got my jack out and set it in place when a scream startled me. It sounded somewhat like a screech owl's trill. I wasn't sure at first where it came from. I looked up and down the road and again heard the voice shriek as if in pain. That time I focused on the woods across the road and saw the woman. She struggled through the underbrush toward the road. I called out and hurried to her. She must've heard me or saw me because she turned her head, thrashed her arms and pumped her legs with renewed vigor. After a few feet, she plunged head first to the forest floor.

"I scrambled to her and saw she had stepped on a rotten stump, fell forward and struck her head. I rolled her to her back. That's when I saw the weal on the left side of her forehead and her wrists bound in a zip tie. The first thing I thought of was how blessed she is to have gotten away from that killer. I called nine-one-one and told them I needed an ambulance. They said it might be a while because of that crash on I-20. I told them to forget it and called my nephew. He got there in five minutes and we rushed her to the hospital."

"Did she speak?"

"Not a word. She moaned several times. That was it. My nephew carried her into the ER. I stayed outside for obvious reasons. He left her in their care and took me back to get my truck. I wish we could have done more for her."

"May God bless you for rendering aid to Sharnee, Mr. Messana."

He gave another terse nod.

Neil stared at the worn rug spread over the floor.

Mr. Messana swigged water from a bottle and cleared his throat. He propped his elbows on his knees and slapped his hands together.

"You carry a heavy load, Neil Caldera, and it has nothing to do with your injured niece. It's eating you. I can see it. Nobody in town knows it either, do they?"

"One knows. One suspects he knows. Other than those two, no. No one knows."

"Secrets and lies, Neil. Both result in trouble for the one who harbors them if relied upon to maintain sanity. People once confided in me until they heard what happened." He rubbed his fingers along the scars on his cheek. "I never betrayed their confidence. That's the way it must be. It's the other kind of secrets that brings trouble. The ones you'd hate for anyone to know."

"You're a wise man, Mr. Messana."

"Tend to business, Neil. Time's wasting away faster than those girls' bodies."

"I have no authority."

Arlo laced his fingers and pointed his two forefingers upward. "We have authority in the talent God gave us. Use yours, Neil." He leaned forward. "That shooting in New York was an accident. You were right where you should have been in your attempt to stop a serial killer."

Neil jerked upright. "How could you possible know that?"

****

A strong odor of wood stain wafted around Huber and Sloane when they got to within ten feet of the house. No footprints or dirt soiled the porch floor painted a pale brown. Sloane glanced behind them at the treads. Theirs were the first feet for the moment to blemish the smooth surfaces. A vacuum cleaner polluted the air with its yammer.

Silence followed Sloane's knock on the cedar siding. "Somebody's at the door," trailed Sloane's second knock. Then another female's voice, "I've got it. You go to your room like I told you."

A woman wearing a blue scrub top, jeans and sandals opened the door. The thirty-two-year-old dental assistant beamed when she saw Sloane.

"Sergeant Azevedo. To what do I owe the pleasure? Come in."

"Hi, Sunny. This is Detective Huber."

They stepped inside and closed the door to a quaint living room. Walls painted beige and furnished with a black leather sofa, matching wing chair and a rocker handmade of blonde wood. A glass-top oval table stood on a black and beige oriental rug in front of the sofa.

Huber acknowledged the woman with a terse nod. Sunny smiled. "It's nice to see you, Detective."

Sloane consulted the vehicle printout and glanced at Huber, who nodded. She took the initiative. "We're looking for a Toyota Avalon registered to this address. It's shown under a different name."

The woman's shoulders drooped. A frown saddened her features. Her eyes glazed. Despair struck her in that moment.

"That's because they registered it in my mother's name."

"May we see it?"

"The bank repossessed it two weeks ago." Sunny sank to a wing chair.

Sloane took a seat in the rocker to Sunny's left. The wood creaked. "It saddens me to hear that. How do you get to work?"

"I'm carpooling with one of the other hygienists."

"What color is the Avalon?"

"It's called Parisian Night Pearl. That's a blue color."

"Any idea where they took it?"

"No, but Leggett came and got it. He towed it away on one of their trucks."

"Davis Leggett?"

Sunny nodded. "He's the one I gave the keys to. He had another man with him I'd never seen before. May I ask why the police are looking for my car?"

"It's potential, not definitive that our focus is on your Avalon. We're talking to every Avalon owner registered in the county."

"But a possibility exists."

"Yes." More probable than possible, Sloane thought, though unwilling to express that opinion.

It depended on the killer's access to Sunny's Avalon.

"Will you let me know either way?"

Huber said, "We still have a lot of work to accomplish before we'll know for sure, but I promise I'll call you when this is over."

****

"You promise?" Sloane said to Huber on their way down Sunny's driveway. "What was that all about?"

"I just wanted to ease her mind. That's all."

"Yeah, sure. You know her, don't you? I saw it on your face once I introduced you to her."

"We dated in high school."

"She's an ex-girlfriend?"

Huber chuckled. "In my dreams. We went out twice. Once to get a taste of what it was like to go on a date with me and a second to get an adequate amount of that knowledge."

"She sure brightened your mood."

"She always did."

"Hence the promise you made. That gives you a reason to talk with her again."

"It's not like that."

"It's exactly that, Huber. You might as well admit it as fact. You're smitten."

"Too much time has passed."

"Whatever you say. Your life. Your choice."

Road and wind noise filled the car for the ten minutes to the address on Durden Road in the south portion of the county. Neither uttered a word until Huber first drove by the address and observed three Toyotas—Avalon, Tundra, Camry—lined one behind another on the circular driveway.

Sloane shielded her eyes even though she wore sunglasses. "Silver. No reason to stop. Head to Leggett's. I want to see if Sunny's car is still there."

"And if it is?"

"We'll have a heart-to-heart with Davis Leggett."

"No way Davis is our killer."

"I agree, but I think he might know who is."

****

The scars reddened on Mr. Messana's forehead and cheek. Neil wondered if he insulted the man by his question. Still, he wanted to know how the man seemed to know details related to the incident in New York City.

"I witnessed it."

"With all due respect, sir…"

Mr. Messana held up his hand. "Let not the fact that I know trouble you, Neil. I identify with your pain. Loss of a person close to you has a way of opening our eyes to life's fragility."

"You speak as though you knew her."

"Two weeks every summer for nine years she stayed with the wife and me. She was my niece. The daughter of my wife's sister. You met her mother at the scene; her father after the unfortunate event. They are the type you want to avoid whenever possible. Angry. Bitter. Ruthless. They would have issued a contract for your death, but I convinced them to change their mind. They accepted my alternative after I told them I would hire someone to investigate you. You had every right to pull the trigger, and you got taken on your investment."

"Friends of friends testified against me on the family's behalf."

"Not so, Neil. I've read the dossier. Friends of your enemies on the force consorted with their faction for personal gain. You trusted them and they betrayed you. Have you ever asked yourself, 'Why Madison, Georgia?' Who do you think prompted the church leadership to ask you to come here?"

Neil arched his brows.

Mr. Messana nodded. "I read your personnel file. Trustworthy."

Gravel crunched beneath vehicle tires on the side of the house. A midnight blue Ford sedan slowed to a stop in front of the garage. The man in the driver's seat opened the door, telephone held to his ear.

Mr. Messana grinned and said, "There's my sleuth."

It was the stranger.

Neil bounded to his feet. The man approached the porch, head high. Lips pulled flat and tight. He ascended the steps and pulled open the screened door. His expression brightened when he saw Neil.

"We meet again, Reverend." He extended his right hand.

They shook. "Call me Neil."

"I'm glad you're here."

"Who are you?"

"Special Agent Declan Gadow FBI. I'm part of the Field Crime Scene Team."

"You reconstruct shooting incidents."

"Yes. The family retained me in an unofficial capacity to look into the death of my cousin."

Neil looked at Mr. Messana.

"My nephew," Messana said.

Agent Gadow continued. "Microanalysis on the bullet shows it passed through an intermediate target before it struck Saniya. This target is different from that first believed or reported by the authorities. It was him, Neil. The projectile passed through the man you pursued and ricocheted off a light standard before striking her. It exonerated you of any negligence. The family also extends their sincere apology for the harm they inflicted on you."

Positive affirmation came from Agent Gadow's statement. Those words brought assurance of release from Neil's chronic self-resentment imposed since the incident. He accepted it without hesitation. The weeds of guilt thrived no longer. Forgiveness never felt so good.

"Thank you." It was the only honorable thing he could think of to say.

"Might I add, those shot placements were beyond belief. Anyone who can chase a guy on foot seven blocks and still put two rounds center mass two-and-a-half-inches apart is a world-class shooter."

Neil acknowledged with a nod.

Mr. Messana lifted his hands. "Well, I suppose I should confess my sins before you now, Neil. I sure as heck have no desire for you to come looking to confront me."

The three chorused a laugh.

"One more thing," said Agent Gadow. "The police commissioner in New York wants you to call him first thing Monday."

****

Neil looked at the caller ID on the screen and touched the button to answer the call. He pulled to the side of Fieldcrest Lane, listened to the caller, and said, "Thanks for your help. I owe you one, big time."

He ended the call, swapped his cellphone for the burner and pressed the number for Sloane. "Hey, I just talked to my contact at the lab in New York. Someone laced the eye drops with ketamine."

"Ketamine?" Sloane said.

"Yeah. Isn't that strange? The same substance in Sharnee's system when they drew her blood at the hospital."

"How is she?"

"No cognitive deficits, thank God. The doctor signed her discharge papers. They're on their way to the hotel where an investigator from Greene County is to record Sharnee's statement."

"That's great. I have some information for you. I learned the identity of our mystery man. He's FBI."

"I know."

A locomotive a quarter mile east sounded its horn, rumbled on its approach.

"Did you say you know? I couldn't hear you above the train," Neil said. "Hold on a minute." He raised the windows. The train rolled west on the far side of intersection where he sat. The freight cars' wheels screeched on the tracks. "Is that better?"

"Still loud, but I can hear you. How did you find out?"

"I met him at Arlo Messana's home. That's not the only thing, either. Arlo Messana claimed he arranged the job offer at the church to get me here in Madison."

"Why would he do that?"

"He never disclosed that information and before I could ask him Gadow showed up. It gets better. The woman in New York was Messana's niece. Agent Gadow is his nephew, a cousin of the deceased."

"There's your reason for being here, Neil. If Arlo Messana arranged the cleric's position for you, he wanted you here. His purpose remains the mystery."

"A favor deserves a favor. Is that what you're saying?"

"He aspired to clear your record, Neil. Job well done."

"You're right. I owe him. When you have time, run his name through the department's records and ask the sheriff's office to do the same. I'm looking for any record of an attack on him that happened around sixteen years ago. Even though the statute of limitations for the assault has expired, I still want to identify the perpetrators."

"He may be waiting for you to ask him."

"Maybe. His choice of words made it sound like he knew only one of the three men who attacked him. He identified the man as one of his peers. How is the search for the Avalon going?"

"We may have located it. Huber and I are on our way to the funeral for Vanessa and Katie. After that we're going to Leggett's place to look at the Avalon repossessed two weeks ago. The color matches the one we saw on the security video."

"I'm on my way to the school. I'll see you there."

Chapter 27

The auditorium at Morgan County High School filled to overflow capacity twenty minutes before 1:00 p.m. Persons without seats lined the sides and across the back. Members of the Flack family followed an antique white casket to the front and took their places on the left side. The Moore family filed behind a pearl rose casket and sat to the right.

An orator lectern equipped with a sound system centered the stage. A row of black padded chairs extended ten feet behind the lectern. Neil took his reserved spot in the third seat. The Madison Presbyterian Church youth minister sat on his left. The Principal of Morgan High occupied the center seat. Members of the school's choral group filled the remaining sixteen chairs.

Neil scanned the faces on the front row. A female in Navy Service Dress Blue uniform sat next to Vanessa's mother. Likewise, a female in Navy SBD sat alongside Katie's mother. Neither attended the funeral in an official capacity. Each one clasped the hand of the mother next to her. Heads lowered. Momentary swipes of cheeks.

At one o'clock, the principal rose to welcome the quiet crowd. The choral group performed the song "Friends" written by Michael W. Smith. Attendees throughout the auditorium smiled, nodded or sobbed at the lyrics.

A hush came over the crowd when Neil stepped to the lectern.

"Today we pay our respects to the lives of Vanessa Flack and Katie Moore and acknowledge their families, friends and the multitude of others they left behind. Often, we do not realize until they no longer live in our midst the influences of others and how their lives at one time or other touched ours. Memories live on and bless those fortunate enough to have known them."

Neil cited Vanessa's and Katie's accomplishments, encouraged their families, and addressed their peers in the words of Paul the Apostle to Timothy paraphrased, "Let no one belittle you or undervalue your opinions because you are young. Show yourselves examples to the world in your speech, faith, and everyday life and may the Lord guide you in each aspect of your lives."

At the cemetery, the parents introduced Valerie Flack and Kylie Holcomb to Neil and Sloane. Valerie wore the insignia of an E-8, Senior Chief Petty Officer. Kylie's patch showed rank of W-2, Chief Warrant Officer 2.

Kylie said, "I understand you consulted with the police on our sisters' cases. Valerie and I wanted to thank you for all you've done to help. We have family obligations to take care of tomorrow but would like to sit down with you later in the week at whatever time might be convenient for us and you. We're scheduled to leave Friday evening."

Neil wrote the burner phone number on a slip of paper Kylie provided and added Sloane's name and cellphone number as an alternative.

"Any time Thursday or Friday works for us. Call

the top number first."

On the way to the car where Huber waited for her, Sloane said, "We still need to go by the church and have a look at that baptistery. Will anybody be there?"

Neil reached into his pocket and came out with his keys. The six keys jingled when he held them up and shook them. "Doesn't matter. I still have a key."

****

A black GMC Acadia turned into the church's parking lot ahead of Neil and Sloane and parked parallel to the side entrance. Neil nosed in at the rear of the Acadia. Sloane pulled the police car to the far side of his Acura.

Nan Wilkerson pushed out of the SUV in a white print blouse and purple pants. She unlocked the door and dropped her keys in a small beige handbag. She waited for Neil to get out of his car. "Good afternoon."

Neil thought the smile on her face looked genuine compared to the face he saw on her at their last encounter Monday morning.

"Nan, this is Sergeant Sloane Azevedo. We'd like to have a look at the harness system and baptistery if you have no objection."

"That's fine by me. I don't imagine it could do any harm just to look." She escorted them inside. "If you don't mind my asking, why are the police interested in our baptistery harness?"

"This is part of our investigation into Miss Flack's death," Sloane said. "I understand she attended services here."

"That's right."

"We believe her killer may have used the baptistery to wash her body."

Nan sucked in a breath. Her left hand shot to her chest. She looked at Neil. "Please tell me that didn't happen. Who would do such a thing in God's house?"

"Hopefully no one, Nan. It is part of their investigation that needs confirmed or ruled out."

"Y'all go ahead. I'm going to my office."

Neil led Sloane through a small hallway on the far side of the choir loft and left through a doorway to a set of steps that ascended to the pool. An electric ceiling patient-lift with a blue lift sling hung at the base of the steps. Long lanyards attached the sling to the trolley.

Sloane took out her Maglite and scoured the beam across and up and down the sling and the lanyard attachments. She opened a DNA flocked swab, wet it with distilled water, and swabbed the seams in the sling. She repeated the process using different swabs for each lanyard attachment. She secured the evidence, labeled and initialed each bag.

When she finished, Neil said, "This is how it works." He pressed a button on the control panel. The trolley hummed and moved along the track.

"Help me unhook it. I'm taking it with me." Sloane handed off the keys to the police car. "I have a box of large bags in the trunk."

Neil retrieved the bags from the trunk. He stopped by Nan's office to let her know they were taking the sling.

Nan said, "I apologize for my behavior Monday. You deserved better than that. No problem if the police need the lift. If asked, I gave permission to take it."

Neil thanked her.

Sloane had removed the sling and lanyards by the time he returned with the bag.

"I called Huber and filled him in on this evidence. He and I are on our way to Leggett's in fifteen."

Neil nodded. "I'll go by home to change and meet you there."

****

The two cars bounced on the uneven surface along the base of a hill to their left along the dirt path cut through the impound property. The rear tires spun on the unmarked detective car ahead of Neil when Huber turned left and ascended the hill. Neil avoided the fresh furrows as he followed the Ford and parked to Huber's right. A V-shaped expanse contained eight cars nosed outward and a Ford crew cab pickup at ninety degrees to the others.

Huber headed straight for the Avalon while Sloane avoided a mud hole, handed off the registration printout to Neil and powered up her camera.

"We eliminated three out of four. The list contains only those registered here in Morgan County. I have a good feeling about this one."

Neil scanned the row of vehicles left to right. Someone parked the Toyota Avalon they sought third from the left between a black Chevrolet Impala and graphite Kia Optima. The brown Ford Focus filled a space on the end to the left of the Impala. Vehicles to the right of the Kia included a Hyundai, a Nissan, two Hondas, and a Dodge. Lack of fresh tire tracks confirmed no movement across the wet soil. Placards hung from rear-view mirrors identified their repo status.

They followed Huber to the Avalon. "How was the owner's demeanor?"

"Direct. No hesitation in her answers. I detected no signs of deception in either her voice or body language."

Huber said, "This is it. The tag number matches the one on the list. No tire tracks suggest it remained here since the storm last night."

Neil peered into the Avalon's windows and saw locked doors. The interior visible to him showed meticulous care by the owner. The driver's seat back was in line with the B-pillar on that side.

"How tall is the owner?" Neil asked.

"I'd say five-four or thereabout," Sloane said.

"A person taller than five-four last operated this vehicle based on seat position."

"Probably the repo driver," Huber said.

"Maybe. Maybe not. If he got in long enough to back it in, he may not have had to adjust the seat rearward. Perhaps he was in a hurry. Throw in a leg. Perch on the edge of the seat. Back it in place. Hop out. Lock it. Done."

Huber rested his arms on top of the car on the passenger side, regarded Neil with brow scrunched. "You not only believe the killer is a female, she has to be extremely tall?"

"A surrogate study will convey the person's height within reason. We can use this car once it's processed. Start with Sloane as our surrogate. If she sits in the seat and discovers it to be in a comfortable driving position with no adjustment, we'll know height within an inch or two, dependent on torso and leg length."

"Impressive."

"Another way would be to have the owner sit in the seat and slide forward after documenting present position of the seat tracks and measure the difference. That should tell us how far rearward the person adjusted the seat."

"If she readjusted it to the same," Huber said.

"Agree. The most accurate is to examine the seat track for Brinell marks on a manually adjusted seat."

"The what?" Huber asked.

Sloane said, "Forensic marks on the upper seat track window made by the locking pawl."

"This car is equipped with power seats." Neil rounded the rear of the car and peered in from the passenger's side.

He backed away to allow Sloane passage, bumped against the Impala and glanced behind him. A mark on the Impala's door registered in his mind when he looked away. He swung his head around, leaned forward. The scratch looked familiar. The curve resembled a half-moon angled from ten to four compared to a clock. Neil studied it for any significance. Why had he remembered it? He leaned his left forearm on the roof rail and tapped the window with his thumb. He paused. Stared at the driver's seat where an image of a person formed in his mind.

Neil straightened. Looked at the Impala front to back along the side and back to the driver's window.

"Detective. Sloane. Look at this." Huber came and stood to Neil's left, Sloane on the right. Neil pointed to the scraped surface. "We need to find the owner and ask when this car was repo'd. I saw this car Saturday evening on my walk to the barn to meet Chad Stoltz."

"How do you know it's the same car?" Huber asked.

"I noticed that scratch while I talked to the driver."

"And who was that?"

"Tess Fleishman."

Huber gave Neil a hard stare. "That's asinine. Tess Fleishman's laid up at home. The chief, her *husband*, keeps us up to date on her condition and that includes her inability to do things for herself."

"Hearsay," Neil said. "Have you any personal knowledge of her helplessness?"

"Well, no. I haven't seen or talked to her lately."

"When?"

Huber's face flushed. "What is your problem, Neil? What do you have against Chief Fleishman? First, you wanted his records and now you're making assumptions about his wife?"

"Facts, Detective. Now answer the question. Define 'lately.' "

"Three or four months, okay? She would've gotten weaker, not stronger."

Sloane said, "Unless she's faking the illness."

Huber flailed his left arm. "Now *you're* calling the chief a liar? Come on, Sergeant. You don't really believe that, do you?"

"Consider the possibility he doesn't know," Neil said. He thought of his conversation with Brita. "What if we can prove it?"

A horrible thought of Vanessa Flack's body lying in the Impala's trunk at the time he talked with Tess assailed his mind. Chad Stoltz found the bloody scene before then. Chief Fleishman reported the discovery of Vanessa's remains afterward. The likelihood sickened him.

Sloane touched Neil's arm. "Are you okay? Your face turned ashen."

"I just realized Vanessa's body must have been in the trunk when I saw Tess. It sickens me to know she was right there." He motioned toward the rear of the Impala. "If only…" He shook his head. He looked at Huber. "You have probable cause. Put a hold on these vehicles."

Huber motioned to the Avalon and the Impala. "These two?"

"All of them."

"There's nine of them."

"Then you know how many to hold."

Neil whispered his intent to Sloane and told her how Sharnee marked the trunk in which her captor put her. He wanted information and knew exactly where to acquire it.

Sloane nodded.

He got into his car and headed to Morgan County Hospital.

****

The door scrubbed the worn linoleum when Sloane pushed inside Leggett's office. The workplace smelled of grease, oil, and old wood. A woman of sixty-four and hair flatteringly gray waved from where she stood behind a desk in an adjoining room.

"I'll be right with you, honey."

"No rush."

The woman pranced out to Sloane in a rose border print patio dress and black flats a minute later. "I'm Madeline. How may I assist you, pretty lady?"

Sloane introduced herself. "Are you in charge of the repossessed vehicles on your lot?"

"That would be Davis, the owner. I'm sorry but he's not available at the moment. He sent word that some guys jumped him at a nightclub and he ended up in the hospital. I'll tell you one thing. If he were my son, I'd put an end to all his gallivanting foolishness. It's bad for business and puts my livelihood in jeopardy."

"How long will he be away from the office?"

"No need for you to have to wait, Sergeant. The records should be in his office. Follow me. You can be my witness that I've not bothered anything in there should he be so inclined to make an accusation of such whenever he gets back here. He's that type."

Sloane said, "I can't say I've spent much time with the man."

They entered an eight by ten room with a table used for a desk and wall-to-wall four-drawer metal file cabinets to the left. Madeline pulled open the top drawer of the leftmost cabinet.

"Neither should you ever want to. I've told him more times than I can count that his attitude hurts business, but like he says, it is his business and he'll run it the way he sees fit. Makes no never mind to me as long as I get to keep working."

"How many people does Davis employ?"

She removed a file and opened it on the table. "Me and two that work part time. He don't trust nobody to give them total run of the business. Everything we have on those vehicles is in here. Would you like for me to make a copy for you?"

"Yes, please."

"Anything else I can do for you?"

"Show me the keys to those vehicles."

Madeline stopped, turned around to face Sloane. A grin played on her lips.

"How long do you plan on holding them? You are putting a hold on them, aren't you?"

Sloane sensed the woman's delight. "Yes. We'll hold them until we complete our investigation. No longer than necessary, of course."

Madeline chortled. "Of course. I'm sure the police wouldn't aspire to inconvenience Davis Leggett any longer than what is absolutely necessary."

"The Department never with intent dares impose any difficulties on the citizens of our fine city."

When Madeline opened the cabinet door, she gaped at the pegboard. "They're not all here." She counted the keys. "Three of them are missing."

Sloane pulled out her pocket-size notepad and pen and opened the folder. She listed the nine vehicles and put a check mark next to the make and model Madeline called out to her. Three remained unchecked on Sloane's list after Madeline identified the final key—Accord, Optima and Altima.

Madeline put the keys to the six vehicles in a nine-by-twelve envelope and copied the repo documents, while Sloane called Huber with an update and told him about the missing keys.

"As soon as you get a search warrant, request the GBI's crime scene techs to process the Avalon and Impala."

"What about the others?"

"For now, get wheel clamps on the three cars with the missing keys. I'll be back out there in fifteen."

"I'm curious…" Madeline stuffed the copies into the envelope containing the keys. "Since you're seizing the vehicles and obviously are investigating Davis for whatever crimes you suspect him of, well, what about his cellphone? Do you want his number?"

"You really take exception to him, don't you?"

"Oh, it's more than that, Sergeant. Much more. Do you have children?"

"None yet."

"I have a sixteen-year-old daughter who I can't let come visit me at work because of that nut job. I made that mistake once and I assure you it'll never happen again. All this has got me to thinking I really don't want to work for him any longer."

Madeline's hand trembled. She tore off a corner of the desk calendar, scribbled numbers in two rows, and offered the paper to Sloane.

Sloane looked at the spiny numbers on the jagged paper. A graphologist would find an analysis of Madeline's handwriting inconclusive when compared to traits from a known sample.

"What is this second set of numbers?"

Madeline shrugged. "Something you might soon need."

Chapter 28

Laughter spilled into the corridor sixty feet away from the nurse's station where Neil consulted with the charge nurse.

"We've had to put up with his outburst since eleven this morning," the forty-seven-year-old nurse said of Davis Leggett. "It's been over four hours and he's still at it. The guy refuses to listen to reason. He's disturbing the patients and my staff is afraid to go in there."

"Full implications of his attitude change will soon be appreciated."

The nurse sniggered. "I'd like to see that."

"Allow me two minutes and witness for yourself the act of compliance."

"Deal."

Neil moseyed into the room. Davis Leggett sat propped up on the bed, shirtless, cellphone in his hands. A bandage covered his right forearm halfway between his elbow and wrist. Billy Ray Haney looked on from the near side. Neither man noticed Neil until he said, "Hi, Davis. Remember me?"

Both men startled. Davis fumbled his cellphone, grabbed at it too late to regain control. The phone slewed off the bed and hit edge-wise on the tiled floor. The IV pole at the head of the bed jangled when Billy Ray backed into it.

Davis scrunched his eyebrows. His eyelids became slits. "What are you doing here? Get out of here now."

"I have a captive audience, Davis. I'm not leaving until you hear what I have to say."

"Is that so?"

"Exactly so."

Billy Ray slinked by the corner to Neil's right. Neil glared at the man. "No. You stay right where you are. Hands where I can see them."

"You can't make me."

"This should do it." Neil jammed the heel of his right foot to Billy Ray's left thigh six inches above the knee. Billy Ray pitched to the floor, hands to thigh, but not quickly enough to brace either hand to the floor to prevent his face impact. He remained piled between Neil and the hospital bed.

"That's an assault," Davis yelled.

"Then I have nothing to lose, do I, Davis?"

"What do you want?"

"Let's begin with your boisterousness."

"My what?"

"Your rowdy behavior disturbs the patients. It stops now."

"What else?"

"The name of the person you are allowing to use your repossessed vehicles for the crimes of kidnapping and murder."

"I ain't doing no such thing."

Neil took a step closer to the bed. "You'll not admit what? Providing the means of transportation or the person to whom you provided them?"

"Neither. And you can't force me. I know my rights."

"You forgot one thing."

"Yeah? What's that?"

"Any arrangements you might have for the rest of your life. You have two choices. You can either give up the information and plan for whatever part of your existence remains after prison or continue on your pathetic path and die in there. Before you decide, you should know the police seized every vehicle you repossessed, your tow trucks, personal vehicles and your business. Oh…" Neil stretched his left leg and slid the cellphone out from under the bed with his foot, picked it up. "…this, too. I'm taking it to the police. You are held accountable for every bit of evidence found and charged accordingly."

"You can't do this to me. I'm innocent."

"How's the arm? I know why you're here."

"You don't know nothin'."

"I recommend you consider the choices I've laid out for you. Those are the only two available to you." Neil held up the phone. "Tell me her name or should I just call her from your phone?"

"Knock yourself out."

Neil swiped a finger across the screen and woke the cellphone.

"Give me the code."

"In your dreams."

"No? Then I'll do it myself." The cellphone responded to the four-digits Neil received in his text message from Sloane and granted access. "How's that for completeness? I'll open your contacts. Scroll through until I get to the number I want to call, or I could look at recent calls and select the correct one. You choose, Davis. Contacts or recent calls? Which shall it be?"

Neil turned the screen for Davis to read the contact's name. Sweat covered Davis's face, dripped off his chin onto his chest. The monitor recorded his pulse at 138. Blood pressure showed 192/140.

Neil heard the whisk of scrubs. The charge nurse's cologne wafted around him. "Shall the nurse call a code, Davis? You'll go into cardiac arrest if you don't relax."

The nurse stepped alongside Neil. "What happened to this one?" She tilted her head toward Billy Ray who sat hunched back to the wall.

"He needed a break."

"Did you get what you came for?"

Neil glanced at Davis who turned his face toward the window. "Yes. Body language expresses more truth than an abundance of spoken assertions. This one won't be giving you any more trouble. If his attitude regresses, call me."

"What about him?" She motioned to Billy Ray.

"Call Security and tell them to escort him off the property with instructions not to return."

"Never mind that," Billy Ray mumbled, pushed up off the floor. "I'm leaving."

****

The late-afternoon sun and humidity in the seventies slammed a double whammy on the uniformed officer who attached the Denver boots onto the driver's side wheels of the three vehicles. The backs of forty-five-year-old hands shined from the sweat. He had secured the Accord and the Optima and worked on attaching a clamp on the Altima when Sloane walked up behind him.

Sloane handed off a bottle of water. The officer rose and twisted off the cap. He chugged half before pressing the bottle to his left cheek.

"If you have no objection, I'm going to sit in the air conditioning for a few."

Sloane pulled on blue sterile gloves on her way to the rear of the Impala. She started on the driver's side and sniffed along the seam of the deck lid for any odors foreign to trunks of vehicles, specifically the ammonia stench of aged urine. One out of the one trillion distinct scents detectable by the human nose by the olfactory cleft at the top of the nasal cavity and because women possess a keener sense of smell than men. The odds of smelling the single scent she wished to find were one in six based on what Neil told her. She retraced the seam twice more. No alerts came from inside the Impala's trunk.

She sidestepped a mud hole to her left and hovered at the rear of the Avalon. She followed the same pattern around the seam. Again, nothing inflamed her sense of smell.

A tone on her cellphone signaled an incoming text message. Sloane looked at the screen. Huber.

—The judge signed a search warrant. The scope includes all structures owned by Davis Leggett on the property and all vehicles under his control.—

Sloane smiled when she read the attached copy. No limits to the search of the nine repossessed vehicles.

Huber added, "GBI on their way. ETA thirty."

No reason for her to look like an idiot sniffing the trunks of cars.

Sloane sashayed to her cruiser and retrieved the envelope containing the keys. The Ford Focus was the first of the nine looking left to right. She inserted the key in the lock and rotated it clockwise. The release thumped and the deck lid raised on its attachment arms. Sunlight lit the trunk mat, including a stain in the midline closer to the bulkhead than the rear. The smell gave no doubt to substance.

Urine.

Analysis of a sample would confirm origin, although she already knew the source.

Sharnee.

Neil answered her call on the first ring. Sloane said, "We have the car. The urine stain is precisely where one would expect it to be."

"Fantastic. I'm on my way to my car now."

"The GBI techs should be here soon. Did Davis tell you anything?"

"Given his limited vocabulary, I got enough. Plus, I perused the contacts and recent calls on his cellphone. That triggered symptoms of a panic attack. Based on smell, the chump should have asked for a bedpan."

Sloane laughed. Neil loved the dulcet tone of her laughter. He loved everything that made her the person he adored and wanted to spend time with.

"Any word on his release?"

"I'm sure it won't be too soon for the staff. They want him out of there."

"His secretary expressed disdain for him. Davis tops her list of reprobates. She'll make an excellent witness in court."

"One step closer. I'll stop by there on my way home. I prefer you hold on to Leggett's cellphone. It's up to you if you want to let Huber know you have it."

"I think I'll hold on to it until tomorrow."

****

The screen lit on Tess's cellphone a split second before the speaker played "Don't Stop Believin'." The number showed contact from Morgan County Hospital.

Tess snatched the phone off the kitchen table. She swallowed the bite of banana sandwich in her mouth and washed it down with black coffee while Steve Perry continued to sing Journey's hit song.

"Why are you calling me from the hospital phone instead of yours?"

"Take a guess," Davis said.

"I'm not playing games with you, Davis. Where's your phone?"

"That preacher took it."

Tess leapt from the chair, slung the coffee mug backhand against the refrigerator. The half-filled mug shattered. Coffee splashed the fridge, the stone-tiled floor, and the cabinet doors below the granite countertop.

"You imbecile. How did he get ahold it?"

"I accidentally knocked it off the bed where I'd laid it beside me while I talked to Billy Ray. Caldera saw it fall and got to it before Billy Ray could pick it up off the floor."

"You had it locked, right?"

"Yeah, it was locked."

Tess sighed, stared at the mess in her kitchen. "Good. At least he can't gain access to anything on it."

No verbal response on the line.

"Are you still there? Davis?"

"I'm here."

"What are you not telling me?"

"He had the code to my phone. I don't know what

to do."

"That's your problem."

Chapter 29

The familiarity of the house felt different the moment Neil crossed the threshold into his kitchen. The same oak table and four chairs in the nook, the same worn leather sofa and chair in the open living room, and the smells of his existence there finally conveyed a sense of home. It wasn't so much the furnishings or the scents, but relief.

Neil's shoes thumped the floor when he removed them in front of the sofa. He glanced at the clock on the mantel—5:47. He fluffed a pillow on one end and reclined in a state of repose unlike any he'd benefitted from in two years. This time when he closed his eyes his mind faded to black and emerged in upstate New York. Sunlit snowdrifts following a protracted blizzard covered the landscape on his maternal grandfather's homestead. Serenity replaced the ominous state of affairs he'd endured since the shooting.

He remained awake. Eyes closed. He thought of his grandparents and the many uninhibited days and nights he lazed in their home and yearned for a future known to encompass a twelve-year-old-boy's dreams. The reverie transported him to graduation day and the way achievement of that one goal brought satisfaction to him. The NYPD awarded a gold shield and then his promotion to Detective Specialist. Fond memories, yet one topped all—the moment he met Sloane Azevedo.

He sensed the touch of her lips. The smell of Sloane's body wash and citrus shampoo in damp hair on his cheeks confirmed the reality of her presence. He opened his eyes. Embraced her. Savored the taste of her kiss.

"You smell nice. How long have you been here?"

Sloane laid her head on his chest. "Five minutes."

"I didn't hear you come in."

"I saw your feet on the arm of the sofa when I stepped up to the door. I eased in so I wouldn't disturb your rest."

"I must've fallen asleep. What time is it?"

Sloane looked at the watch on her left wrist. "Six fifteen. Can I get anything for you?"

He took her hand in his. Felt its softness and warmth. "I'm glad you're here."

"How did it feel when you opened your eyes and saw me?"

"Better than any words I could ever choose to describe it. But if I must select one—perfect. More than I deserve."

"We could spend our lives in a search for what we deserve and still miss the most important thing in the world."

The truth in Sloane's words defined a path through the randomness of life to a place of certitude. A high-quality life was what he'd always wanted along with the right person with whom to share it. Neil saw both in Sloane Azevedo. Beautiful. Caring. Loving. No way could he ignore his feelings and take a chance on losing her.

"My search has ended, Sloane." He kissed her hand, pressed her palm to his chest. "I know you feel it, too."

"I do. You shower and I'll start our dinner."

"Deal."

****

The sound of Neil's padding feet faded after he turned into his bedroom. Sloane picked up the pillow and pressed where his head had lain to her face and inhaled. The familiar scent triggered a favorable reaction, one she experienced in his presence. The smell enhanced her readiness for him.

The sound of water whooshed through the pipes. Sloane lowered the pillow to her thighs and ran her fingers across the surface. She imagined Neil stretched out on the sofa, his head on her lap. Hair wet from the shower. The touch of her fingers on his skin while she explored every inch of his face before gliding her hand along his neck to his chest.

Sloane propped the pillow on the arm of the couch and moseyed down the hall. She paused at the bedroom door and listened. The shower head hissed. Water splashed. She slinked into Neil's bedroom. The first time she'd entered his room was the day she removed articles of clothing from a hamper to satisfy Huber's interest in them relating to Katie Moore's murder. That day she rushed in and back out and had not taken the time to appreciate the neatness she now observed in there.

What she saw was nothing like she expected from a bachelor's bedroom. The bed made, covered with a blue and beige bedspread. No pillow shams on the bed, but she expected none. Personal items arranged in an orderly manner on the nightstand and dresser. No articles of clothing scattered on the floor.

Sloane crossed to the foot of the bed. No demur. She conjured up an image of Neil stepping out of the shower, and his reaction to seeing her looking at him. Her breast rose and fell beneath her shirt. She clasped her hands. Closed her eyes. Pressed her right thumb to her left palm and massaged it.

The water shut off.

Sloane opened her eyes. She took a deep breath and stepped to the bathroom door.

****

Neil threw open the shower curtain. He grabbed a towel off the rack and stepped onto a brown bath rug. When he lowered the towel from his face, he saw Sloane in the doorway. He stilled, towel grasped in hands under his chin, watched Sloane's head lift slowly from his feet to his face, her blue-green eyes lock onto his while water streamed down his body and soaked into the rug.

Sloane broke the silence. "I want your word of honor."

The woman he adored clothed in a black form-fitting shirt, jeans and sandals watched from the doorway.

"Always."

"I have to tell you how I feel." Sloane stepped into the bathroom. "I love you, Neil. I'm in love with you."

"I love you too, Sloane. I have for a long time."

"What we decide this evening establishes our future. That's why adherence to fidelity is so important."

"I agree unequivocally." Neil vowed long ago to meet all conditions of a total commitment. He would know when the time came.

"Are you ready to take that step?"

The next step channeled life for Neil in a new direction. Sloane released two buttons on her shirt. She took his hand and pressed his palm between her breasts. The psychological reaction evinced his desire to be with her.

She backed into the bedroom while she kept her hand on his. At the foot of the bed, she removed her hand. Neil slid his hand to her neck, around to the nape, and pulled her to him. He brushed her lips with his and kissed her.

****

A two-inch stripe of sunlight shone through a gap in the drapes. Its course ended on Sloane's right shoulder as she propped on her left forearm. Neil's left hand traveled up her arm to the beam of light.

"The sun shines on you, Sloane."

He propped on his elbow and kissed her. She pushed him to his back and rolled on top of him. Her blue-green eyes locked onto his. An eye color blessed upon fewer than five percent of the world's population.

"That means we have the rest of the evening ahead of us. Shall we go for number two?"

"I have no words, Sloane," Neil said afterward.

Sloane laid her head on his chest. Her left hand squeezed his shoulder.

"Your passion showed me everything I needed to know, Neil. I'd call that success."

Neil's stomach growled.

Sloane lifted her head. "Sounds like time to satisfy another hunger."

He pulled her to him. "Another five minutes."

"I wish every woman could know this. A lot of

women never experience a complete state of sexual fulfillment. They and/or their partner care nothing of the art of making love. The transference of true feelings shared with one another before and after the fact is foreign to them. Not here. Not with us. This was the way I believe it should happen. Talk to me, touch me, and taste me beforehand. Cuddle me, caress me, and chat with me afterward. That's ideal for any sexual relationship. For me, that's the crème de la crème that gives total gratification."

"It's much better that way. That's for sure."

"Of course, there will be those moments when spontaneity justifies a quickie."

They chorused a laugh.

Sloane stroked Neil's lips with the pad of her thumb. He took her hand and kissed her palm.

Neil said, "I wonder if Adam felt like I do now when he saw Eve for the first time."

"Eve was the original model of perfection. I'm—"

"A God-made original, Sloane. Just like Eve."

A tear formed in her left eye. The tear remained there until another formed and both dove onto her cheek. "That's the sweetest thing anyone's ever said about me."

Ten minutes later Sloane and Neil dressed and ambled to the kitchen. Sloane switched on the oven and removed the foil from the two entrees she'd prepared for their dinner. Dover sole in lemon-butter sauce, artichoke hearts, tomatoes and zucchini.

"That looks good," Neil said.

"After twenty minutes in the oven you'll taste how good it is."

She slid the pan on the middle rack once the oven

pre-heated to the set temperature and turned to the counter where she'd set a white cardboard mailer on her arrival. She handed it to Neil.

"I printed a copy of everything I could find related to the attack on Arlo Messana."

Neil pulled a chair away from the oak table, sat, and removed nine pages of file material. He scanned the top page of the Madison Police Incident Report on which identified Arlo Messana in the section categorized "Victim." Neil skipped to the "Narrative" in the middle of page two and began to read.

"At 1130 hours Reporting Officer [RO] responded to a report of an alleged assault on Ferrell Lane, Madison, Georgia. The complainant, Thomas Mahaffey, told RO he observed the victim, Arlo Messana, crawling on the railroad tracks headed toward Fieldcrest Lane. RO found the victim laying on the back seat of Mahaffey's Ford pickup truck with copious amounts of blood soaking a towel wrapped around the victim's face and head.

"RO tried to question the victim to find out what happened to him. The victim spoke clearly in spite of his injuries to his face. He gave RO the names of three individuals who he said stopped to chat with him while he walked on Ferrell Lane earlier this date. He claims the three individuals (James Barber, Harlan Price and Louis Robinson) grabbed him and forced him at gunpoint into the woods where they beat him and left him to die.

"RO assisted the victim to an ambulance called to the location and followed said ambulance to Morgan County Hospital ER where they treated him for his injuries. The victim provided no additional information

pertaining to the incident.

"Case pending further investigation."

Neil laid the initial report face down next to the file. "I recognize one of the three named, but not the other two. Harlan Price is a deacon at the church. Arlo mentioned 'peer' when he told me about the attack on him. Do you know if either of the other two is a minister?"

"Barber was and I think still may be pastor of a church on Atlanta Highway. Robinson owns an insurance business here in town."

Neil waded through the next three pages of investigative notes he thought inadequate to the seriousness of the crime and came to a single page typed statement given to police by the complainant, Thomas Mahaffey. Vagueness defined the two paragraphs. Neil guessed someone must have redacted the statement before making it a part of the initial report. It read almost verbatim to the reporting officer's narrative.

"Are these officers still on the force?"

"No. The officer who initially took the call now works for Athens's Police. The other one moved to somewhere in Alabama."

"They call this nine-page file for an aggravated battery case complete? Those men scarred Arlo Messana for life. The police investigation into this matter is laughable. It's a deceptive cover-up. What they did is not just a shame, it is criminal."

Sloane nuzzled Neil from behind. "I agree. Dinner's on in two minutes."

Neil tilted his head back. His right cheek pressed to the softness of Sloane's left cheek. "Wow. That's aromatherapy at its best."

"Call it aphrodisiac aromatherapy. The herb butter adds a specific quality to our dining experience."

He pulled Sloane around to his lap. "The food smells fantastic, but I was talking about you."

Sloane smiled and kissed him. "C'mon. Let's eat."

Chapter 30

Tess Fleishman clenched and released her fingers around her phone. Neil had gotten his hands on Davis Leggett's cellphone. Rob had called to tell her of a mandatory meeting with the city council. He told her he wasn't sure how long it would last or what time he would be home. No mention of any plans made for their anniversary coming up on Saturday. Not that she would have enjoyed a night out with him. Her interest turned elsewhere after she discovered his infidelity.

She swiped the screen on her phone and touched the contact for the hospital. A woman answered. Tess asked to be transferred to Davis Leggett's room.

"Mr. Leggett is in the process of discharge and no longer occupies the room. Is there a message I can take for him? He may still be on the premises."

"That's all I need for now, thank you."

She let her phone drop to her lap and stared out the window at her bare flowerbed, a section of driveway and her Traverse parked in the garage. Her thoughts rambled to places and persons beyond what lay outside the window.

Her focus settled on her SUV. Availability to use the impounded vehicles now taken from her forced her to resort to the Traverse if she went out anywhere.

But perhaps not.

Tess grinned. Another avenue existed for her if she

willed to take it. That information, along with Rob's excuse for staying away from home for the evening, afforded an opportunity for her to end a business relationship with someone she considered a loose end.

She called a local convenience store and asked if they sold helium-filled balloons. They did. There to purchase three balloons and a small packet of loose balloons and back to the house took Tess seven minutes.

Tess threw open her footlocker and removed a camouflaged ozone gear bag and her duffle. She crammed two changes of clothes and miscellaneous necessities in the duffle and dressed in night camo taken from the gear bag.

She admired the glint on the blade of her CQC-6 knife and secured it in its sheath behind her back. She would feel a loss after she planted it, but she preferred it where she needed for use later. Tess holstered a SIG Sauer P226 stolen from Heslar Armory in Indiana before its discontinued use in 2015 and pocketed an SRD9 suppressor.

Next, she opened the package of balloons, poured three ounces of gasoline into three, tied the ends and attached them to the strings two inches below the helium balloons. She added a foot of safety fuse to each.

Ominous thunderheads blocked the sun's descent in the west. By eight fifteen, twilight on that Tuesday evening grayed Madison.

Time to go.

This evening she wasn't a killer of innocence. This evening Tess became a soldier on a mission. The trail of mayhem and murder behind her stretched too far for her to turn back. No regret. Just a reminder of the one week of hell prompting an Other than Honorable Conditions Discharge.

Her stratagem to confuse the authorities seemed to work. Living with the chief of police worked to her advantage. Rob fed her bits of information without going into any details, but those casual references were enough to let her know none of the evidence they had collected implicated her.

Tess shut off the Traverse's headlamps and drove by the yellow light cast from sodium-vapor streetlamps the last quarter mile. Someone parked Davis Leggett's Tundra at an odd angle to the corner of his residence. She turned in on the downside of the driveway, paralleled the two hundred feet in the grass through a stand of pine trees.

Tess rolled down her window, killed the engine, and listened for any activity in or around the house. Crickets chirped in the distance. No discernable sounds came from the house. Time of day, a thick bed of pine needles underfoot, and enhanced training in stealth strategies assured her success. She grabbed the balloons and a lighter and crept to the house.

Furrows in the gravel revealed hard braking and right steer as if Davis sped up to the house and slid to a stop. The front fender on the driver's side loomed inches away from the corner of the house.

Tess slinked by the truck to the rear corner and around the back of the Cape Cod home. Light formed a rectangle of the sparse lawn fifteen feet out from the rear wall. Tess looked up to see a window lit on the second floor. She waited. The sound of water drained down a pipe inside the wall. The window darkened. The lit rectangle on the lawn melded with its darkened surroundings.

Four additional steps put Tess at a casement window hinged to swing into a finished sixteen-by-twenty-foot recreation room in the basement. It pleased her to see the latch in the same position she'd moved it to on her visit one week earlier. She pressed the frame six inches above and below the lock with her gloved thumbs. The window swung open without a sound.

Tess flicked the lighter. She lit the safety fuses and released the balloons. The rate of burn gave her thirty seconds before fire rained on the house. She dropped through the window opening and crossed the brown synthetic carpet cushioned by a foam pad. The same carpet led up the stairway. She ascended the stairs and waited at the door for Davis to react to her surprise.

The wait lasted twelve seconds.

Davis yelled a stream of obscenities. Feet tramped across the hardwood floor, to a window, she surmised.

Tess drew the pistol and pushed through the door.

Davis leaned forward, hands on the windowsill, neck craned as he looked out the window. Tess raised the pistol, aimed at the back of his head, and fired. High-velocity blood spatter and brain matter soiled the curtains and sheetrock wall on both sides of the window. The body crumpled to the floor.

Tess picked up and pocketed the brass shell casing. She exited the house through the front door at the first flash of lightning. Flames danced on the shingled roof and lapped the faded cedar siding. Blue-white lightning forked in its descent to the earth. A loud boom shook the ground.

How appropriate. Tess grinned at the thought and

backed the Traverse to the road where she feasted her eyes on orange and yellow flames while they consumed the house along with Davis Leggett's body.

The bullet had passed through Davis's head and out the window into the darkness. Given that fact and the ensuing fire, Tess presumed once the fire department extinguished the fire and firefighters or police discovered the body's location and conducted their investigation, no one would suspect any cause of death other than the fire. They most likely would figure Davis ran to the window in his attempt to escape the fire. He perhaps stuck his head out the window—which would explain the lack of carbon monoxide in his system—where he collapsed and therefore sustained thermal burns and charring of his body, including post-mortem heat fractures of the skull.

Therefore, no one could connect her with the murder or the fire even if they suspected her.

Ahead, dime-sized hail fell, struck, and bounced on the asphalt. Hailstones plunked her hood and the top of the SUV when she drove into the torrent.

Chapter 31

"We're back at the hotel." Brita's words came out loud on the burner phone Neil set on the table to include Sloane in the call. Neil pressed the button to decrease the volume. "It's been a long twenty-four hours so I think Sharnee and I will stay in this evening and order room service for dinner. Any news on your end?"

"We found the car."

"I'm impressed."

"The vehicle was one of several repossessed vehicles stored at an impound lot here in Madison."

"Repossessed? So that means you have no suspect in custody." Disillusionment squashed the fervor in Brita's speech.

"Not in custody, yet," Sloane said. "We have a viable suspect. The GBI processed the cars we believe she used during her crime spree. We'll get her, thanks to Sharnee."

"You found the car? The one I peed in?" Sharnee's voice shrilled in the background. "That's freakin' awesome. When are you going to arrest the woman?"

"Soon," said Neil. "The police have to sort through all the evidence to put together a tenable case."

Brita said, "Thank you, Sloane for working so diligently for Sharnee and me. We appreciate everything you've done. I have one more request of you, Sloane."

"Anything."

"Take good care of my brother."

Sloane reached over and took Neil's hand. "It'll be my pleasure, Brita. I'll keep you updated on the case."

After Brita and Neil discussed plans for Wednesday afternoon and everyone said their goodbyes, Brita ended the call.

"They sounded pleased." Sloane pushed up from the table and carried their plates to the sink. Neil followed with their glasses.

"To the extent you now have friends for life."

Sloane rinsed the dinnerware and glasses before putting them in the dishwasher. Neil looped a knot in the top edge of the garbage bag and started for the door. A lightning flash prompted Neil to pull open the door and look out. Cloud-to-ground lightning issued a threat he wasn't about to challenge. Thunder cracked and its boom rattled the walls and windows. Sloane dried her hands on a dish towel, stepped away from the sink.

"I guess I'm staying put for a while," she said.

Neil shut the door. "Good idea." He joined her where she stood in front of the bay window.

"I hope the techs found enough evidence in the Impala to link Tess and Vanessa and the Avalon to her and Katie. You can testify to Tess operating the Impala on the evening of Vanessa's murder, and the store video shows Katie getting into an Avalon. The evidence Sharnee left in the Focus cinches that one as far as the car." Sloane sat on the sofa, her back to the arm, left leg tucked under her right thigh. "We have three vehicles. Three victims. One suspect."

Neil perched on the other end of the sofa, his back

to the corner. "Yeah, one suspect having no alibi except physical limitations purportedly incapacitating her. I have my doubts. What's her background?"

"Military. She and Rob both served in the Navy at Naval Station Norfolk. He was a chief warrant officer. I believe she held the rank of Lieutenant. I'm going to request her records."

"Tess's military status explains the knife and her physical ability to subdue the girls."

"That's another link we've yet to establish. How did Tess woo Vanessa and Katie? We watched Katie get into the car at an arranged meeting place. She showed no hesitation. Katie knew Tess and trusted her enough to get in the car with her that night."

"Katie's cell phone?"

Sloane shook her head. "Not yet recovered. They told Huber to subpoena the records for hers and Vanessa's. Attempts to track them failed. I'll call Huber and set up a session for tomorrow morning."

"Let's set it someplace other than the station. I prefer no interference."

"How's eight o'clock at Perk Avenue sound?"

"Perfect."

While Sloane chatted on the phone with Huber, Neil rested his right arm on the back of the sofa and watched her hand gestures, listened to her inflections. Her gaze fixed on him and stayed there from the time she put the phone to her ear until she ended the call. He believed he'd found someone. The person to whom he could confide and tell his secrets, not that he had any she hadn't uncovered on her own.

Sloane set her cellphone on the floor, shifted to her left knee and slinked to him.

"Hold me. I've had enough re-living moral injustices and criminal behavior committed by evil-filled people. I just want to relax for a while."

Neil shifted supine. Sloane placed a pillow behind his head and shoulders and lay on top of him. He kissed the top of her head and rubbed her back. Her breathing slowed. He felt her body relax. Fingers twitched on her right hand.

He closed his eyes and pictured Sloane's face the first day they met, how her pupils dilated beneath long lashes and the smile that followed their introduction. The way her eyes lit that afternoon and every time they saw each other thereafter mesmerized him. Their future defined once their bodies merged in intimacy. Now she slept on his chest.

Sloane awakened him hours later when she stirred and ran her fingers through his hair.

"What time is it?"

Sloane tilted her head and looked behind him. "Five forty-five." She kissed him. "I have to go. I'll see you at eight."

****

Neil bade Sloane goodbye, showered and pulled on a gray T-shirt with NYPD on the front in bold navy letters and knock-around pants. He sat in the worn chair next to the table on which he kept waiting-to-be-read novels and his spiral-bound notebook.

Neil flipped open the notepad and scanned down his list. The first entry—Reason—remained a mystery. To date, no link connected Tess with either Vanessa Flack or Katie Moore.

He moved on to Location, penned an update of what they now knew: Katie parked her POV, personal owned vehicle, at the Quick Shop and got into a car believed driven by Tess Fleishman.

Neil wrote *Ketamine* beneath the next heading.

Three of the repossessed vehicles seized from Leggett's impound lot provided Tess the means of transportation. Neil listed the vehicles in the order he believed Tess use them: *Vanessa in the Impala; Katie in the Avalon; and Sharnee in the Focus.* Though not yet confirmed, they surmised the Intermediate Site to be the church where Tess washed the bodies in the baptistery. He planned to discuss the issue with Huber at their powwow.

****

"I called the chief to let him know what we are doing this morning," Sloane said when Detective Huber ambled to her and Neil outside Perk Avenue Café & Coffee House. "He told me Tess is gone."

"Gone?" Huber looked surprised.

"She wasn't at home when he returned after the city council meeting and she stayed away all night. No luck so far tracking her vehicle. Come on. We can talk about everything inside."

The lock bolt clicked on the front entrance at eight a.m. A female in a white and black print smock-waist maternity top and black leggings pushed open the front door. "Welcome to Perk Avenue," she said.

Sloane entered first, followed by Huber and Neil. Coffee and cinnamon scents dominated lesser aromas of baked goods. "We'd like the table there at the front window if that's okay." Sloane motioned to the far table left of the front door.

"Sure. Anywhere you'd like is fine. I'll get menus for you."

Neil waited for Sloane and Huber to place their order and he asked for a large black coffee.

Sloane said, "Are you not having anything to eat?" She looked to the server. "Add a side of buttered grits and white toast to my order." She turned back to Neil. "You need to eat. It could turn out be a long day for all of us."

Neil nodded.

"Great. That's settled," Huber said. "Now we should discuss the facts of these two homicides and figure out how much more we need before we have a strong enough case to get a warrant and question our suspect."

"Is your focus now on Tess or someone else?" Neil wanted to know.

Huber sucked in his lips, averted his eyes to the front window. "As bad as I hate to admit it the evidence shows me something I don't want to see and I can't ignore it. Tess is the only viable suspect we have. It looks worse for her now that she's gone. How am I going to tell the chief I'm about to arrest his wife for murder?"

"You're not," Sloane said. "The way we handle this is to conceal the fact until it's time. I'll accept any ramifications."

"What particular evidence swayed your opinion?" Neil asked Huber.

He glanced at Sloane. She shook her head. By that he knew she had yet to show Huber the cellphone.

Huber lifted his eyebrows and nodded. "I sent several pictures of the two portraits in the barn to an expert for analysis and told her what I was looking for. She mentioned the structural signature and some new software they have analyzcs art based of visual cues and puts it in a specific group. She compared the images from the barn to known artwork painted by Tess. In her opinion, within a reasonable degree of scientific certainty, Tess Fleishman painted the images on the barn wall."

Neil removed the spiral notebook and flipped open to his notes. He turned it for Huber to read. The detective hunched forward.

"What is this?"

"This is a fact sheet related to the two murders based on the Scientific Method, which follows techniques from knowledge acquisition to hypothesis to confirmation. Scrutinize each entry listed here. At first, each section mostly remained unanswered. We begin by inquiry. We gain knowledge. Form a hypothesis based on the gained knowledge. Test the hypothesis. Make adjustments or corrections as necessary and confirm. After you complete the cycle, you will know whether you will or will not have a prosecutable case."

"Mind if I take a picture of this?" Huber pulled out his cellphone.

The two pages tore away from the wire binding with a low-to-high zip when Neil ripped them from the notebook.

"You may take these. Some entries we've yet to confirm such as the intermediate site. Sloane and I agree it has to be the church. It's also a place Tess had access to."

Sloane placed a paper bag containing Davis Leggett's cellphone on the table. "There's still more."

"What's in there?"

"Davis Leggett's cellphone."

"Where did you get it? We searched his truck last night. It wasn't in there."

Neil said, "I got it from him at the hospital yesterday."

"You stole his phone?"

"He surrendered it."

"Davis gave his phone to you?"

"The phone fell to the floor when he dropped it."

"You picked it up and refused to let him have it back."

"No. I picked it up and gave him a choice."

"And what choice was that?"

"Tell me the name of the person to whom he supplied the cars or I would scroll through the phone and call myself."

"I guess you bluffed him and he just gave it up."

"No bluff."

Sloane said, "I sent him the code to unlock the screen."

"How did you get that?"

"Madeline gave it to me."

"Recent calls list many contacts between Tess and Davis over the last three weeks."

"Unbelievable," said Huber. "Now she's gone."

"We'll find her," Sloane said.

The server brought their meals. Steam rose from each entrée and Neil's bowl of grits. She refilled drinks and waddled back toward the kitchen. Her left hand pressed on her abdomen. They ate amid the clang of flatware on dishes and chatter of other patrons. Neil slid his empty bowl aside.

He leaned to Sloane when Huber left the table to visit the restroom. "I need to send a link to your phone from my security system. It's just a precaution in case I need you." He pulled up the link and sent it to her cellphone. A tone signified a connection.

"When do you expect this need and my response?"

"Tonight, or early tomorrow morning. Those are the two most likely times anyone will figure I will be at home."

"What do you expect will happen?"

"Tess."

Sloane's cellphone signaled a text message. She opened it and looked at Neil. "The chief wants to see you."

"Is he in his office?"

"He's at home."

Chapter 32

Two squad cars were parked side-by-side on Fleishman's driveway. The one nearest the house faced the street. Neil pulled the Acura to the shoulder. The department's lieutenant met him halfway to the front porch. The African-American extended a thick hand.

"Thanks for coming, Caldera."

They shook. "How is he?"

They strolled to and up the front steps to the porch. "I've never seen him like this before. He's all messed up inside and won't talk about it with none of us. I think that's why he asked you to come over. Maybe you can get through to him."

"Has he heard from Tess?"

"Uh-uh. Nary a word."

Rob Fleishman sat in the same chair Tess occupied during Neil's visit two days earlier. The chair angled toward the window.

"He's here, Chief."

Rob got up and rotated the chair to face the couch. He returned to his seat and acknowledged Neil with eye contact.

"It smells like her." He rubbed the chair's arms fore and aft.

"What can I do to help, Rob?"

Rob dismissed the lieutenant and the patrol officer. He waited until they exited and closed the front door.

"First, I apologize to you for my conduct at the barn and for what I now realize was a snap judgment on mine and the deacons' part. I overreacted to the word of one man whose aversion for you I now know was without merit."

"Let me guess—Harlan Price."

"You're a lot smarter than people give you credit for, Neil. Harlan pushed to have you removed and even retained the services of a PI to investigate you."

"I saw Birdie with Beth at Perk Avenue. Birdie came up to me and blabbed on her dad. The PI sat at a table a few feet away. I squashed his probe from the start when he followed me away from the church an hour later."

Rob shifted forward on the chair and leaned forward. "May I ask you about your background?"

Neil hunched and supported his forearms on his knees. "Thirteen years on the job. NYPD."

Rob's eyes widened. "You're the one."

"That's me."

Rob straightened in the chair. He shook his head. "All this time I wondered why Arlo Messana recommended you. Now I know."

"What's that?"

"You refuse to kowtow to anybody. I respect that. I think Tess picked up on that from the start. She adored you, Neil. I could see it in her eyes."

"Tell me about her. Any changes in her you've noticed in the past weeks?"

Rob glanced out the window. "It hasn't been just the past few weeks. This is something that's been brewing a while. She refused to talk to me about it. I had to find it out on my own this morning." He paused, inhaled and sighed long with a deep shoulder droop. "The problem stemmed from an incident involving a chaplain at Naval Station Norfolk three months before Tess and I wed. Tess had just returned from a special assignment when she filed a harassment complaint against the chaplain, which included one comment pertaining to her 'well-put-togetherness' quoted in the official report."

"What became of it?"

"Out of a dozen or more females questioned, two of them sided with the chaplain. They claimed Tess instigated the sexual contact. Tess told me they fabricated evidence. That evidence resulted in Tess receiving an Other than Honorable Discharge."

"Because of false allegations."

"False or not, those claims ruined Tess's career in the service. I'd never met any of the parties involved and never even knew their names until this morning. Last night I called a friend in NCIS and asked her to look at the file. She called me back this morning and told me the names of the two so-called witnesses. Everything made sense.

"Late yesterday Huber told me you claimed to have seen Tess last Saturday evening driving the repossessed Chevrolet Impala seized yesterday morning. I told him you were mistaken because of her medical disability. I thought it impossible until now. I searched for any medical records Tess might have kept here and found none. I called the oncologist's office in Covington and they denied ever treating her."

"Do you think she faked her illness?"

"No doubt in my mind. I know she did. This whole ordeal started before we even left Norfolk. I often wondered why she chose this town. Madison, Georgia never entered my mind until she approached me two months after our wedding and showed me an ad for the chief's position. She insisted I apply for it. Rather than reenlist, I applied for the job and was accepted. I thought she just needed to distance herself from the reminders of everything around there. Man was I duped. She planned the events of this week four years ago."

"The murders?"

"Yeah. She planned to kill Vanessa Flack and Katie Moore long before she ever met them. I have no—"

"Hold it right there, Rob. You believe Tess plotted to kill Vanessa and Katie before she ever approached you to move here?"

Rob leaned back in the chair. "The whole plan hinges on her two accusers."

It made sense after seeing Valerie and Kylie at the funeral. "Valerie Flack and Kylie Holcomb. Two fellow service members linked to Vanessa and Katie. I met them after the funeral."

"Once I heard their names, I figured you would have at least seen them there. Valerie is Vanessa's eldest sibling, and Kylie is Katie Moore's half-sister from their mother's previous marriage."

Neil gazed into Rob's eyes. "You will distance yourself, correct? Let Huber do his job?"

"As bad as I hate to, I have no choice."

"Where is she, Rob?"

Rob glimpsed at his cellphone on the table next to the chair and looked out the window. "I wish I knew."

****

A picture of Tess came on the screen a moment before Rob's cellphone vibrated on the table. Neil's eyes shifted from the face on the screen to Rob. Rob broke his stare out the window and picked up the phone.

"It's Tess," he said. "I'll put it on speaker."

Neil gave a terse nod.

"Rob?"

"Where are you? I called you several times, and they all went to your voice mail. I've been worried about you."

"I needed to get away. It gets old staring at four walls all day long every day."

"I try to understand, Tess. I really do. I've put you on speaker. Neil is here with me."

"Oh. Hi. Thank you for being there for Rob. I had hoped this might ease some stress but I fear my sudden departure added to it."

Neil said, "We're concerned for your wellbeing, Tess."

"I believe you, Neil. I'm just not so sure about anybody else."

"I care, Tess. You know how this past week's been for me. I have two murders to solve and little to go on. The families deserve better."

"I know this is bad timing, Rob. I feel for those families. I can't imagine losing a child like that. This is just something I needed for me."

"Will you be back by Friday evening? I have anniversary plans for us."

"Go ahead with your plans. I'll surprise you. I promise."

The screen signified the call ended.

"What do you make of that?" Rob said.

Neil shook his head. "It's difficult to judge the tenor of her voice on the phone. You know her much better than I do, but her absence is no coincidence."

"I agree. Suspicious behavior is not enough. I need evidence."

It might be a trap.

Chapter 33

Low humidity in the thirties blessed Georgia that Wednesday afternoon. It was a welcomed departure from the average low in the fifties, which made it feel somewhat cooler even in the sun than seventy-eight degrees. Neil admired the cloudless sky on his way to the hotel's entrance. A whitetail doe in her late gestation period browsed the greenery along the tree line.

A Greene County Deputy Sheriff engaged in a chat with the concierge a few feet inside the lobby. The lissome deputy broke off her conversation when the door opened and Neil strolled in.

"Excuse me. Are you Neil Caldera?" she said in a congested drawl. "Tapley" engraved her brass name tag.

"Yes."

"Do you have a minute to talk?" The deputy motioned to a seating area to the right of the main entrance. They sat in chairs angled at ninety degrees. The deputy opened a black leather portfolio and handed seven photos to him. "These images were taken by the security cameras night before last at Gaby's. I'd like for you to look at them and tell me what you see."

The pictures were eight-by-ten matte prints in black and white consistent with ones captured by an infrared camera. The high-resolution camera performed better than most he'd seen. Neil studied the images shown in each photo. Back-angled, side, and left-front-angled views showed Sharnee facing and while in the clutches of her abductor. The abductor looked similar in height to Sharnee, whom Neil knew to stand at five-eight-and-a-half.

"The top photo is of Sharnee. She's sitting on the table facing the lake consistent with the statement given by Kyle, a server at Gaby's. The second photo shows Sharnee off the table face-to-face with a second person on the far side. The person fits the height of our suspect." He set the photo aside and studied the next one. "This one captured the abduction. The abductor held something in her right hand up to Sharnee's neck."

"We figured chloroform, but that's not any kind of cloth and it's not covering her nose and mouth."

Neil touched the picture. "That has to be a syringe. Sharnee's lab work was positive for ketamine. When injected, the effects last around thirty minutes. Effects by other means of ingestion last much longer. That explains how Sharnee woke up and managed her escape."

"Detective Huber in Madison called me and told me they found the car."

"That's correct. The car was one of nine repossessed vehicles stored at a local impound."

"Huber did not mention a suspect."

Neil thought it best to withhold any information pertaining to Tess. "The GBI techs searched the vehicle for evidence. Analysis is ongoing."

"So it's fair to say they have a suspect, but no physical evidence to tie the person to the crime."

"You know how it works. Evidence collected in a

few hours may take the crime lab days or even weeks to analyze and issue a final report."

The deputy nodded. "Unfortunately, I do."

"Anything else you need from me?"

"That's good for now. I'll stay in touch with Huber."

****

The king club suite overlooked the lake. Brita led Neil to the balcony where she and Sharnee lounged while awaiting his arrival. Sharnee leaped out of her chair and hugged him.

"One of the Greene County deputies stopped by to interview Sharnee."

"She waylaid me in the lobby." He touched Sharnee's right cheek. "Let me have a look at your neck."

Sharnee tilted her head leftward. "It's been sore."

"The deputy asked me to look at photos from the security footage. I saw something in one of them I want to confirm."

"Like what?"

"Needle mark." Neil located a red injection site at base of the neck on the right. No contusion around the site. "There's one right here." He touched a finger to the spot.

Sharnee flinched. "That's where it's sore. I remember feeling the sting. I didn't remember it while I was in the hospital." She returned to the chair, tucked her left leg under her right.

Brita sat. "Any progress to report on the car you found?"

"According to the suspect's husband she didn't come home last night."

Brita straightened. Her chin dropped. "It's Tess, isn't it? That woman is the suspect in those murders. She's the one who—"

"Who is Tess?" Sharnee asked.

"Somebody your uncle knows," said Brita, eyes trained on Neil. "Why did you not tell me you suspected her? Are you protecting her?"

"No, I'm not protecting her. I want her put away for what she's done. You know that about me. The problem is the lack of tangible evidence."

Sharnee gasped. "You know the person who did this to me? This Tess whatever her name is?"

"Fleishman."

"The police have the car Sharnee was in. What about that evidence?"

"We're waiting on the crime lab."

Brita threw up her hands. "Wait, wait, wait, wait, wait. That's all you ever hear these days."

"They'll get her, Brita. When they do, she'll spend the rest of her life in a cell."

"I hope so."

"Have I ever let you down?"

"No, and you'd better not. Ever. Enough of that talk. I want to enjoy the afternoon here in this lovely setting with you and Sharnee."

No phone calls or text messages interrupted Neil's time with Brita and Sharnee between three o'clock and when the waning glow of light scattered the surface of Lake Oconee. They munched on red grapes, kiwi, brie and cheddar cheese, crisp bread and butter-flavored crackers.

"I love this place," Brita said. "Thank you for suggesting it. Sunsets at home are nothing compared to this."

"I'm glad you two came to visit."

"We've missed having you in the neighborhood. Leya and Shina cried when I told them we were making the trip. They miss their brother, too. I think it's time for you to come home."

****

Neil sneaked room-to-room and found nothing out of the ordinary other than a trace of the scent along the hall to his bedroom where it was strongest. Locks were engaged on the doors to the outside and every window.

Satisfied he was alone, and curious about the perceived presence, he opened his laptop and perused the security footage since the time he left home that morning.

No person or unlawful entry into the house caught on camera.

Neil shut down the computer and got into bed.

Chapter 34

The call Neil expected to receive from Valerie Flack and Kylie Holcomb before their departure on Friday came as a conference call Thursday at 9:45 a.m. All parties agreed to meet at noon in the Oak Room at the James Madison Inn.

Sloane stayed on the line after Valerie and Kylie disconnected long enough to tell Neil she was to call him on the secured phone. Neil hurried to the bedroom where he had set the burner phone on the nightstand.

He picked up on the first ring, sat on the side of the unmade bed and laid back.

Sloane said, "Tess returned home late last night."

"That blows the theory that she went into hiding."

"She must figure avoiding attention by being at home is better than raising too many questions by her absence. It seems to have worked to her advantage."

"It may not after today. I'm curious to hear an account of events from Valerie and Kylie."

"We might have just received a break in this case. Leggett was murdered. The pathologist confirmed a gunshot to the head. The sheriff's office is sending an investigator to his house…"

Neil ran his hand beneath a pillow while he listened to Sloane. His fingers trailed off the end of the mattress. His focus sidetracked when the tips of his fingers brushed a hard object attached to the mattress.

Something he knew wasn't supposed to be there. He flipped the pillow aside and tugged the mattress away from the headboard.

"Neil, are you listening to me?"

"I found something. I need you to get over here now."

"What is it?"

He told her.

****

The marked police unit nosed downward and rolled to a stop behind Neil's Acura within five minutes of his call. Sloane shoved open the door, darted to where Neil stood and enfolded him in her arms.

Her body trembled at the sight of a CQC-6 tactical knife. "I imagined…"

"What might have happened?" Neil finished for her.

"Yes. That thought seized my mind from the moment you told me."

Sloane eased back. Her hands lingered on his shoulders and then slid down his chest until only her fingertips touched him.

Neil took her hands in his. "I have an idea. The only way it will work is if you stay here tonight."

"You could have just asked me."

"Would you mind staying here tonight?"

"I'd be delighted."

They went inside to the bedroom. The left corner of the mattress jutted off the box springs. Sloane leaned forward and looked at the head end.

"This is menacing," she said. "How long do you think it's been there?"

"My guess is late yesterday. I rotated the mattress

and changed the sheets before I left here. It wasn't there then."

"Did the cameras not capture anything?"

Neil rubbed his neck. "That's what disturbs me. She somehow defeated the system."

Sloane pulled on a pair of powder-free purple nitrile gloves and removed the Emerson CQC-6 knife with blade open from its hiding place. She slid aside the drape and held the knife in the natural light. Examined both sides of the handle and blade.

"There's a partial print on the base of the blade."

"Identifiable?"

"I think so." She laid the knife on the dresser. "I'll get the camera and an evidence bag."

Sloane took photos of the bedroom and mattress. She photographed the knife, switched the setting on the camera to macro and took close-ups of the latent print.

"Ridge detail looks promising," Neil said, looking at the digital image.

"I'll run it through AFIS. We know her prints are in the system. Do you have a safe?"

Neil opened the closet. A black fire safe was bolted to the wall and floor on the inside corner.

"That will work," she said. "I want to leave the knife in there for now."

He recognized Sloane's objective and opened the safe. He closed it after she deposited the knife inside.

She kissed Neil. "I'll see you at the inn."

****

Southern charm greeted guests at The James Madison Inn in historic downtown Madison. Its pine floors and antique doors and windows enhanced its appeal.

Valerie and Kylie met Sloane and Neil out front in the shade of a crape myrtle filled with buds. Valerie wore a triple-color-block-striped blouse and black denim jeans with white sandals. Kylie had on a pink short-sleeved V-neck chiffon blouse, jeans and flats.

After greetings, Kylie escorted them to room 106 in the Marrol House. Kylie and Valerie sat on wingback chairs at the foot of the bed. Straight backs reflected their military training. Sloane and Neil took the two slipper chairs covered in rose cloth brought in for the meeting.

Kylie looked at Neil. "Valerie and I discussed the things we want to talk to you about. We have a lot of questions for you."

"Before you begin, we've had some developments in the cases. I believe it will answer some, if not most, of your questions. Then we have another subject we'd like to discuss with you."

Kylie and Valerie looked at each other. Kylie looked back at Neil and nodded. "Our main concern is finding out who murdered our sisters."

Sloane said, "We're investigating a person we believe murdered your sisters. Have either of you served with a female by the name of Tess?"

Valerie startled. "Tess Adair? Is she here? Do you think Tess Adair is the person who killed Vanessa and Katie?"

"That's the other matter we want to discuss with you," said Sloane. "Tess Adair is now Tess Fleishman. She's married to Rob Fleishman, Madison's police chief. We'd like to hear about the incident at Naval Station Norfolk involving the chaplain."

"I often wondered what happened to that hussy."

Kylie frowned and shook her head. "She tried her best to railroad that chaplain with her claim of sexual harassment. I can provide the details if you'd like."

Sloane waved her right hand. "The details we'd like to hear involve you two and why Tess received the Other than Honorable Conditions Discharge."

"That's classified," said Valerie. "The case was sealed."

"You know Tess tried to seduce him," Kylie said to Valerie.

Valerie glared at Kylie. "You know we can't say anything, Kylie. We're under orders."

"We'll be doing ourselves and our sisters a disservice if we keep silent. Tess got away with her atrocious acts, not to mention her attempt to defile and shame a good man. You know what she did. Tess Adair stripped, got into the chaplain's bed and waited for him to get there. When he refused her advances, she threatened him and his career and painted that awful picture of him on his car door. The MPs found the chaplain's wife's finger hanging from the rear-view mirror with her wedding rings still on it, for goodness' sake. You witnessed a lot of her behavior yourself. We both did. You know Tess cut off that woman's finger even though the police never proved it."

Sloane glanced at Neil.

Valerie grinned and said, "That was smart, Kylie. You didn't tell *them* anything."

Sloane said, "Tess painted a portrait of the chaplain?"

"She sure did. She painted it on the door of his car. It was hideous looking, but you could tell it was supposed to be him."

Neil pulled out his cellphone, touched an icon. He selected a picture and turned the screen for them to see.

"Was it anything like this?"

"Exactly like that except…that looks like you," Valerie said.

"I'll bet you've had other things happen, haven't you?" asked Kylie. When Neil said nothing, she continued, "I'll take that as a yes. Expect things to escalate. Tess won't stop until she gets what she wants." She turned to Valerie. "Sound familiar? He has become another object of Tess's desire."

Valerie looked at Neil before her eyes settled on Sloane. "There's something else you should know about Tess. She was SWCC—Special Warfare Combatant-craft Crewmen in Little Creek, Virginia. Her team worked with the SEALs and their training was like that of the SEALs. She was one of their best."

Chapter 35

Tess sneaked to the side door of Neil's house a few minutes before midnight. She pushed off her shoes and inserted the key. The door swung open with no sound. The kitchen smelled of orange cleaner. Moonlight peered between slats in the blinds and formed angled planes to the living room's hardwood floor. Darkness blanked the house beyond the hallway.

She pushed her top off her shoulders and let it fall to the floor. Her wet hair brushed her shoulder blades. The flow of air under the ceiling fan aroused her. She stepped out of her panties and tiptoed to Neil's bedroom.

Her pupils adjusted to the darkness. The bedroom door stood open. Dim light filled the room. Tess settled on her heels. She closed her eyes and inhaled. Neil's scent filled her lungs. She caressed her torso. Imagined his caress the way she craved his touch. She opened her eyes and scanned the room. The silhouettes of furniture lacked detail. She focused on the king-size bed. The headboard abutted the far wall. A comforter crumpled on the floor at the foot.

A sheet covered a form lying on the right half of the mattress. Face turned to the wall fifteen feet away. No movement. Tess listened. Soft breath sounds came from the bed. A clock ticked to her left.

Tess gripped the jamb. She slithered forward. The

pad of her left foot glided across the hardwood. She followed with her right foot. Neil's bedroom walls enclosed her. Her body quivered. Warmth flushed her. Someone to make new memories awaited her.

Two strides put her even with the foot of the bed, one foot away. Tess leaned forward and felt the sheet's border. High thread-count soft. She ran her fingers along the edge before parting the sheets and sliding between them. She spooned behind the warm body and draped her arm across Neil's chest. Tess inhaled his scent. The touch of his bare chest excited her.

"Hello, Neil." Tess pressed her body to his.

"What are you doing here, Tess?"

"I want you, Neil. Make love to me."

Neil turned to face her. His left hand touched her face, swept her hair back. His hand lingered five seconds on her right cheek. Tess kissed his palm and rolled to her back. She inhaled short breaths the minute his hand slid to her neck. The passion increased once his hand glided to her shoulder and down her right arm.

The second Tess lifted her hand to grasp Neil's she felt the slap of cool stainless-steel clamp her right wrist. Neil rolled away before she crooked her left arm around his neck.

The lamp on the nightstand lit.

Tess craned her neck and saw Sloane Azevedo standing next to the bed.

****

Neil swung his legs off the bed and tugged on a pair of khaki pants. He grabbed a blue tee off the floor and pulled it on.

Tess rotated away from Sloane, pushed upward on the bed, and leaned on the headboard. She rested her left hand on top of the sheet. She looked at Neil.

"You want to cover yourself?" Neil said.

"What I want is you, Neil."

"That will not happen. Ever," Sloane said.

Tess looked at Sloane. "Why not? He can choose me or you or anybody else. I need this, Sloane. You may even join in if you'd like."

"No, Tess," Neil said. He rounded the foot of the bed.

Tess locked eyes with Neil. "Will you at least hold me?"

"No."

Tess clutched the sheet, tugged it to her chin. "I did all this for nothing." She flopped to her right side and drew her knees up to a fetal position. The cuff rattled against the wooden headboard post.

Sloane said, "What have you done, Tess?"

"I'm sure you'll hear soon enough. Have you identified the person responsible for the girl's deaths?"

"Yes."

"Have you made the arrest?"

"Not yet," said Sloane.

"Why haven't you?"

Neil said, "We'd prefer she turn herself in."

Sloane's cellphone chirruped. "Huber," she said, touched the screen and held the phone in front of her.

"We have a double homicide on Four Lakes Drive. We need your response ASAP."

"Thirty minutes."

"I don't mean to tell you what to do, Sergeant, but we really need you here. One of the victims is Chief Fleishman. This whole scene's a bloody mess. It looks like the perpetrator took a shower before leaving.

Bloody shoe prints on the carpet lead from the side of the bed to the bathroom."

Neil kept his eyes on Tess. She remained motionless even after Huber mentioned Rob Fleishman's death. He knew she killed her husband and his lover. A shower explained Tess's damp hair and the fresh scent of soap.

Sloane said, "Have you recovered a weapon?"

"The chief has a knife in his chest."

"Request a GBI team. It will best serve us if they process the scene. Has anyone notified Tess?"

"One of ours is on the way over there even as we speak."

"Advise the officer to disregard. She's not home. Tess is here with us."

"Us?"

"Neil and me."

"I guess you'll tell her?"

"Tess heard you. I have you on speaker."

Tess remained silent and motionless. Eyes open. No change in facial expression.

"Okay. I'll call the GBI."

Sloane ended the call. "What is your plan now, Tess?"

"You care to reconsider my offer? May I experience what I want just once?"

****

The news of Chief Rob Fleishman's murder prompted responses from every major news agency in the Atlanta and Augusta markets. Reporters jostled for position among their peers and fifty or more townspeople outside Madison Police Department to see and attempt to garner a response from any person they deemed important or relevant to the murderous rampage.

Tess Fleishman sat in a holding cell most of the night to early morning, charged with four counts of murder, pending further results of Morgan County Sheriff's inquiry into the murder of Davis Leggett. She had yet to answer questions posed to her.

At eight that Friday morning, Sloane Azevedo stepped behind a lectern set up at City Hall dressed in her uniform. Neil sat to the left between the mayor of Madison and the police captain. Sloane stood poised, introduced herself as spokesperson and began, "Early this morning Madison Police arrested Tess Fleishman for the murders of Vanessa Flack, Katie Moore, Rob Fleishman and Nadine Thorne.

"Tess Fleishman is a former military officer married to Madison Police Chief Rob Fleishman. The Madison Police Department chooses not to discuss motive or specifics related to any evidence linking Tess Fleishman to the crimes for which she is charged.

"I want to thank every officer involved in the investigation, particularly Madison Police Detective Darren Huber and the many GBI agents called on to assist, for their time and efforts in bringing the investigation to a successful conclusion. A debt of gratitude also goes to Neil Caldera for his persistence after being asked to consult on these heinous crimes.

"While we wait for the Crime Lab's results of analyses, Tess Fleishman, upon transport, will remain in custody of the Morgan County Jail until such time the evidence is presented to a grand jury for indictment."

Hands flew up at the end of Sloane's statement.

The room filled with exuberant chatter. The noise ebbed somewhat when she fielded the first reporter's question.

Neil sidled through the nearest door. Someone called his name before he turned up the sidewalk. Neil turned to see Arlo Messana in a white shirt, red tie, and black dress slacks slide out of a midnight blue Ford sedan parked on the far side of the street. FBI Agent Declan Gadow sat behind the wheel.

Neil jaywalked to the other side. "Mr. Messana. It's a pleasure, sir."

Arlo Messana extended his right hand. Neil felt strength and sincerity in the handshake and suasive smile of the man who earned his respect and trust. "You're welcome in my home anytime you care to come by."

Mr. Messana got back in the car. Agent Gadow acknowledged Neil with a bob. A well-dressed man sat on the rear seat. A fedora shaded the man's face, but Neil sensed familiarity.

He watched the sedan drive away and called Brita with the news.

"Is it truly over?"

"Yes."

It wasn't over.

Chapter 36

That evening Sloane and Neil lounged on the pontoon out on Lake Oconee in the cove where they anchored one week earlier.

"I'm surprised Tess made no move to retrieve the knife," Neil said after they watched the sun disappear and clouds in the western sky change from deep rose to purple.

"Not me. Not after what I witnessed. It is obvious Tess meant you no harm. She wanted you to acknowledge her existence more than anything else. You remained strong throughout or you might've fallen victim to her predatory instincts. Tess is a beautiful woman. I had a hard time watching her body pressed to yours."

"The only way I got through it was to focus on what she had done, not what she was doing."

"Every woman has a certain level of them."

"What?"

Sloane leaned on her forearm, put her left hand on his chest and gazed into his eyes. "Predatory instincts."

Neil pulled Sloane to him and kissed her. Their chemistry felt right. Unlike the way he felt when Tess tried to seduce him. The touch of Sloane's lips triggered his hormones. The moans she emitted conveyed her feelings for him.

Sloane's cellphone trilled two seconds before a text

message tone sounded on Neil's. The alerts repeated a second and third time before they broke their embrace and read the message sent from her captain.

—*Tess Fleishman escaped during transport. Huber and one deputy dead.*—

They looked at each other as if thinking the same thought—we have to get to Brita and Sharnee.

Sloane scrambled to the operator's seat and fired the engine. The boat tilted in the U-turn and surged forward, skimming the water's surface the half-mile to the dock. Neil looped the rope and secured the boat in the slip. They sprinted to Sloane's Jaguar. The tires squealed out of Blue Springs Marina's lot. Sloane at the wheel.

Neil called Brita. The call transferred to voice mail. He left a message to call him and tried Sharnee's phone. Same result. Neil dialed the burner phone. No answer. He called the hotel. The desk clerk transferred the call to Brita's and Sharnee's room.

The Jaguar sped along Parks Mill Road. Neil looked at Sloane. "No answer and they're not in their room."

"I'm sure they are okay, Neil. Just in case, there's a Glock 19 in the glove box."

Neil pressed the release button. A bulb lit the glove box interior. He removed the pistol from its black leather pancake holster. The same model he once carried on the job. The model he had fired and killed a serial killer and Saniya Carta.

He wondered if Brita or Sharnee or both faced a similar fate.

He checked the pistol's balance.

"You never forget the feel, do you?" Sloane said.

"No."

"Then you know what to do if necessity dictates it."

Seven minutes later Sloane wheeled up to the Ritz-Carlton Reynolds. Neil bounded through the front entrance. He ran to the check-in desk where three employees assisted guests. He showed a photo of Brita and Sharnee on his phone's screen to the employees and guests.

"This is my sister and niece. They are guests here. Have any of you seen them this evening?"

The three employees denied having seen them within the past three hours. One guest, a teenage boy, asked to take a second look at the picture.

"Yeah, um, I saw the girl a few minutes ago headed toward the pier. She was with somebody but I don't remember who. It might have been the woman. I don't know."

"Which way?"

One clerk pointed. "Through those doors and follow the walkway straight to the lake."

Sloane caught up to him before he reached the doors. "They're here?"

"This way."

He pushed open the doors. They followed the walkway to the pier, looked around. No sign of Brita or Sharnee.

After searching the beach and the smaller private horseshoe lounging areas, Sloane said, "There. The second one."

"I see them." He let out a sigh.

"What are you two doing here?" Brita said on their approach. "I thought you would be out celebrating."

"I've been calling you."

Brita's face blanked when Sloane looked at Neil. She sat upright on the lounger. "What's wrong?"

"She escaped."

"What?" Brita leaped off the chair. "How?"

Sharnee left the company of two college-age girls and joined them. "Mom?"

Brita put her arm around Sharnee. "Everything's fine, dear. Sloane and Neil came by for a visit on their way to dinner."

"That's a relief. I thought they were here with bad news. I'm going back to talk with my new friends. Nice to see you again, Sloane."

"Me too, Sharnee."

They waited for Sharnee to get beyond earshot before either of them continued.

Brita said, "What next?"

Neil felt his cellphone vibrate a second before it rang. He looked at the screen, tilted it for Sloane to see a number unfamiliar to him.

She shrugged.

He touched the speaker icon and answered.

"Neil." It was Tess.

Brita's eyes squinted.

"Hello, Tess."

"I guess by now you've heard. I wanted to let you and Sloane know I harbor no animosity against either of you. You both treated me better than I expected or deserved and therefore I have to reason to inflict any harm to either of you or your families."

Neil remembered Sloane's statement about predatory instincts. He mouthed, "She's lying," and scanned the grounds. Every second or third person he saw focuscd on a cell phone.

Tess continued. "I am the victim, Neil. It began in Virginia and continued here. Rob made a mockery of our vows by his infidelity." Someone sneezed off to their left. The sound came from the trees between the parking lot and the end of Cottage Cove. Loud enough to hear through the phone. "I crave love, Neil. I need someone to love me, not use me. I saw what I believed was an opportunity with you. Sloane knows the desire, don't you Sloane?"

Neil handed the phone to Sloane and melded into the trees. He looked for light emitted from a phone. Nothing. He guessed Tess must have routed the call through a hands-free device to avoid detection. A rumble coming from an outboard motor flowed over the terrain. A red laser beam pierced the darkness from forty-five degrees to Neil's right, aimed at a dark silhouette hunkered at the base of a pine tree between where he stood and the incoming boat.

The shape leaped out, arms raised, and yelled "Ha," in front of Neil who pressed the pistol's muzzle to the teenager's chest. "I'm sorry, mister. Please don't shoot me."

"Scram."

The teen ran off through the trees.

A female's voice almost inaudible behind Neil said, "Drop the gun."

Neil pulled the pistol in close, flexed his wrist, and slid the muzzle around his side beneath his left arm. "I think not, Tess."

A sting at the level of his right kidney bowed his right side. His right index finger twitched on the trigger guard. His mind flashed back to Bleecker Street in New

York where a bullet from his gun struck and killed Saniya Carta. Behind him, dozens of tourists roamed the hotel grounds. He dared not risk a shot at Tess.

"Walk."

Neil took a step toward the lake. "I should have expected you might come here. You don't give up, do you?" Another sting hit his back. Tess's left hand eased into the cleft of his arm and side and latched onto the pistol's barrel.

"A woman knows what she likes, Neil. You have presence and intentionality. Let go of the pistol. You won't risk a shot at me. Not here. Not after what happened in New York."

The ejection button clicked and spat out the magazine. Tess released her hold on the barrel but pressed the knife blade against his spine. Neil cleared the chamber, dropped the cartridge into one pocket, and stuffed the magazine in another. He stuck the pistol in his waistband and turned to face her.

Neil expected to see Tess in her prior haggard and frail state. Instead, evil expressed an undeniable beauty. She wore a deep V-neck ruffle blouse. Her hair shined and skin glowed where a moonbeam peeked through the canopy.

"Why Tess? Why did you have to kill Huber?"

"Do you like the way I look? I cleaned up for you. I have access to a house on Martin Oaks. It's fifteen minutes by water and the scenery is divine on clear nights. Come away with me, Neil. Make love to me. One night is all I ask. I'm no longer a married woman."

"True, but you will always be a murderess."

"I promise to be good for you and to you."

A grisly figure came into view like a ghost ten feet

behind Tess. Moonlit ridges and shadowy valleys ominous to most anyone else who saw the man became a welcome sight to Neil. The man who possessed impeccable timing tilted his head rightward.

Tess nudged Neil. "What are you looking at?"

Neil gave a terse bob. "Have a look behind you."

"Tsk. Tsk. I'm not a fool who falls for antics, Neil."

Neil shrugged. "Consider it a warning, Tess." He sidled a half step to his left.

Tess swiveled to her right. Arlo Messana extended his right arm and clamped his right hand around her knife-filled hand. His left hand seized her neck. "Any resistance is ill advised, Mrs. Fleishman. Drop the knife."

Tess wriggled and spouted, "Take your hands off of me."

Arlo held on unmoved, as if Tess were a child. "Criminal enterprise imparts malice no person can learn in academies and universities. In my old world, you have no rights. Do as you are told or suffer the consequences."

Tess Fleishman calmed. The knife dropped to the pine-straw-covered ground. She put her left hand to Neil's cheek. "Will you promise to visit me?"

Neil removed her hand. "So long, Tess."

He nodded to Arlo, who let out a shrill whistle. Dark-clad masked individuals closed in on them from the lake and parking lot. They formed a half circle ten feet out.

A latecomer wearing a charter hat broke through the line, bypassed Arlo and Tess, and strode up to Neil. The man removed his hat. Guido Carta extended his right hand and held out a folded newspaper in his left.

"I wanted to be the one to give this to you. Reading the article delivered a great deal of pleasure as I know it will to you, Caldera, but the headline cinched it for me." Neil shook Carta's hand and accepted the paper. Guido Carta waved the masked squad forward and returned the hat to his head. "Look me up when you return to the city. I'd like to discuss future possibilities. Arlo."

Arlo nodded. "Guido." The group led Tess to a waiting pontoon. "No need to fret," Arlo told Neil. "They're all Feds."

"Guido?"

"Consider his invitation a victory. Accept it. He invites a person only once."

"What about you?"

"My life is here. Although, I might be persuaded by someone's insistence."

Neil grinned and opened the folded newspaper. The headline, "Exonerated," resonated off of the *New York Post*. "This piece changes nothing."

Arlo placed his hand on Neil's shoulder. "Life in the past rarely does, my friend, but…" He gave a terse nod toward Sloane. "A good woman changes everything."

A word about the author...

Steve Rush is an award-winning author whose experience includes tenure as homicide detective and chief forensic investigator for a national consulting firm. He worked with the late Joseph L. Burton, M.D, under whom he mastered his skills, and investigated many deaths alongside Dr. Jan Garavaglia of Dr. G: Medical Examiner fame. His specialties include injury causation, blood spatter analysis, occupant kinematics, and recovery of human skeletal remains.

Steve's book Kill Your Characters; Crime Scene Tips for Writers was named finalist in the 2023 Silver Falchion Award for Best Nonfiction and Honorable Mention in the 2023 Readers' Favorite Awards. Steve won joint first prize in the 2020 Chillzee KiMo T-E-N Contest and longlisted in the 2022 Page Turner Awards.

He lives in Metropolitan Atlanta, Georgia, with his wife Sharon.

www.steverush.org